Sea of
Memories

OTHER TITLES BY FIONA VALPY

The French for Love

The French for Always

The French for Christmas

Sea of Memories

FIONA VALPY

LAKE UNION
PUBLISHING

Published by Lake Union Publishing, Seattle

www.apub.com

Amazon, the Amazon logo, and Lake Union Publishing are trademarks of Amazon.com, Inc., or its affiliates.

ISBN-13: 9781542046657
ISBN-10: 1542046653

Cover design by Emma Rogers

Printed in the United States of America

In loving memory of my grandmother
E.T. ('Milly') Macdonald
1906–2008

souvenir (n) memento; item given, kept etc.,
to recall the past.
[French, inf: to come to mind;
se souvenir vpr to remember]

I remember that day, cut from a cloth of gold,
When the silk-smooth sea unfurled to the far horizon
And the breeze brushed the blonde beach-grass,
One hundred strokes to make it shine.
We walked the strand-line, bathing our feet in waves
As pure as promises, that sighed upon the sand.
A shell, bright amongst the dark kelp ribbons,
Held the sun, the moon and the stars within.
I keep it still in my coat pocket, its curves
Hold safe that day for ever more.
Ella Dalrymple

2014, Edinburgh

'Welcome to the Drumbeig Nursing Home'. The words on the sign belie the fact that I'm standing in the pelting rain, on the wrong side of the glass door, stooping slightly to bring my ear nearer to the Entryphone in the hope that someone's heard me press the buzzer and will respond. I huddle in closer, trying to flatten myself against the wall beneath the shallow overhang of the guttering, which drips even more water down my back. The wind tears handfuls of yellowed leaves from the plane trees that encircle the grey stone building and throws them against the windows, where they plaster themselves for a moment before being washed to the gravel by rivulets of raindrops. I check my watch, impatient, my mind already on home – *Will Dan be coping? Will he have remembered Finn's medication?* – then press the buzzer again, a longer and more assertive ring this time.

'Sorry to keep you waiting. If you could just sign in for me.' The receptionist hands me a clipboard and a pen. I slide off my sodden coat so the sleeve won't drip on to the polished surface of her desk. 'Have you visited us before?'

I shake my head, signing my name and the date. In the column headed 'Visiting', I write my grandmother's name, 'Mrs E. Dalrymple'.

She turns the sheet to read what I've written. 'Ah, you're here to see Ella? That's nice. She's settling in well, and her son comes to see her regularly, but it'll be good for her to have some more visitors.'

Guilt makes me bristle slightly. I want to tell her that I've not been able to come before – *I work full-time as a teacher, you know, my son has problems, it's not easy to make the time* . . . But I leave my excuses unsaid and force a polite smile back, raking my fingers through the wild strands of my hair that are already turning to frizz in the hot-house air of the nursing home.

It was the call from my uncle, Robbie, that prompted this visit. 'She'd love to see you, Kendra, if you can spare the time. There's something she wants to ask you. But I have to warn you, she's not so strong these days. You'll see a change since you last saw her at the house. Her mind's wandering a great deal more now.' His tone was gentle, although there was a hint of insistence, which increased my sense of guilt in not visiting her before. But my mother isn't close to Granny Ella – some complicated, never-spoken-of mother–daughter strife – and so there wasn't much contact when I was growing up. It makes visiting all the more complicated. I doubt I'll tell Mum that I've been to the nursing home today. It might feel like a kind of betrayal, even if I'm not sure why. I know if I mentioned it in passing, no matter how casually, there would be a sniff and an abrupt change of subject at the other end of the phone.

'Second floor, go right along to the end. She's the last door on the left.' The receptionist directs me with a professional smile.

There is a thick, oppressive smell of cooking cabbage, which seeps from beneath the dining-room doors to mingle and clash with other scents of air freshener and disinfectant. My footsteps make no sound on the thick blue carpet. I decide the lift would be even more claustrophobic and take the stairs, a reminder to be grateful, suddenly, for the use of my legs. By the time I've climbed to the second floor, I'm sweating and my scalp prickles with the heat of my own body. I pull the high neck of my woollen jumper away from my skin, hoping to cool down a little, trying to breathe. *How is my grandmother adjusting to living in the stifling atmosphere of this institution*, I wonder, *no matter how clean and warm it*

2

may be? Are the nursing staff kind? Is she well cared for? Does she miss the independence of her solid Morningside home, the generous, high-ceilinged spaces, the rooms filled with a lifetime of belongings? Or does all of that no longer matter to her? Has she forgotten it, as she forgets so much these days? Her mind seems to be discarding memories in the same way that she's discarded so many of her possessions, paring back her life to just the bare essentials. Downsizing not just her accommodation, but her life, her whole being, as her days draw to a close.

The last door on the left has the number 12 stencilled on to it and a name card beneath it in a little metal frame: 'Ella Dalrymple', printed in neat, rounded handwriting. A young hand, not her own elegant italic script which waves and trembles these days on the cards she sends out at Christmas.

The noise of a television, the volume turned up high, emanates from the room on the opposite side of the corridor. But, as I pause outside Granny Ella's door, there's nothing but silence on the other side of it. I tap softly. Maybe she's asleep. I can leave a note, creep away without disturbing her, get home in good time to check on Finn, start supper, get on with the marking I've brought home with me: thirty-one essays on 'Who's to blame for the tragedy in Macbeth?' I suspect that some of those essays may well turn out to be tragedies in their own right.

The urge to turn and leave is strong. After all, I could honestly say now that I'd tried to visit, and my conscience would be clear. But at the same time I can't help registering my reluctance to go home. I always seem to feel that way these days, knowing that as I come through the door I'll be wary of meeting Dan's eyes in case I catch another glimpse of the look of defeat that flickers there now, overshadowed by the guilt he can't conceal at seeing me coming in, tired, from another day's work. We'll both try to pretend that it's fine. He'll put on a brave face and try to be positive about the latest job application he's just sent in, and I'll make an attempt to be bright and breezy about my day, dredge up a smile and a funny story about something one of the kids at school said. But we'll both know. Despite trying to protect one another, we're worried sick about our current financial predicament and even more so about the future. Whatever lies out there for our beautiful, unreachable son? Finn was a difficult baby from the start, and the doctors put his listlessness, which alternated with terrible, terrifying fits of rage, down to colic or teething or some vague, undefined 'virus'. And then when he was two years old they realised that, in fact, there were 'significant developmental delays' and started referring us to the specialists who finally diagnosed his autism. Every day since has been an exhausting struggle, whether we're trying to help Finn through his anger and terror or whether we're battling with the authorities to try to get more help for him. And while Dan and I both put a positive gloss on things during the day, there'll be that awful chasm again later tonight, when we lie in bed, miles apart. It feels like each of us is drowning in our own sea of worries, unable to reach across and pull the other to safety. We're drifting further and further apart, unable to summon up the strength, any more, to fight the undercurrents that are dragging us both down.

A nurse comes out of the room opposite carrying something covered with a towel. She shoots me a brisk, no-nonsense smile and I turn back to Ella's door and tap again, a little more firmly. My grandmother's gentle voice, as cracked and age-worn as the old seventy-eight gramophone records that she used to own, invites me to 'Come in'.

'It's me, Granny, Kendra. Just come to see how you're doing.' My voice sounds false to my ears, with the over-brightness of a guilty conscience.

I don't know whether she'll recognise me. There was that one time when I went to see her at the house and she called me Rhona, her lined face breaking into a radiant smile of joy and relief, thinking her daughter had come back to see her at last. 'I'm not Rhona, I'm Kendra. Rhona's daughter, remember? Mum will come and see you one of these days, though, I'm sure.' *And it's high time she did, before it's too late*, I didn't add. She hasn't been back to Edinburgh for years, refuses to see her mother and has left it all up to Uncle Robbie, even the move to the nursing home and clearing out the house to put it on the market.

But I can see that today's a good day. Granny's eyes are bright, her mind sharp.

'Kendra, dear, how lovely. Come in and pull up that chair. But you're soaked! Here, hang your coat by the radiator to dry out a bit. It's a foul day out there.'

I give her a hug, noticing how frail she is, how fragile the skin of her cheek feels against that of my own.

I drag a chair closer to hers and take a good look around. Robbie and his wife, Jenny, have done a good job, arranging the few belongings that could be brought from the house so that the room, with its bland, magnolia-painted walls and beige carpet, has been transformed into something a bit more comforting, more personal.

Ella's paintings from home have been hung, with my favourite one – the beach scene with the sailing boat – on the far wall, where she can see it from her bed. There are a couple of the old rugs on the floor, their colours still jewel-like despite being a little threadbare here and there with the passage of thousands of footsteps down the years. And her books and ornaments are arranged on the shelves that Robbie made to fit around two walls of the room, and beneath the window that looks out across the treetops to where Edinburgh Castle floats in the distance, illuminated, as though sailing on the storm-tossed sea of branches in the foreground.

On the cabinet at her bedside sits a delicate, deep-blue bowl, shot through with a vein of pure gold like a bolt of lightning, containing a handful of seashells. Those shells are particularly poignant somehow. There's nothing special about them; they are a beachcomber's modest pickings. And yet, for her to have kept them like this, they must be more than they appear: treasured memories of holidays long ago, perhaps, reminders of days gone by spent on far-flung beaches awash with sun, wind and sea. I swallow the emotion that rises suddenly in my throat.

'How are you settling in, Granny?'

I know this move has been hard for her, that she sees it as an admission of defeat, an ending, and I glimpse the look of sadness that flickers around her eyes at my question. But she quickly composes her features, a customary calm smile on her face as she replies, 'Oh, fine really. This place wouldn't be bad at all if it wasn't for the fact that it's full of old people.'

I nod, grinning back at her. 'I see. And at the age of ninety-four, you're excluding yourself from that description, I take it?'

'But of course.' She raises her eyebrows in a look of mock innocence. 'Despite appearances to the contrary, I'm really only seventeen you know. I have a theory, you see, that, when you've lived as long as I have, your memory chooses whichever age it wants to be; and today my mind has been back in my eighteenth year again.'

I look at her a little askance, worried that she's having another one of those lapses where her brain loses its connections to the more recent memories and transports her back into the past, stealing her from us, little by little, with this cruel trick of the aging mind.

But her eyes are clearly focused, watching my face intently. She must have seen the giveaway flicker of concern in my expression because she reaches for my hand and holds it in both of hers.

'Don't worry, Kendra, I'm teasing you. I'm all here today.'

My cheeks flush and I put my other hand over hers, turning to face her more squarely. The realisation that she knows – that she's aware of her lapses of memory, the frightening, dark flickering of a candle flame that had always burned so steadily up until now – hits me suddenly, bringing a lump to my throat again that silences me.

'But,' she continues, 'I do know that I'm losing my marbles.' She squeezes my hand as I try to find the right words to protest, to say *No*, *that's not true, you're fine*, as if those lies would make it better for both of us.

'No, dear, I am. There's no point in pretending otherwise. And so I want to ask you a favour. You're good with words, and now that I'm in here' – she nods at the room around us, which is all that remains for her – 'I have a great deal of time on my hands and a head full of memories. So, before I forget them all and there truly is nothing left, I want you to write them down for me. To tell my story. Would you do that for me? I remember you used to say you wanted to be a writer. Here's a chance for you to exercise that talent.'

'Yes, well you know what they say: "Those that can, do; those that can't, teach." But, of course, Granny Ella. I'd be happy to write down your memories. The only problem is time. I can only come and see you after school, although I suppose I can come more often in the holidays. But there's Finn too . . .'

I trail off, feeling guilty again. Of course, I could try to make a bit more time, but Dan's so stressed out right now, stuck at home all day with our lovely, challenging boy. I know he finds it all so hard, the constant reminders of how 'different' Finn is, the agony of worry about what the future might hold for him . . . How will his autism develop as he grows older? Who will look after him when we're gone? And then, by way of light relief, Dan spends any spare moments he has trying to send off more job applications, with little hope of any success. The only news is bad these days; ex-colleagues who've been made redundant too now, as well as the all-too-frequent letters of rejection which have plunged my husband into an all-time low.

Ella nods, relinquishing my hands as she turns to open a drawer in the bedside table behind her.

'I know how busy you are, dear, and I don't want to make any more demands on you. So I got Robbie to bring me this.' She brandishes a hand-held tape recorder. 'What I'm proposing is that I will speak my

7

memories into here and then give you the tapes so that you can transcribe them in your own time, in the comfort of your own home. I'll give you these scrapbooks to take away too – perhaps they'll help you to be able to picture it all, bring the people and the places to life.'

There's a shoebox tied up with string and a larger cardboard box on the floor beside the bed, holding what looks like a pile of board-bound photo albums. I pick up the top one and open it at random. A photo of my mother as a young girl gazes out at me seriously from the black page. Written beneath it in white ink – she must have had a special pen for the purpose – in Granny Ella's neat handwriting, the caption reads 'Rhona, aged 8'.

I raise my eyes to meet Ella's again, wondering, as I so often do, exactly what *did* happen to create the distance between my mother and my grandmother. It sits there like an ice-field, chilly and uncrossable, riven with the unfathomable crevasses that life has driven between them.

Ella lays her hand on mine again, her grip stronger this time, a note of urgency in her voice.

'Please, Kendra. My time is running out. Before it's too late, before I forget it all and there's no one left to tell it, please would you write my story?'

I glance again at the photo on the page, of a girl in a neat white blouse and striped school tie, her straight blonde hair held back from her face by a plastic hairband, her dark eyes enigmatic. And I realise that my grandmother isn't just asking something of me. She's offering me something too. Explanations, perhaps. Insights, certainly.

Looking at the box of albums, I realise how little I know about my grandmother's life. Because of the rift with Mum, I didn't see that much of her when I was young, and it was only when I came to Moray House to do my teacher training, and then met and married Dan, that I began to see my Edinburgh granny more often. Caught up with my own life, with all its distractions, I'd never seen her as more than an elderly relation, there in the background to weigh on my conscience now and then, whenever Robbie and Jenny were away or otherwise engaged.

So, I have to admit, I'm intrigued at the prospect of looking through the albums and poring over pictures from my mother's and Uncle Robbie's past. There'll no doubt be pictures of my grandfather too, a dimly remembered figure from my childhood who died when I was seven. I remember the long drive north from London for the funeral; a draughty Scottish church; my mother sobbing, my father unable to console her; shortbread and orange juice at Granny Ella's house afterwards. We didn't stay the night there, although there were lots of spare rooms. 'I'd rather stay at Robbie's,' I'd heard Mum telling Dad, her voice suddenly too high and too loud . . .

I drag my attention back to the here and now, seeing my grandmother's expression which is a mixture of questioning and invitation.

'Okay, it's a deal.' I smile at Granny Ella and she beams back with relief.

'I was hoping you'd say that! Here are the first two tapes, and I got Robbie to buy a second one of these gadgets so you can play them back at home.' She puts a lumpy envelope on top of the albums in the box. 'And, Kendra, tell it your way. Take my words and the pictures and write it properly. Use that talent of yours. So that others can read it and understand.'

I nod again slowly, once more aware that there's an underlying urgency in what she's saying.

Suddenly aware, too, of the two pairs of eyes that are on me, appraising me expectantly: Ella's own and, from the photo in the book on my lap, those of my mother as well.

PART 1

1938, Île de Ré

A girl stood on the jetty, watching as the ferry that would carry her across to the island ploughed steadily through the blue waters towards her.

Setting down the cream leather travelling case, she slipped her jacket from her shoulders, releasing herself from the confines of its neat tailoring and letting the warmth of the French sunshine caress her skin. Her arms were pale after the long northern winter and there'd been no spring at all to speak of that year; she felt like a butterfly, emerging from its slug-like chrysalis, suddenly discovering its wings and spreading them wide to soak in heat and light and colour.

A breeze – the soft breath of the wide Atlantic Ocean that extended to the other side of the world beyond the low-lying island – lifted her honey-coloured hair where it fell over her shoulders, cooling her neck and her flushed cheeks.

It had been a long journey from Edinburgh, full of new and exciting experiences. She'd have been tired if she weren't so nervous at the prospect of meeting her hosts, and the approaching ferry was now bringing that hurdle ever closer. On the overnight sleeper to London, Mother, who – despite Ella's protestations that, at the age of seventeen, she could manage perfectly well on her own – had been chaperoning her as far as the boat train, had slept the sleep of the just in the other berth. Her slow regular breathing mingled with the clatter of the wheels over the rails and the occasional startling roar of another train passing in the darkness.

But Ella, who was used to the silence of her bedroom in the leafy suburbs of South Edinburgh, had hardly slept a wink. Not that she'd cared. She had been too excited, her head too full of the journey before her, the summer abroad stretching in front of her like a promise. So she had lain, swaying in her narrow bed with its stiffly starched cotton sheets and grey woollen blanket with LNER stitched on it in red, and practised French phrases in her head. It was one thing to have been top of her class at school, earning approving nods from Mademoiselle Murray, but Ella suspected that her teacher's accent had had a strong twang of Morningside about it. French had certainly sounded very different on the gramophone records that Mother used to play, smiling dreamily as she listened to Maurice Renaud sing and reminiscing about the time she'd seen him perform when she'd stayed in Paris as a young girl. 'You know, Ella, it's essential to spend time in a country if you really want to be able to speak a foreign language,' she'd declared. 'Not to mention being able to understand the culture.'

And so, last Christmas, her mother had written to her old friend Marianne Martet to enquire whether it might be possible for Ella to visit for a week or two.

'Even better than a fortnight in Paris, she's inviting you to come and spend the whole summer with them at their holiday house on the Île de Ré! Six whole weeks with the twins! Imagine, you'll be speaking French like a native.'

Ella was secretly a little disappointed. She'd been looking forward to the promise of the sophistication and elegance that Paris held, having pored over the *Picture Post*'s feature on the famous World Fair, which the city had hosted the previous year. She'd never even heard of this island. A consultation of the heavy *World Atlas* showed that it was one of a few tiny slivers of land that looked as if they'd been chipped off France's Atlantic coastline and fallen into the sea. But still, an adventure was an adventure, especially for a girl who'd never been further than Fife before now.

The planning had taken weeks: visits to Jenners for a holiday wardrobe which included three bathing costumes, a suite of new undergarments, and fittings for several light, cotton dresses, prettier than any she'd owned before.

'You'll need to keep well covered up with your fair colouring,' Mother had fussed. 'And don't forget to wear your sun-hat all the time, otherwise you'll get freckles and then you'll be sorry!'

Father had presented her with the little travelling case the day before she left. 'I'm told every young lady who travels to foreign parts needs one of these,' he'd said with a smile. The key, which she wore now on a ribbon around her neck, unlocked the brass fittings to reveal a shot-silk interior of the deepest cherry red, which held several silver-topped bottles and jars and a brush-set with a little oval mirror, each item held in its place with fine leather straps. There was just room for her night things and the few spare items she'd need for the journey. Everything else had been carefully folded, wrapped in tissue paper and packed into the big suitcase.

The ferry slowed as it neared the jetty and there was a bustle of activity suddenly in the port. A deck-hand carried her suitcase on to the boat for her, giving her an appreciative glance over his shoulder as she picked up her smaller case and followed him on board. A man with a beret settled a crate of clucking chickens in the shade of the wheel-house and smiled at Ella as he sat down on the hard wooden bench that ran around the edge of the boat. And then, with a shout and a wave, the ropes were cast off and the ferry began its return journey to the island, the turnaround fast to make the most of the tide.

Ella went to stand near the prow, looking out towards her destination, a pale smudge of land which lay low amongst the waves. *In a storm it must almost get swept away,* Ella imagined. Mindful of her mother's warning words, she clamped one hand firmly on to the straw hat that shaded her face from the sun as the breeze strengthened a little across the water and threatened to snatch it from her head and send it bowling away over the waves. She licked her lips to moisten them and tasted salt.

The sky was a heady blue overhead – very different from the Edinburgh grey that she was used to – and she tipped her head back to follow the trajectory of a sea-gull as it soared high above.

Tilting her head to follow the arc of the gull's flight, Ella glanced back at the mainland receding steadily beyond the foaming wake of the ferry. For a moment, she had the unnerving impression that she'd stepped off the very edge of the earth, that the bustling staging-posts of her journey – Edinburgh, London, Paris – might still exist back there in some other universe, but now she'd left that world behind.

The boat ploughed its way onwards and the white sands of the Île de Ré drew ever closer, reminding Ella of the paintings by Turner that she'd studied in art lessons at school. In the wash of the light of an early summer's evening, the sea shimmered with shifting tones of lapis and turquoise and the island seemed forged from white gold beneath its thatch of dense green pine branches. Taking a deep breath of the salt air, Ella suddenly wished the crossing would last forever, that she could live her life in this state of suspension, flying as free as the birds that soared in the dizzyingly blue sky above her.

But then, all too soon, the ferry was drawing alongside the passenger jetty on the edge of a port where the gangling, awkward arm of a crane swung cargo into the hold of a larger ship, to the accompanying cries of men and sea-birds.

The ferry's passengers surged forwards, gathering up bags and parcels. The man with the beret balanced the crate of chickens on a bicycle and wheeled it down the short gangplank, safely on to dry land.

Ella picked up her cases and made her way, a little lopsidedly, off the boat. Marianne Martet had written that they'd be there to meet her, but Ella had no idea what *they* looked like. Mother had described her old friend as being very beautiful and vivacious, with big eyes and dark curly hair. And, in her letters, Marianne had said that her twins – Caroline and Christophe – were now eighteen years old and were looking forward to the company of another friend for the summer, especially one so near their own age.

As the crowd cleared and the cars that had driven off the ferry moved away down the dusty road, Ella became aware of a donkey-cart drawn up at the far end of the jetty. Standing on it, so that they could see over the heads of the crowd, and waving their arms in her direction were two young people, a girl with a cascade of auburn curls and a boy whose fringe fell low over his dark eyes. The light caught the planes of his face, high cheek bones casting shadows which emphasised the hand-some set of his features. There was a completely unselfconscious and relaxed beauty about the pair, which made her warm to them immediately, dispelling any apprehension she'd had at the thought of spending the summer with strangers. The girl wore a short-sleeved shell top and pedal pushers that left her tanned calves bare, and the boy had on a cotton smock, the sort a fisherman might wear, over loose trousers. All at once she felt constrained and overly prim in her neat, tailored jacket and full-skirted dress.

Christophe and Caroline jumped down from the cart and came to greet her. Ella held out a hand to shake Caroline's, and blushed awkwardly as Caroline leaned in under the hat at the same time to kiss Ella on both cheeks. Flustered, her hat pushed askew, she turned to Christophe and paused, unsure of the correct etiquette now. And her cheeks flushed an even deeper shade of pink as he, too, planted a kiss on each of them. To cover her embarrassment, Ella clamped the crown of the hat firmly back on to her head, grateful for its wide brim.

'Eleanor Lennox. You are welcome!' Christophe's eyes were alight with amusement as he stooped to pick up her large suitcase.

'Please, call me Ella, everyone does unless I'm in trouble.' She was relieved to find she could understand his French and, although she spoke hesitantly at first, she was able to find the words to reply.

'I don't believe a girl such as you could ever be in trouble,' he laughed. 'You look far too neat and tidy for that! *Oh là là*, and this case is clearly full of more such *costumes*. It's going to be far too heavy for poor Anaïs to pull. We'll have to walk alongside the cart.'

'Please don't listen to him, he's only teasing.' Caroline took Ella's hand in hers. 'Your dress is beautiful, and so is this travelling case. You must excuse us, we are always so very *décontractés*, so relaxed, when we're on the island. It makes such a nice change from life in Paris. We forget what civilised people look like!'

'Ah yes, but what is civilisation, truly?' Christophe paused, setting down the heavy suitcase in the dust behind the donkey-cart. 'I would argue that the way we are on the Île de Ré is how life really should be and the posturing and posing of Paris is the sham. There are plenty of people in the city who could be said to be the very opposite of civilised. And as for the wider world,' he continued, warming to his theme, his eyes blazing suddenly, 'we have the Fascists in Spain killing their own brothers and the Germans ignoring every promise they made at Versailles and rearming, then annexing Austria. They are intent on expanding their empire – who knows for what purpose? – but it surely cannot be an innocent one. Refugees are flooding into Paris, our own relations have been displaced through fear of persecution. The whole of Europe is in turmoil! How can any of that be described as "civilised"?'

From beneath the brim of her hat, Ella watched his attractive face, which became even more animated with youthful passion as he spoke. He gesticulated with his strong, sun-tanned hands, emphasising the point with sudden force.

'Come, Christophe,' Caroline spoke gently, laying her own fine, equally tanned fingers on his arm, 'now is not the time for a political diatribe. Eleanor must be so tired after her long journey and *Maman* is expecting us at home.'

With a sigh of resignation, Christophe bent to pick up the suitcase once again and, with some effort, heaved it on to the back of the small wooden cart with a bump that made the fawn-coloured donkey look up from where she was tearing mouthfuls of grass from the side of the road and gaze around at them with dark eyes and a look of dreamy bewilderment.

'Anaïs, meet Miss Eleanor Lennox and her enormous suitcase,' Christophe announced with a mock flourish and then went to caress the little donkey's soft ears and muzzle, gently taking hold of the harness so that he could lead her in a broad circle to turn the cart in a homeward direction.

'Hello, Anaïs. You're beautiful.'

'Climb up, Miss Eleanor Lennox. Your carriage awaits.' Christophe's eyes danced, belying the stiffness of his invitation.

'Please, as I said, it's Ella. And I think I'd rather walk actually. I've been sitting on trains for so long, I'd prefer to stretch my legs.' Secretly, Ella was anxious that perhaps her suitcase really *was* too heavy, but she wasn't about to let this laughing French boy know that his teasing had found its mark.

He was looking at her now with what seemed to be a glimmer of admiration as she stood up to his jesting. She was aware of him taking in the graceful line of her waist and arm as she held her hat firmly on her head, defying the mischievous, snatching breath of the sea-breeze and fixing him with her clear, green-eyed gaze, but she couldn't know that his fingers were itching for a pencil and a sheet of paper on which to capture those flowing curves and the way the wind blew those strands of her hair. His expression grew serious suddenly and he nodded. 'Alright then. Ella it is. And Anaïs thanks you for your thoughtfulness.'

As they left the harbour, the road they turned on to was scarcely more than a dirt track, a dusty lane scratched by the wheels of passing carts into the mat of beach-grass that bound together the shifting sands beneath. Ella's leather shoes pinched her feet and grew dull with the scouring of the sand as she walked. She glanced, enviously, at the soft canvas slippers that Caroline and Christophe were wearing, which left faint imprints of their rope soles in the dust alongside the deeper, more invasive prints of her raised heels. It had seemed so important, back there in that other world, to choose the right wardrobe for this summer's trip, and Ella had sensed her mother felt so too, as she conceded, perched on a chair in the Morningside Shoe Shop, that the pair with the small heel – a feature normally frowned upon in their Presbyterian family – did look *chic* enough for France. But already, just minutes after arriving, Ella was realising that this 'right' wardrobe was all wrong for the Île de Ré.

The three of them walked alongside the donkey-cart, following the road which ran in a straight line across the island, unhindered by hills or valleys, on the flat, low-lying sliver of land. In the evening light, dusk-softened now, tall spikes of hollyhocks glowed against the white render of the fishermen's cottages clustered here and there along their way. The colours of the flowers – raspberry pink, lemon yellow, dark plum and soft apricot – seemed particularly vivid, as if there were a clarity in the light here that was lacking on the mainland. Ella tipped the brim of her hat low over her eyes, dazzled by the setting sun ahead of them which, even this late in the day, still bathed the island in far more warmth than she'd experienced on even the most clement summer's day in Scotland. Her body seemed to be expanding, like a seedling unfurling in a hothouse, in response to this sudden surfeit of heat and light. Again, she felt the sense of constraint in her tailored dress and jacket, her stiff leather shoes, her hat and gloves.

They came to the little town of Sainte Marie de Ré, and Ella began to wonder how much further they had to go. A blister had begun to nip on her heel and she was starting to regret not having taken up the offer of a ride on the cart. Finally, of her own accord, the little donkey turned into an even smaller lane, almost hidden between two white-washed cottages.

'What are those plants?' asked Ella, pointing at the lush greenery which ran in perfectly straight rows to either side of them.

'They are vines,' said Christophe. 'See, the bunches of grapes are just beginning to form.'

'I didn't know grapes grew so close to the sea.'

Christophe nodded. 'Some of the best vineyards in the world are near to the coast-line. The sea-breezes are good for the health of grapes as well as people.'

Ahead of them, beyond the sparse tufts of sea-grass that thatched a low-lying line of dunes, the ocean was suddenly visible again, redoubling the light as the sun's long rays strewed diamonds across a million tiny wavelets. Off to the right sat a pretty two-storey house, a little larger than most of the cottages they'd passed, rendered the same dazzling white, but with shutters painted the blue of a soft sea-mist, framing tall sash windows that seemed glazed with gold in the light of the setting sun.

Opening a gate in the low wall that surrounded the house's flower-filled garden, Christophe led Anaïs round to the front door which, like the windows, stood open, allowing the ocean breeze to blow through and gently lift the edges of the fine white muslin curtains that Ella glimpsed through an open doorway inside.

Christophe grunted with the effort of heaving the suitcase from the back of the cart. 'Leave it there for the time being. I'll bring it in after I've seen to Anaïs. Come on old girl, let's get you out of this contraption.'

As he led the donkey around to the back of the house, a tall, smiling woman appeared in the open doorway. She had the same warm eyes and cascading curls as Caroline and held out both hands to take Ella's in hers.

'Ella, *bienvenue*. You are most welcome. I'd have recognised you anywhere – you are the spitting image of your mother! Please, call me Marianne, there is no formality here. You must be so tired after your long journey, but now you are here at last and there will be no need to travel much further than the beach or the village for the next six weeks.

Caroline will show you to your room and you can freshen up a little before supper.'

Ella followed Caroline down a corridor of bleached oak floor-boards, craning her neck to try to take in the rooms that they passed. This house by the sea couldn't have been more different from her own Morningside home with its heavy velvet curtains and dark mahogany furnishings. The rooms she glimpsed were awash with light, their ceilings lofty with lime-washed beams, and what furniture there was had a rustic simplicity – a disparate collection of unmatched objects, yet the overall effect was one of elegant harmony.

The girls climbed a broad wooden staircase which creaked quietly beneath their feet, and then Caroline flung open a door to the left of the softly lit upper corridor. Another set of white muslin curtains billowed as they entered the room, and Ella had the sudden impression that she was standing on the deck of a boat in full sail as her travel-weary body swayed slightly, still unaccustomed to being back on terra firma.

A faded rag rug softened the wooden floor-boards, adding a splash of colour to the whitewashed room. On the bedside table, a bunch of honeysuckle and roses breathed its sweet scent into the evening air. Ella took off her hat and sank, thankfully, on to the cotton quilt that covered the bed. She eased off her shoes and wriggled her toes, still encased in their white silk stockings, luxuriating in the sudden freedom. Against the far wall of the bedroom, the mirror of a wooden dressing-table reflected the last of the day's sunlight, making it dance amongst the curtains. Above the wrought-iron bedstead hung a watercolour painting in a fine gilt frame, a sailing boat skimming across an aquamarine sea towards a line of low-lying dunes.

'That's wonderful,' Ella pointed. 'You can almost feel the wind and the sunlight and smell the sea.'

Caroline nodded, sitting down on the bed alongside her. 'It's one of Christophe's. Combining the two things he loves best, painting and sailing. He's really getting to be rather good at both these days, only don't tell him I said so or it'll go straight to his head.'

The two girls giggled as they heard a loud thumping on the stairs. Christophe pushed the door wide, dragging Ella's case behind him. 'Don't tell who you said what?' he asked with a broad grin. Without waiting for an answer, he flung himself on to the bed alongside his sister. 'Phew, well, Anaïs and I are both mightily relieved that that's the last we'll see of that thundering great millstone for a few weeks!'

'Ella was just admiring your painting of *Bijou*,' Caroline nodded towards the picture.

'Tomorrow we'll take you out in her,' Christophe smiled. 'She's a beauty.'

Ella was struck by the way in which his face seemed to change with each utterance, his emotions writ large across his features. His dark eyes could go from laughing to brooding and back again in the course of just a few sentences, like a squall blowing across the sea, clouds chasing across the sun and then the sky clearing once again. She was accustomed to concealing her feelings, following the lead of her parents in suppressing overt displays of emotion at all times, even within the privacy of the family home. But the twins seemed unfettered by such constraints, and Ella felt her own heart expanding a little, yearning to experience a far greater range of sensation than had hitherto been available to it during her safe – and, she now felt, rather dull and monochrome – Edinburgh childhood. Once again, she had a sensation of expansion, just under her ribcage this time, and was overwhelmed with a sudden urge to unbutton her jacket and loosen her dress to make room for whatever it was that was happening to her heart.

A delicious scent of something savoury being cooked on the stove downstairs came wafting up into the room.

'*Allons*, Christophe. We must leave Ella alone for a few moments to rest and unpack before supper is ready.' Caroline smiled at Ella. 'There is no need to change, unless you feel like it after your journey. We will stay as we are. I meant it when I told you we are very relaxed here. If you want to freshen up, the bathroom is the next door on the right, just across the landing there. Come down when you're ready. We'll be in the kitchen, or sitting outside on the terrace behind the house. When you come through the kitchen, you'll see the doors.'

After hastily hanging up her clothes in the tall *armoire* that stood in one corner of the bedroom, and piling her neatly folded under-garments into a pretty chest of drawers, painted cream and decorated with garlands of pink roses, which was pushed against the far wall, Ella went in search of the bathroom.

She brushed the wind-blown tangles out of her dark blonde hair until it fell in a smooth curtain on either side of the serious, oval face that gazed back at her from the age-misted mirror hanging above the basin. Despite her determined attempt to adhere to her mother's warn-ing and keep her hat firmly on her head, the sun and wind had evidently still managed to creep in beneath the brim and weather her cheeks with a faint golden glow. Peering a little more closely in the fading evening light, to her dismay she counted at least five freckles scattered across the bridge of her nose. She shook her head at the frown that appeared on the face in the mirror. 'There's no point spending the next six weeks worrying about freckles,' she told her reflection firmly. 'We are *très décontractés* here on the Île de Ré.' She smiled. 'And your *accent Français* is already much improved, *Mademoiselle* Lennox.'

She washed her hands with the small bar of creamy soap that sat beside the basin, drying them on a white linen towel afterwards and noticing how soft they felt. Then, hanging her formal jacket in the *armoire* back in her room, she draped a soft cotton cardigan over her shoulders, in case the evening air grew chilly, and hurried downstairs, passing through the kitchen to the terrace beyond.

At the back of the house, a generously proportioned garden was enclosed by high whitewashed walls. Honeysuckle, from which she supposed the sprigs in her bedroom had been picked, scrambled up and over them, scenting the air, its perfume mingling with that of the jasmine, which trailed in starry tendrils across a wrought-iron pergola above the terrace. Through an open gate at the far end, Ella glimpsed Anaïs cropping the grass contentedly beneath the trees in a small orchard. Marianne, Caroline and Christophe sat at a broad wooden table, laid with a white cloth and ivory-handled cutlery. Blowzy, deep-pink roses spilled from a painted earthenware jug in the middle of the table, and a cut-glass pitcher of water sat alongside a bottle of red wine. Carrying on the calm evening air, the bell on the clock-tower of the church in Sainte Marie could be heard tolling eight o'clock.

Christophe was leaning on one elbow, his chin cupped in his hand, drawing something in a sketch-book which he shut hastily and pushed to one side as Ella approached.

'Come.' Marianne patted the chair next to hers. 'Sit here, Ella, and tell me all the news of your mother. It's been many, many years since I last saw her, but having you here brings back happy memories of my stay in *Edimbourg* when I was about your age. Caroline, pass Ella that bowl of olives. Will you have a glass of wine with us? Perhaps mixed with a little water if you're not accustomed to drinking it both before the meal and as an accompaniment to the food, as we do?'

The dark wine turned a clear ruby colour in the heavy crystal glass as Madame Martet topped it up with water from the pitcher and handed it to her. Ella sipped it hesitantly, trying at the same time to adopt an air of sophisticated nonchalance, as though every evening the boiled beef or mutton that tended to be the regular fare for suppers at her house, was washed down with a bottle of Château Talbot, the name engraved on the label of the bottle sitting on the table before her. Even watered down, the wine was heady and rich, and Ella felt the last knots of tension, born of her long journey and her even longer anticipation of this summer, dissolve and fade with the last of the light as night fell over the island.

In the glow of the candle lantern that Marianne had brought to the table, along with a platter of *blanquette de veau*, Ella glanced surreptitiously at Christophe. The shadows played across his features and his eyes seemed to shine with an inner light of their own. He glanced up and met her gaze, and she felt the flicker of a connection between the two of them. To cover her confusion, she turned her attention gratefully to the plate of food in front of her and to Caroline's questions about life in Scotland.

Finally, a faint chill in the night air made Ella shiver and yawn. Noticing this, Marianne said, with a smile, 'Come, it is time for bed. I think we are all tired tonight after the excitement of Ella's arrival. Even you are a bit quiet this evening, my talkative twins. Leave the dishes, Sandrine will be in in the morning. Get a good night's sleep, my dears. The barometer is set fair, so tomorrow you can take *Bijou* out for a long sail. I'll make you a picnic lunch if you like.'

Upstairs, Ella lay between smooth cotton sheets, her eyes wide in the darkness of her room. At the open window, the night air crept in through the shutters, stirring the curtains with its salted breath. Through a gap where the shutters didn't quite meet, she watched as a full moon rose, casting a beam of silver light across the floorboards and on to the cotton coverlet of her bed. The vast ocean, out there just beyond the dunes, reflected the bright moonbeams, creating a strange twilight, a dream-like dawn at midnight, and the gentle sighing of the waves whispered promises of the summer ahead.

It isn't really dark at all, was Ella's last thought before she fell asleep, her mind drifting away on a soft island moored in a sea of light.

She was awoken by the sound of someone – Christophe, she supposed – whistling the *Marseillaise* as he went downstairs and then being hushed by someone else – Caroline or Marianne, presumably.

A bright line of sunlight, straight as a rule, slanted in through the gap in the shutters, a golden replacement for the moon's silver beam the night before. She jumped out of bed and crossed the rag rug to pull open the heavy metal arm that held the shutters closed and threw them wide. A warm breeze enveloped her bare arms and made the fine lawn of her nightdress flutter around her ankles. Unimpeded now, the sun's rays flooded the room with sudden heat.

Ella pulled on a skirt and blouse, brushed her hair, and all but ran downstairs.

The French windows in the kitchen stood open again, as they had last night, and a stout, grey-haired lady wearing a white apron over skirts made of striped cotton ticking came in from the terrace, carrying an empty tray in one hand, her wooden clogs clacking on the terracotta tiles. '*Bonjour, mademoiselle. Enchantée.*' She shook Ella's hand formally, with a strong, work-roughened hand, but the broad smile never left her face. Caroline, following in her wake, introduced her as Sandrine, and then the lady turned to busy herself at the sink.

'Come, Ella, breakfast is on the terrace,' said Caroline, picking up a pair of broad-lipped pitchers from the kitchen table. As they emerged into the jasmine-shaded daylight, she announced, '*Voilà,* Ella and coffee.'

'There you are, my dear. Did you sleep?' Marianne passed Ella a basket of bread, as Caroline did the rounds, pouring treacle-dark coffee into small rounded bowls for each of them and topping up the rich-smelling brew with hot, creamy milk. More accustomed to a bowl of porridge and tea served in genteel cups and saucers, Ella paused, unsure how to proceed. She followed suit, gingerly, as Marianne picked up her bowl with both hands and sipped from it. The coffee was delicious and invigorating, as was eating breakfast outside in the heady sea air. Christophe tore his bread into chunks which he dipped into his coffee bowl, but Ella followed Caroline's example and spread hers thickly with white butter and cherry jam.

'So today we'll take you out in *Bijou*,' said Christophe, in between mouthfuls. 'Have you ever sailed before?'

She shook her head. 'Never.'

'Don't worry. She's a beauty, and easy to sail. We'll teach you.'

'I'm worried that you might spoil your pretty clothes though,' Marianne said, smiling kindly. 'Caroline, could you lend Ella something of yours? And we must get you a pair of *espadrilles* from the market this weekend. They are perfect for the beach and the boat.'

An hour later, Christophe nodded approvingly as he helped Ella climb into the little rowing dinghy which he held steady in the water against the side of a rough slip-way. Bare-footed, holding the sandals that she'd just slipped off, she took the hand he was holding out to her and stepped down into the small wooden tender that would ferry them out to where *Bijou*, a pretty daysailer, bobbed on her mooring. 'You look almost French in those clothes,' he said with a smile, only releasing her hand once she was safely settled on one of the wooden seats. She had changed into a loose navy blue top, striped with white, and a pair of cotton shorts that Caroline had lent her. Her hair was tied back from her face with a navy ribbon, which fluttered in the breeze.

Ella smiled back at him, her new outfit lending her a feeling of relaxed confidence. Speaking a different language, wearing different clothes and setting out on an altogether new experience all combined to heighten her new-found sensation of freedom; the liberty to be someone entirely other than her Edinburgh self.

Christophe reached up to take the picnic basket and a capacious, leather-handled straw bag full of towels and jumpers that Caroline was passing down to him. He helped his sister into the dinghy in her turn and then set the oars in the rowlocks, pushed off from the slip-way and turned the bow towards *Bijou*'s mooring.

Once on board the sailing boat, Ella felt awkward and clumsy. The other two busied themselves with easy assurance, readying the yacht and stowing the picnic in the tiny cabin below decks. *Bijou* really was a beautiful boat, her lines sleek and elegant, her deck made of oiled teak and the boards of her clinker-built flanks pristine under their coat of white paint.

'She's an original, there's no other boat exactly like her,' Christophe explained with some pride. '*Grand-père* had her specially built, ten years ago. *Maman* inherited her, along with the house, when he died. She's been coming to the Île de Ré since she was an infant. It was *Grand-père* who taught us all how to sail. But *Papa* doesn't really enjoy the sea, and *Maman* would rather spend her time tending to her beloved garden, so I'm looking after *Bijou* now.'

Caroline cast off from the mooring buoy and, as Christophe drew the tiller towards him, *Bijou* turned her bow towards the open sea and the wind caught her sails. They edged out slowly at first, picking their way between the other boats that were moored in the shelter of the harbour, until they were clear. Ella felt the wind pick up suddenly, making her hair-ribbon flutter against the nape of her neck.

Then, all at once, they were flying.

Sparkling wavelets, their crests speckled with white, rose up playfully before them, sending up a shower of fine sea-spray as *Bijou*'s bow ploughed through them. A kittiwake, white as blown cherry-blossom against the dizzying blue of the sky, soared on an updraught, its ink-tipped wings wide-spread, and Ella felt her heart soar with it, transported by the sense of exhilaration and pure, unadulterated joy that suddenly surged through her body. She tipped her head back to follow the gull's flight and then closed her eyes for a moment, letting the rays of the sun caress her face, all thoughts of sun-hats and freckles completely forgotten now.

Christophe steered them on a long reach that took them south from the island. Settling back against the transom of the boat, he nudged his sister. 'Look, Caroline, I think our guest is enjoying herself.'

Ella beamed back at the two of them. 'It's terrific! It feels as if we're flying through the water.'

Christophe nodded. 'I always think of it as a dance. The ocean is a formidable partner. Today, her mood is gay and upbeat – see, she's wearing sequins. We're dancing a quickstep. Some days she's gentler, more romantic, dressed in silk, and then it's a waltz. Occasionally, she can be moody though. When she dances a *paso doble* or a tango, full of anger and passion, we must be careful and use all *Bijou*'s skills to match her.'

Caroline laughed. 'And when she turns into a whirling dervish, when it's really blowing a gale, then we leave her to dance alone. She may be a dancer, but she's a powerful one. In this case, she is definitely the one who leads.'

'Get ready to tack,' ordered Christophe, shading his eyes with one hand.

Caroline loosened the jib sheet and motioned to Ella. 'When he says "ready about", we hunker down like this to let the boom swing across. You don't want to get hit on the head by it.'

Ella followed Caroline's lead, scrambling under the boom and across to the port side, and *Bijou* changed direction, pointing landward once more so that the low line of the island's dunes was ahead of them again. The sun's rays warmed Ella's back now, permeating the soft cotton of her top. Her skin glowed with the warmth and the wind and the exhilaration of the sea-spray that filled the air each time another wavelet rose up to meet *Bijou*'s prow.

Thinking about Caroline's words, Ella felt a shiver ripple through her, despite the sun's warmth. The sea was a benign, playful dance partner today, but the small wooden boat seemed suddenly vulnerable as it skimmed across the ocean. Beneath the sparkling surface, the water was mysterious and dark, fathoms deep with powerful, unseen currents.

How silly, she thought, to have such dark thoughts on a day like this. A day filled with sunlight and beauty and youth and freedom. The wind whipped a strand from her long ponytail across her mouth and she shook her head, to shake off both the hair and her thoughts. She stretched one arm out over the side of the boat, extending her fingers towards the waves' lacy caps, the spray cooling her skin until goose pimples, like grains of golden sand, formed over its smooth surface.

She turned to look back at the frothy white train left by their wake and caught Christophe's dark gaze fixed upon her. Like the ocean, his eyes seemed to have hidden depths, sparkling with inner light one moment, suddenly stormy the next. She felt her cheeks flush, but met his gaze steadily with her own. In that moment, she sensed something powerful between them, last night's moment of connection trans-forming itself into a surge as strong as the pull of the tide. She knew, instinctively, that there could be no point in trying to swim against it. Like a force of nature, it was something far beyond anything she'd experienced before, something she knew she would not have the power to fight even if she'd wanted to. And she discovered she didn't want to at all.

With a calmness that belied the turmoil she felt inside, she smiled at him and said, 'Do you think I really could learn to sail *Bijou*?'

For a long moment he made no reply, his eyes still fixed on her as though mesmerised. Finally, he shifted across on his seat, making space for her to slip in and take hold of the tiller. She was acutely conscious of his strong, brown arm behind her, helping to hold a steady course.

'Small movements, nothing sudden. She will respond to whatever you ask her to do. Try pushing it slightly away from you – yes, there, you see how she turns into the wind? And we lose a little speed? You need to play it a little, you will feel it when you catch the right spot. Where the wind catches the sails perfectly. Watch that ribbon against the canvas: you want it to blow straight rather than fluttering or flapping. That's it, good.'

An hour later, they sailed into a bay tucked into the sheltering arms of the dunes, and dropped anchor. Apart from an occasional fishing-boat chugging purposefully about its business in the distance, there was no one else in sight. *Bijou*, her sails loosely furled, bobbed quietly at the end of her anchor. The breeze seemed to have dropped now and the sun was high above them, almost directly atop the mast.

'Let's swim first and then we'll eat lunch.' Caroline was already pulling her top over her head to reveal her bathing-costume underneath. Christophe did likewise and, with a whoop, dived from the side of the boat, the line of his body long and lithe as it sliced into the surface of the water with scarcely a splash. Ella wished she'd had the foresight to put on her own bathing-costume beneath her borrowed clothes. She pulled it from the straw bag and stood awkwardly for a moment.

'You can go down below and change in the cabin.' Caroline showed her, and Ella clambered down. She changed quickly, and re-emerged moments later, tying the halter-neck of her own costume at the back. It was one of her purchases from Jenner's, white with yellow daisies, much prettier than the utilitarian navy-blue one that she had worn for her swimming lessons at the Warrender Baths.

She perched on the side of the boat and then swung her legs round so that they dangled over the water. Little waves rose playfully beneath her feet as if trying to catch her toes and pull her in. Whilst she had been one of the best swimmers in her class at school, she felt apprehensive now. There was a great deal more water both around and beneath her, for one thing. And no solid side within easy reach to cling to for a rest if needed. Where was Miss Campbell, the games mistress, when you needed her?

She swivelled round, taking firm hold of the side of *Bijou*, and lowered herself into the sea. Ella gasped as the chill water enveloped her sun-warmed body, but a moment later she felt nothing but a blissful coolness. She pushed off from the boat and tried a few tentative strokes. The salt water made her strangely buoyant and so, her confidence growing, she struck out towards Christophe and Caroline who were floating a little further out, watching her progress.

'It's heavenly!' she gasped, as she reached them and turned on to her back to float, as they were, looking back towards the land.

A slow smile dawned on her face as she realised what she was looking at. 'Why,' she exclaimed, 'it's the painting, isn't it? The one above my bed? I recognise the line of those dunes there and the way the beach curves back on itself.'

Christophe nodded, pleased. 'It is.'

'You have a good eye, Ella,' Caroline said, treading water. 'Have you studied art?'

'Only at school. But I enjoy visiting the galleries and exhibitions in Edinburgh.'

'Maybe you should think of pursuing it as a career, as I am going to do in Paris. I'm applying to several galleries and museums for a *stage* next year to learn about picture conservation.'

'I didn't know such a thing existed. I wish I had though, it sounds a lot more fun than the course at secretarial college that I'm going to be starting in the autumn. Mother thought it the most suitable qualification. With my French, I might even be able to get a position in the Diplomatic Service. I don't think I'm good enough at drawing to do anything in the art world though. I'm not sure what my parents would say if I told them I was contemplating a change of tack and a career in picture conservation! And you, Christophe, what will you do? Apart from becoming a famous artist, of course,' she teased. 'Are you going to work in a museum like Caroline?'

His eyes darkened, becoming unfathomable. '*Non*,' his answer was terse, a bitterness that she'd not heard before creeping into his voice. '*Papa* has decreed that art is something for girls to dabble in whilst they are waiting to be snapped up by some eligible man. I have to follow in his footsteps at the bank. It's already arranged. But anyway,' he continued, 'let's not spoil the day with such thoughts. Back to the boat for lunch. *Allons-y!*' and he set off in a fast crawl that made the girls squeal as he splashed them thoroughly, drenching their hair and dispelling the gravity of the moment.

They climbed back into *Bijou* over her stern, Christophe hauling himself effortlessly out of the water and then reaching back to extend a hand to each of them in turn. As Ella towel-dried her hair, Caroline and Christophe set out a picnic on the fore-deck from the wicker hamper. Suddenly, she discovered she was absolutely ravenous.

The three of them sat in contented silence in the shade of a makeshift awning that Christophe had rigged up over the boom, devouring golden-crusted bread spread thick with soft, pungent cheese and topped off with slices of the reddest, juiciest tomatoes she'd ever seen. Nothing had ever tasted so good, Ella thought.

They washed it all down with cool water from a stoppered earthenware bottle and then Caroline handed them each a sun-warmed peach, with sweet, white flesh so ripe that the juice trickled over Ella's chin and fingers.

Afterwards, they lay, sated, in the shade, drowsy with sunshine, sea air, the warmth of the afternoon and so much good food. Ella gazed up into the impossible blue of the sky, one arm shielding her eyes against the light, listening to the sound of the waves murmuring quietly against *Bijou*'s hull. She felt the little boat rocking gently beneath her and closed her eyes for just a moment . . .

She had no idea how long she'd slept, but the sun's angle had changed and *Bijou* had swung a little at the end of her anchor so that a ray of light was creeping in beneath the awning, illuminating the strands of hair – still just a little damp from their swim – that fell across one shoulder and twined themselves across the daisies on her costume. She licked her lips, tasting the tang of salt, and turned her head to find the others. Caroline was sleeping too, curled on her side, breathing softly. Christophe sat with his knees bent up, intent upon the sketch-book that he rested against them. His pencil moved rapidly, whispering across the rough paper, drawing lines that were swift and sure. He glanced up and his dark eyes met hers again. He looked startled, as if he had been lost elsewhere while the girls slept, and her awakening had brought him back to the real world with a jerk. Wordlessly, she smiled, bringing one finger to her lips with a glance towards Caroline, and he nodded, smiling back. She held out one hand, silently asking him to pass her the sketch-book. He flushed and shook his head, closing the book's board cover, but she insisted, her hand still extended, her eyes refusing to leave his. Reluctantly, he handed it over and she held the little book above her face as she began to turn the pages.

The first sketches were of scenes from the island: a sea-scape with dunes and sea-grasses in the foreground; a row of fishermen's cottages with hollyhocks clustered against the white walls; the orchard at the back of the house, with Anaïs cropping the grass beneath the trees; Christophe's sister and mother sitting on the terrace, Caroline deep in a book, his mother intent on a piece of sewing in her lap. But then she turned a page and found a sketch of a young girl, standing on a jetty, with one hand holding her wide-brimmed hat on her head, her skirts blown by a sea-breeze. And on each page that followed was another sketch of Ella. Some were just a few simple pencil lines which caught a gesture or expression that she recognised as her own.

Others were more detailed where he had evidently spent time working on them.

The final drawing in the book was of her asleep just now, the crook of one arm covering her eyes, her fingers curling open in a gesture of abandonment, innocent and trusting, and so tenderly drawn that it made her catch her breath.

Caroline stirred, waking, and Ella quickly closed the book and handed it back to Christophe. He stood, stretching the cramp out of his legs, and then prodded his sister with his bare toes. 'Come on, you two sleepy-heads. It's time we headed for home.' And with that he busied himself, unfurling the sails and making ready the boat, his movements followed with thoughtful distraction by Ella's wide-eyed gaze, as she absorbed the truth and the beauty of what she'd just seen.

2014, Edinburgh

'Are you sure you're warm enough, Granny?' I arrange the fine woollen shawl around Ella's shoulders before sitting down on the bench beside her.

'I'm fine. Stop fussing, Kendra! This is just lovely, what a good idea.'

On this autumn afternoon there's still a little gentle warmth in the air and the sky is a surprising deep blue. The yellow-brown leaves that remain on the trees are perfectly still on this rare, wind-free day. I was the one to suggest we venture out into the nursing home's garden for once, rather than staying inside in the stifling cocoon of Ella's room, a suggestion which evinced a surprised smile from the receptionist as she dug in a drawer for the key to unlock the back door, but one which Ella accepted with alacrity. We sit with our backs to the grey stone wall that encloses the patch of neatly trimmed lawn and the angular rose beds where one or two late blooms cling on doggedly and raise our faces to the low-angled sunlight.

Ella sighs with pleasure. 'What a treat. Somehow it seems all the more precious when one knows it won't last much longer.'

I'm not sure whether she's referring to the fact that winter's just around the corner or whether it's something more final that's on her mind. I take her hand in mine, meaning to comfort her, but finding that the touch of her gnarled, age-worn fingers gives me reassurance instead. There's a lump in my throat, all of a sudden, and I'm not sure whether it has more to do with the thought of losing my grandmother or the kindness of her touch. Now I come to think of it, I can't remember the last time Dan and I held hands or touched each other with anything more than a perfunctory peck on the cheek in passing. Her touch reminds me, too, of how I long to be able to hold Finn's hand in mine; what it would mean to be able to give him that reassurance of love and support. I swallow hard and squeeze Ella's hand gently in return.

She smiles, looking down at our clasped fingers. 'Look at your lovely smooth skin, so unlike mine. These awful age-spots. All that sunshine takes its toll over a lifetime. But, oh, it is so wonderful to feel it again!'

She closes her eyes, and I wonder whether the sensation of the sun's warmth on her face transports her back to those heady days of her first summer on the Île de Ré.

As if she can read my mind, she says, 'How is the writing coming along?'

'Well, I think. Would you like me to bring it with me next time and read you what I've written so far?'

She releases my hand with a soft pat and rearranges a fold of the shawl. 'No, I trust you. And I want you to write the story your way. You can read the whole thing to me once it's finished. But feel free to ask me any questions. Some of my memories are a bit sketchy these days so I may have missed things out when I've been rambling into that machine.'

I shake my head. Her recordings are coherent and fluent, making it easy to weave the threads of her story; and the photos help me to picture it all just as it must have been. In fact, her words on the tapes come across as stronger and more confident than her usual speaking voice, making her memories seem more real, more firmly rooted in her mind, than her life today.

Closing her eyes again, Ella speaks softly now. 'Sometimes it takes time to get to know people – and some we can never really know. But others you can know in a heartbeat. That's how it was with Christophe and Caroline. I suppose innocence helps . . . childhood friends, first loves. Life gets a lot more complicated as it goes along. But it was life itself that I fell in love with that summer, Kendra, not just the island and the Martet family, but all the possibilities and the hope that that awakening brought with it. It opened my eyes to what life could be.' She glances at me, a look that is penetrating, as if she can see beneath the surface and into my soul. 'Have you ever felt that way?'

In the clear autumn sunlight, her eyes are a vivid green flecked with gold. *Just like Finn's*, I think, and I know that she glimpses the sadness that flickers across my own face before I can disguise it beneath another smile.

'When I first met Dan, yes. I'd had a few boyfriends before him, but no one special. But when I met him I knew. In a heartbeat, like you said. And we were both full of the confidence and hope of youth then too. But, like you say, life happens. The hope gets buried under all the other stuff that comes along. And the confidence gets eaten away . . .' I tail off, my throat constricting again suddenly. I don't often admit to anyone – least of all myself – just how difficult things are at the moment.

We sit in silence for a moment. And then Ella takes my hand again, giving it a squeeze. 'Never lose hope, Kendra. Even when everything else is gone. Life without hope is a living death. Hope is what makes us human. Without it, we are in danger of losing touch with what it is to be alive.'

I nod. 'But sometimes it's just easier not to. Hope hurts.'

She glances at me again, with that deep green gaze of hers. 'I know it can do. But in my experience, when you've lost so much, feeling that pain just might be better than feeling nothing at all.'

Her words – and her look of profound sadness as she utters them – make me think again of her estrangement from my mother. Does Ella still hope for a reconciliation? Before it's too late? Writing her story seems to be linked to that somehow, although I still don't know how or why. But maybe the act of sharing it with me and of knowing it will be there on paper after she's gone gives her hope of some sort too. At the very least, perhaps it gives her a sense of purpose – or is she simply doing this as a way of trying to encourage me to heave myself out of the rut I've found myself in? I thought I was supporting her in coming to visit, but I have the distinct impression that I am gaining far more than I'm giving . . .

The last rays of sunlight slip down behind the wall and the shadow that has been creeping across the grass towards us veils Ella's face. She shivers slightly. 'Come on, that was nice while it lasted, but it's time we went in now.'

I help her to her feet and offer her an arm as we walk back towards the door. 'I'll see you back to your room. It's nearly supper time anyway.'

'Thank you, Kendra. For the fresh air as well as for coming to see me. I have another tape for you. Oh, and I found some more of Caroline's letters that you might like as well.' As we reach the back door, she pauses and turns to look back at the deepening shadows where one or two white roses glimmer. 'Do you think Finn would like this garden?' she asks. 'You could bring him with you sometime perhaps?'

'If the weather is good he might. He loves going to the allotment with his dad. But he needs to be introduced to new places gently . . . Anything unfamiliar makes him panic. We'll have to see.' I know he'd hate the nursing home, with its strange smells and narrow corridors and unknown people, all of which he'd find terrifying.

Ella doesn't push it. But she smiles as she says, gently, 'Well, I hope I'll see him again sometime.'

1938, Île de Ré

Day after day, Ella settled into the easy rhythm of summer on the Île de Ré. When they weren't sailing off the island's sand-soft beaches, they were criss-crossing its dusty roads on bikes, until the landscape of salt-pans and sand-dunes felt more familiar to her than her home and her life in Edinburgh.

The steeple of the church in Sainte Marie beckoned them homewards from their outings on land and sea, pointing skywards amongst lush green vineyards and golden cornfields inlaid with swathes of scarlet poppies. The watercolour wash of sea and sky imprinted itself on her very being, honing and refining her eye for beauty. She loved it all, from the white fisherman's cottages to the vast citadel by the beachfront in St Martin; from the spires of hollyhocks that spilled into the narrow cobbled lanes in the villages to the tapestry of wildflowers – scabious and cornflowers, Queen Anne's lace and sea-holly – which lined the lanes; from the oyster beds to the salt-marshes, where the precious white drifts of finest *fleur de sel* were raked into heaps to bleach in the sunshine and where the little shaggy donkeys, Anaïs's kin, that worked the salt-pans wore curious striped leggings to protect them from the scouring salt and the biting flies, giving them a sweet, clown-like air.

Cycling through La Flotte one day, they passed a *préventorium* where children lay on ranks of canvas stretchers in the sun, presided over by a stern-looking matron in a starched cap and apron. 'They come here to benefit from the island's healthy climate,' Caroline explained. 'Some may be recovering from tuberculosis, others from anaemia. The sunshine and sea air is the very best cure there is.' The three waved as they cycled onwards and the children cheered, before being hushed by their disapproving nurse. And Ella felt sure that those children could be in no better place to regain their strength: she herself glowed with well-being, her hair bleached blonde and her skin tanned golden by the wind and sun that were constant companions on their outings.

News from the world beyond the island was intermittent: the occasional letter arrived from Ella's mother, enquiring how her French was progressing and giving news of her parents' annual visit to Fife for the golf and the bracing walks on the beach at Elie; and sometimes, in the hallway, the muffled sound of the radiogram could be heard from the drawing-room, to where Marianne retreated from working in the garden, to escape the heat of the afternoon. When Caroline asked her mother what news there was from Paris, Marianne would shake her head and smile a smile that never quite transformed the sadness in her dark eyes. 'More of the usual craziness,' she once remarked.

But their days were carefree: sailing in *Bijou*, picnicking on the beach or exploring the island on three slightly rusty bicycles. It was as though the slender stretch of water separating them from the mainland were an impenetrable barrier, one which nothing from the outside world could cross.

Christophe, Caroline and Ella were inseparable, spending every waking moment together. And whilst the powerful bond between Ella and Christophe continued to draw them together, Caroline was always there too, a welcome member of the trio with her air of gentle calmness and her steady loyalty to them both, chaperoning them unobtrusively on their outings.

Sitting in the dunes beyond the house one day, she put into words what each of them had sensed. 'It's funny, before you came, Ella, I always felt that Christophe and I made up two halves of a whole. But now I realise that you were missing from us, and I can't imagine life without you in it.'

Ella nodded, her oval face solemn. 'I feel the same way. I don't even want to think about how it'll feel to leave you at the end of the summer. Promise me you'll write, both of you? And I promise I'll write back to you in Paris when I'm home in Edinburgh.'

They hatched plans, for the twins to come and visit her in Scotland sometime, and for Ella to come back again next summer. 'And all our summers for evermore,' declared Caroline, drawing a heart-shape in the sand at their feet. She wrote their three names inside it, in a circle. 'There, look I've made a magic spell, so it will come true.' She turned to Christophe, her eyes shining suddenly. 'I know, Ella must come and stay in Paris next year. We'll actually be spending most of the summer in the city anyway once we both start work – sadly, there'll be no more lovely long holidays for a while. We can show you the city and you can keep improving your French – although you are pretty much fluent now already. Perhaps you might even decide you like it enough to contemplate working there once you have completed your secretarial course.' She jumped up, dusting sand from her shorts. 'I'm going to go and tell *Maman* to write to your mother immediately, inviting you. Then we'll have that to look forward to already.'

Christophe rolled on to his stomach and smiled his long, slow smile at Ella. They were rarely alone like this, just the two of them, and she felt suddenly self-conscious.

'Will you come and visit us, Ella? It would make returning to Paris almost bearable if you promise you will.'

With the sharp edge of a razor shell that she was holding, she retraced the outline of the heart Caroline had drawn. The wind was already catching a few of the grains of loose sand, softening and blurring the letters of their names, reclaiming the beach as its own.

For a moment, at the sight of those names fading away, she felt an upwelling of emotion so strong it made her throat constrict, making it impossible to speak. As if unable to help himself, Christophe reached out and traced the line of her jaw with his finger. She raised her eyes to his, then took his hand in hers, stroking the skin across the back of it in her turn, where it was brown and smooth.

Finally, she smiled. 'I promise.'

All at once, it was the last full weekend of their summer on the island. This time next week they'd have packed up and be setting off on the journey back across the water to their real lives, in the real world.

The August heat was oppressive today, the usual breeze from the ocean having died away for once, leaving the air still and heavy. A dark cloud-bank, thick with foreboding, was gathering out at sea.

Ella sensed a change in the atmosphere around the breakfast table that had nothing to do with the change in the weather. The twins' father was arriving later on that day, and it seemed that the prospect had made Christophe's mood equally brooding. Monsieur Martet would be joining them on the island for the final week of the holidays, his work at the bank having kept him in Paris during the rest of the summer. Marianne and Caroline, whilst not as evidently morose as Christophe, seemed strained as well, talking just a little too brightly of the plans for the coming days while Monsieur Martet was there. The week would culminate with the social event of the season, a *soirée dansante* at the former Governor's house in Saint Martin to raise funds for the charitable *préventorium* it had now become. Marianne wanted to check that each of them had something suitable to wear.

'But Christophe, I asked you to pack just one suit. You know it means so much to *Papa* to go to the ball. It's for a very good cause, and so many of his business associates will be there.'

'But why do *I* have to go? None of *Papa's* business associates will want to talk to me. It's so stuffy and formal. And it'll be our last night on the island, so why can't we choose to spend it as we wish?'

'You know that this year, of all years, it's important that you attend. You'll be joining the bank in a few weeks' time and those business associates will be useful connections for you to have made. They will expect to see you there with your family. Please, Christophe, for all our sakes, don't upset *Papa* on the day of his arrival. He has so few days of holiday anyway, let's make sure the week is a pleasant one . . .

'Now,' Marianne continued, her tone firm, brooking no further argument, 'I'm sure there's an old suit of yours hanging in the *armoire* in my bedroom. I think you probably left it here last summer. I may be able to let the trousers down a little. Hopefully, we can get away with it. You can borrow a shirt and cravat from *Papa*.'

'I will look ridiculous, dressed up like a performing monkey!'

'Well, if you do look ridiculous then that will be entirely your own fault,' his mother retorted, exasperated.

From out over the ocean, a low rumble of thunder rolled in, soft but threatening.

'Damn this weather!' Christophe's frustration spilled over and he tore angrily at the *brioche* on his plate, reducing it to a heap of crumbs. 'We can't even go out for a sail today.'

'Why don't you take the bicycles and a picnic and go to the lighthouse? I don't think you've seen it yet, have you, Ella?'

'Not from dry land. We've glimpsed it in the distance from *Bijou*. It would be interesting to climb to the top and get a different view of the island.' Ella seized the opportunity Marianne had created to change the subject, trying to divert Christophe from his ill humour.

They returned late, hot and tired from their lengthy cycle ride, pedalling hard on the journey home, through air that felt, to Ella, as thick as porridge. As they wheeled their bikes around to the back of the house, the smell of cigar smoke met them on the evening air, overpowering the usual evening scents of honeysuckle and jasmine. Monsieur Martet stood on the terrace, formal in his dark suit, an ambassador from the real world, and it seemed to Ella that he had invaded their island idyll, unwittingly bringing with him unwelcome reminders of the world outside.

He turned to survey them, but made no move towards them, preferring to wait while they leaned their bikes up against the wall of the small outbuilding which housed Anaïs's cart, the oars for *Bijou*'s tender and a few gardening implements. Under his silent gaze, Ella felt dishevelled and unkempt as she approached the terrace. Nervously, she wiped her dusty hands on the sides of her shorts and then tucked her hair behind her ears in an attempt to make herself a little more presentable. She wished she had been more formally attired for her first encounter with the twins' father.

Caroline reached him first and stood on tiptoes to kiss him on either cheek. Christophe stood off to one side, awkward and aloof, as his sister made the introductions. '*Papa*, this is Ella.'

Monsieur Martet extended a hand and shook her rather damp one. '*Je suis ravi de faire votre connaissance, Mademoiselle Ella.*' She noted that he addressed her using the more formal '*vous*'; and yet, at the same time, when he smiled his eyes crinkled in a not unfriendly manner. In fact, she thought, he looked more tired than severe at close quarters.

Marianne appeared from the house behind him. '*Oh là là*, you are so late back. I wondered whether you'd cycled right off the end of the island and into the sea! Go and clean yourselves up for dinner. But before you do, you'd better put those bicycles inside. It looks as though we may be in for a storm tonight.'

As if in agreement, a flicker of lightning licked the sea beyond the dunes, quick as a viper's tongue, followed a few seconds later by a growl of thunder that seemed to make the sultry evening air tremble.

They ate dinner outside. 'Let's risk it,' Marianne had said, 'and if the storm arrives we will pick up our plates and make a run for it.' Darkness fell, but brought with it none of the customary coolness that Ella had come to expect. If anything, the air seemed to grow hotter and heavier, and she found she had little appetite for her plate of *bar au beurre blanc*.

'What news is there of cousin Agnès?' Caroline broke the heavy silence that pressed in on them, adding to the weight of the sultry night air.

Monsieur Martet shook his head, wiping his moustache with his napkin. 'Nothing more yet. As you know, the French authorities have all but closed the border now. It's so much harder for refugees to enter the country. But I am still writing letters and am confident that, through some of my contacts at the bank, we will succeed in getting the family to Paris.' He patted his wife's hand consolingly.

Caroline turned to Ella to explain: '*Maman*'s cousins from Austria are coming to stay with us for a while. Things in their home country are very difficult now that it is a part of Germany. So they are planning on moving to France.'

Christophe helped himself to another potato from the plate in the middle of the table. 'It's so tedious. Cousin Agnès is completely neurotic and her husband is a bore.'

'Well it's only until they find a place of their own in Paris. Anyway, the children are very sweet, no matter how annoying their parents may be,' retorted his sister.

'And, in any case, you'll be out at work for most of the time.' His father's words fell heavily on to the table, silencing them all once again.

Tentatively, to try to change the subject, Ella ventured, 'I wish I'd been able to see the World Fair when it was in Paris last year. Did you all visit the *Exposition*? Was it really as magnificent as they say?'

Monsieur Martet dabbed at his moustache again with his napkin before replying. 'It was impressive alright. But what a ridiculous edifice the Germans constructed! It sat next to the Eiffel Tower as though trying to dwarf it, in a face-off with the Russian pavilion. Some people thought it elegant and *moderne*,' – he pronounced the word with disdain – 'but I find that grand Nazi architecture inhuman, both in scale and in atmosphere. It was certainly a show of strength, which is what they intended, I suppose.'

'We visited the Spanish pavilion,' Christophe chipped in eagerly. 'There was a painting in it by Pablo Picasso, which was utterly revolutionary.'

His father shook his head. 'I thought it was awful. It hardly made sense, all angles and barbarism. And I don't see the point in representing something so horrible in a work of art. A brutal massacre in the Spanish Civil War is hardly a pleasant topic to gaze at.'

Christophe retorted. 'Surely the point of art is to be able to tell a story when words are not enough? And Monsieur Picasso certainly does so with *Guernica*.'

A long, low rumble of thunder made the glasses on the table rattle, and Marianne glanced up at the sky apprehensively, raising a hand. 'Was that a spot of rain?'

Ignoring his wife, the look Monsieur Martet gave his son was reproving. He sighed. 'We've been over this before. A little less time spent thinking about art and a little more reading the business papers would stand you in good stead, *mon fils*. Your desk awaits you at the bank. Come the autumn, you won't have time to think about anything other than your career. It's time you put away your sketch-books and concentrated on more worthwhile pursuits.'

Christophe drew a sharp breath, about to argue back. But suddenly there was an almighty flash and, almost simultaneously, a thunder-crack that made them all jump. Ella spilt the glass of water she'd been holding, dampening the skirt of her dress, and as she tried to dab at it with her napkin she realised more spots were appearing alongside it as fat raindrops began to fall.

'*Vite!* Inside!' Marianne began gathering up plates and the rest followed suit, rushing to escape the downpour which had begun as suddenly as the turning-on of a tap.

As Ella lay in her bed that night, listening to the thunder and the drumming of the rain, which drowned out the roar of the ocean beyond the dunes, a kaleidoscope of thoughts whirled in her head. The summer was drawing to an end. But how could she return to the chill, austere greyness of Edinburgh with its soot-encrusted buildings, where the autumn leaves would already be beginning to fall? All at once, she couldn't bear the thought of being incarcerated in a fusty room in front of a typewriter. And who would she be when she got back there? Certainly not the same Ella Lennox who had set off from Waverley Station all those weeks before.

At the thought of leaving Christophe, her heart constricted with pain that her slight frame could hardly contain. They'd never really kissed, other than the chaste pecks on the cheeks that the French exchanged simply by way of saying hello. There seemed to be an unspoken promise between them – that tidal flow pulling them inexorably towards one another. And when he'd run his finger along the line of her face that day on the beach, she'd felt a jolt of electricity pass between them, as powerful as a lightning bolt.

She kicked back the thin cotton sheet, her limbs hot and heavy in the storm-filled air.

It seemed impossible to leave. And yet she knew it was impossible to stay. This summer had changed everything, and the safe, certain future that had been mapped out for Ella in Edinburgh had gone with the wind that blew in across the Atlantic, making the sea-grass in the dunes sway and dance.

'Think about Paris next summer . . . just that and nothing else . . . we *will* be together again . . .'

The storm seemed to be weakening and, finally, she fell into a hot, restless sleep, tossed on a sea of troubled dreams.

'Come on, Christophe! Benoît is here!' Caroline was hopping with excitement, watching at the front door for Sandrine's husband, who would hail them occasionally from his fishing-boat, while tending his lobster pots when they were out sailing in *Bijou*; but this evening, at Monsieur Martet's request, he had hired one of the island's new rental cars from the local garage and was driving them to the ball. 'Oh, Ella, you look beautiful!'

'Thank you. So do you, Caroline.' The full skirts of the girls' evening gowns swished about their ankles, emphasising their slender waists as they twirled one another in the narrow hallway, their feet already tracing a few dance steps while they waited impatiently for the party to assemble. Caroline's dress was a deep coral silk and she had tamed her unruly curls with a pair of tortoiseshell combs. Ella's frock, in pale *eau-de-nil* satin, brought out the gold flecks in her eyes – or perhaps it was just the anticipation of the *soirée* ahead and the chance to dance in Christophe's arms that made them shine so.

The girls posed, arm in arm, as Monsieur Martet took their photograph with his latest acquisition, a brand new Leica camera that was able to capture pictures in colour.

'*Papa*, we must get a copy made for Ella so that I can send it to her when we get back to Paris,' declared Caroline.

Her father, dashing in his white tie and tails, looked a little more relaxed after his week on the island, and his greying hair contrasted with his face, which was sun-tanned now. But Ella couldn't help noticing how, as he watched the two girls chatter and laugh in their party finery, his eyes grew sad. Twenty years before, he had witnessed the horrors of a war, the like of which he'd hoped the world would never experience again. She knew that he had seen enough of the darkness of war to know that moments of light and beauty should be treasured; so now he seemed to be engraving this one on his memory, like the photograph he had just captured with his camera, storing it away against the threat of darker times to come.

As the church bell in Sainte Marie could be heard chiming seven o'clock, Ella watched as Marianne descended the stairs with regal grace and, pulling himself together, her husband helped her on with the gold lace cape, which matched her flowing evening gown. With infinite tenderness, he drew aside one of the tendrils of her dark hair, which had escaped from the *chignon* at her neck, and then bent to kiss the pale skin which lay beneath it. Saying, 'Come, my beautiful wife, your carriage awaits,' he offered her his hand.

Picking up their long skirts, Marianne, Caroline and Ella made their way down the sandy path to where Benoît waited.

'Come *on*, Christophe!' Caroline called again, more impatiently this time, glancing back over one shoulder.

Finally, a thundering on the stair heralded the precipitous arrival of her brother. He wore a dark suit, which Marianne had altered so that it fitted him well enough for the evening, but his feet were bare and his shirt was open at the neck. In one hand he carried a pair of black leather shoes and in the other a tie and collar studs. He scrambled in beside the girls and began assembling the final parts of his outfit.

'Sorry,' he mumbled, fumbling to fit the studs into their fiddly openings. 'I just lost track of time.'

His father frowned.

Marianne took the final stud from him and deftly fastened the wayward shirt-collar, then ran her fingers fondly through her son's hair to tidy it a little where it fell over his eyes. 'There. Now tie your shoelaces before you trip over them and go flying across the dance floor.'

As they drove through the sturdy fortifications that surrounded the town and into the narrow streets of St Martin, the sun lay low in the sky, casting long shadows from the clustered buildings of the port. The late August air was warm and in the silver-blue evening sky above them, swifts darted and whirled in their never-ending summer flight.

They pulled up before a set of handsome gates, through which other elegantly clad guests were hurrying into the grounds of the *Palais des Gouverneurs*. Ella shook out the folds of her dress, smoothing the delicate green satin and at the same time trying to calm her excitement.

Monsieur Martet took his wife's arm to lead her up the avenue to where the doors of the mansion stood open. Parodying the grown-ups' formality, Christophe offered an arm to each of the girls, which they took, laughing at his mock pomposity, and joined the procession of arriving guests.

The white walls of the former Governor's Palace were offset by dark yew hedges, clipped with precision into geometric topiary, but the formality of the gardens was softened with drifts of lavender and marguerites, whose pale flowers stirred in the evening's breeze. The building had been sold off by the state some years before, and had been bought by a wealthy family from Champagne, who funded a summer camp here for city children from poor backgrounds whose health benefited hugely from a few weeks' sea air and sunshine. Its young guests having been returned to their homes now, the building lent itself to one final end-of-season party, the price of the tickets helping to raise funds for the next year's camp.

Inside, the mansion's tall windows stood open, to allow the evening air to breathe some coolness into the high-ceilinged ballroom, where a string quartet's soft strains were in danger of being drowned out by the rising hubbub of chatter as the guests assembled.

Waiters circulated with trays of champagne *coupes*, whose sparkling contents only served to raise the volume of the laughter still further until it reverberated from the intricate cornicing high above their heads.

Ella leant close to Caroline, straining to make out what she was saying as she pointed out various faces in the crowd whom they knew from Paris. Christophe stifled a yawn. '*Ah, oui, le Tout-Paris*. Why do we have to waste our precious final evening talking to them here when we're all about to go back to the city where we'll be seeing them in any case?'

Marianne materialised at his side, just as he was reaching for another glass of champagne from a passing waiter. 'Put that back, Christophe.

I'm sure I've counted you drinking at least two already. *Papa* wants you to come and meet one of the directors of the bank. *Allons-y!*' She took his hand firmly in hers and threaded her way back through the throng with her son following meekly in her wake.

Ella gazed about the room, taking in the sumptuous arrangements of white lilies that flanked the great stone fireplace at one end, beyond which could be glimpsed a long table, draped with snowy linen, laden with vast platters of oysters.

'So much plenty,' she thought, 'after all those years of austerity. On a night like this, it's hard to believe the world could ever know want again.'

Caroline nudged her. 'Why so serious?'

She laughed, shaking her head. 'It's nothing. When do you think the dancing will begin?'

'Soon. We will listen to the Director of the *préventorium* making his speech and then, once the proper formalities have been observed, the band can strike up . . .'

Just then, as if on cue, the musicians in the corner fell silent and a ripple of applause spread through the room as their hosts took centre stage and began to welcome their guests.

Ella was gratified to note that she could understand almost every word of the Director's speech. Her summer on the island had certainly paid off. By next year she should have passed her secretarial diploma. Perhaps she really could try to find work in Paris, find suitable lodgings, somewhere near Caroline and Christophe. She pictured herself walking briskly through Parisian streets, wearing an elegant *couture* suit, high heels clipping the pavements as she made her way to an important meeting at some embassy or other. She felt a flicker of doubt as she wondered how her parents would greet this suggestion. But that bridge would just have to be crossed once she got back to Edinburgh.

Ella's attention was brought back to the room by another ripple of applause and she realised that the Director had finished his speech. The ballroom cleared as guests surged towards the buffet of food and out on to the terrace beyond, where little tables had been set for the partygoers to enjoy their supper, washing it down with yet more champagne.

The musicians reassembled, joined by an accordionist, and they struck up a waltz. Suddenly, Christophe appeared at Ella's side and he slipped a hand around her waist. 'Let's dance,' he said, 'now, while everyone else is busy filling their plates and we have the floor to ourselves.'

He led her to the centre of the room and, with the scent of lilies mingling with the warm sea-breeze, the two of them floated across the floor in a private dance all of their own. The musicians smiled at one another and played with renewed feeling, moved by the sight of such youthful beauty and grace, and the pure tenderness with which Christophe smiled as he lost himself in Ella's gaze.

'Your eyes are viridian, the colour of the ocean out beyond the point where it deepens suddenly,' he whispered, for only Ella to hear. 'Sea-green, flecked with golden sunlight. I would gladly drown myself in them if it meant we could dance like this for evermore.'

She smiled and squeezed his shoulder with the fingers that rested there, and he pulled her a little closer as they waltzed on.

The evening passed all too fast for Ella, intoxicated as she was on happiness, love and a single glass of champagne.

Christophe danced with his sister and his mother, and Monsieur Martet gallantly escorted Ella around the dance-floor in a neatly executed fox-trot, but the whole evening she was aware that Christophe was never far from her and that he reappeared at her side at every available opportunity to dance with her again.

At last the throng of guests began to thin, and Monsieur Martet, consulting his pocket watch, declared it was time to leave.

They were quiet on the drive home, each lost in their own thoughts; memories of the evening, perhaps, and the final plans for packing up for the return to Paris the next day.

'Goodnight, goodnight, and thank you for a wonderful evening.' Ella kissed Monsieur and Madame Martet at the foot of the stairs and then glanced about, looking for Christophe so that she could bid him goodnight as well. He was nowhere to be seen, so she climbed, on dance-weary legs, to her bedroom.

She slipped off her shoes with relief, her feet having grown unaccustomed to being so constrained after a summer spent either running barefoot or wearing her soft canvas *espadrilles*. Still in her evening gown, she picked up her hairbrush and began to smooth the waves out of her hair, which was streaked with pale highlights now after her weeks in the sun.

A rattling sound at the window made her pause and set down her brush. Again, there was a soft clatter against the wood of the shutters, as if someone was throwing pebbles. She pushed them open and looked out. Down below, in the moon's pale light, Christophe gazed up at her. He held a finger to his lips and then beckoned to her.

Barefoot, she gathered up the skirts of her dress and tiptoed back downstairs. At the door, he caught her hand in his, his eyes shining in the moonlight.

'It's our last night, and far too beautiful a one to be asleep in bed. Come to the beach with me!'

Hand in hand, they ran along the sandy path, picking their way through the dunes, to the beach where the dark waves sighed as they cast themselves on to the silver sand.

The moon was full and it lit the ocean with a path of light that shimmered from the far horizon to where the waves bathed their feet on the shore. 'Look, she's wearing a sash of white silk tonight,' Ella pointed. 'I feel as if we could step out on to it and dance with her all the way to the other side of the world.'

'I wish we could,' murmured Christophe. 'But I'd rather dance with you instead.'

He held out his arms and she stepped into them, letting fall her satin skirt and not caring that the hem trailed on the damp sand and would surely be ruined by the sea-water. They waltzed in the moonlight, serenaded by the hush of the waves and the occasional fluting cry of a curlew, Ella's head resting on Christophe's shoulder.

When they finally came to a stand-still, he bent down and picked something up from the sand at their feet.

'For you,' he said, handing it to her. The moon's rays picked out the finely etched lines on the white shell in the palm of her hand, a clam-shell whose two halves were still held together by their central hinge.

They wandered back up the beach on to the drier sand alongside the dunes and sat down. Christophe took off his jacket and draped it over Ella's shoulders, and she rested against him, his arms around her as he leaned back on to the flank of the dune. His voice was soft, shushed by the waves as they washed on to the sand below them. 'What is it about you, Ella-from-*Edimbourg*? Why is it that you make me feel this way? As if, at last, I can see that there is light in the darkness after all. Maybe, even, that my calling in life is to be something more than just a clerk in a bank. You make me believe that I should fight harder for the things I am so passionate about.'

She nodded, her head cradled in the dip between his shoulder and his heart. 'I feel it too. This summer has made me wake up and open my eyes to all the possibility that there is in this world. Made me realise that I want to live a bigger life than the one I'd imagined up until now . . . up until I came here . . . until I met you.'

Her eyes shone in the moonlight as she tilted her face upwards and they kissed. The softness of his mouth against hers made her head spin and she felt, suddenly, as though they were soaring out over the moonlit ocean, like sea-birds in flight.

The sea-grass whispered as the night breeze brushed through it, and Ella opened her hand to inspect the shell he'd given her again.

Christophe touched it gently, turning it over so that the smooth inner surfaces of the shell's two halves were face up.

'My mother calls these "Neptune's lockets". You see, it is just like a locket you would wear around your neck. I wish I could give you a silver one and then we could put our two likenesses in it and you could keep us together that way, even when we're apart.'

'Neptune's locket. I like that.' Ella nodded. 'I shall treasure this one just as though it were made of silver.'

He wound a tendril of her hair around his finger, stroking its silk-smoothness with his thumb.

'I've just realised who it is you remind me of!' he exclaimed suddenly. 'From the first moment I saw you on the jetty all those weeks ago it's been bothering me, something just beyond the reach of my memory that you bear such a likeness to, a quality I've been searching for in every sketch I've drawn of you . . . And now I've remembered. It's a painting by Botticelli. *The Birth of Venus*. Have you seen it? The young goddess, born of sea foam, is standing on a shell like this one, being blown on to the shore of a magical island. Just as you were blown here, to the Île de Ré, across the water so that we would find each other. You are my Venus, and one day I will paint a picture of you, just as Botticelli did, a picture that will make people understand that all that really matters on heaven and earth is beauty.'

She smiled. And then lifted her face to his in the moonlight and kissed him again, sealing their hearts together so that, like the shell which she clasped in one hand, they became two halves of a perfect whole.

2014, Edinburgh

It's been a good day today: a day without tantrums and screaming; a day without Finn's terrified withdrawal from a world that makes no sense to him, which leaves him tearing at his hair and clawing at his face in a panic, drawing blood sometimes. A normal day, almost, for most other people, but for us, days like this are so few and far between that they become the remarkable ones.

Dan's found a community project, which he heard about from someone at the allotments one day when he and Finn were working there. It's council-funded, based on a patch of derelict land just outside the city, building a garden for children with special needs.

'Finn's always so much calmer when we're outdoors,' Dan enthused as we sat at the kitchen table eating our spaghetti bolognese this evening. 'Digging and planting seem to steady him; they seem to be activities that make sense, that he can understand. Perhaps working with the earth roots him as well as the plants.'

It's late now. I'm shuffling through some more of Ella's letters, as Dan finishes drying the spaghetti pan, wiping his hands on the teatowel before hanging it over the handle of the oven door.

Beside him, on the kitchen-dresser, alongside a bunch of keys and a pile of bills, there's a framed photo of my mother with me and Finn shortly after he was born. We'd brought him home from the hospital and within days I was at my wits' end, trying to get him to eat and sleep.

It all sounded so simple and logical in the baby books I'd bought, so why couldn't I do it? Why did my tiny son scream with pain and rage when I brought him to my breast? Why couldn't I console him and settle him with my hugs and songs and hours and hours of walking up and down with him held on my shoulder as I gently patted his back? Mum came up on the train straight away when she heard my frustrated, exhausted sobs after I'd called her to admit defeat with my attempts at breast-feeding Finn. And, as usual, her calm presence reassured me as she made up bottles of formula and gently helped me to find ways to soothe my baby boy. She gave me back my confidence, just as she always had done when I was young. From the perspective of being a mother myself now, I remember how she would alternately cajole and cheer me through the soap operas of school friendships and fallings-out, and how she encouraged me, quietly, but firmly, through the awkward, terrifying stage of adolescence and exams. In the photo, I am holding Finn who is, thankfully, asleep. And my mother is perched on the arm of the sofa beside me, a supportive arm around my shoulders. I am smiling – just a little wanly – towards Dan as he takes the picture; but my mother, Rhona, is gazing down at her daughter and her grandson with an expression of utter love.

I find it hard to reconcile the two facets of Mum's character: how can someone who is so warm and loving have shut her own mother out of her life? As I look at the framed photograph, I realise that she must have been hurt very badly indeed to have resorted to protecting herself in such a drastic way.

Dan follows my gaze and reaches out to straighten the photo slightly. I smile at him as I rub the knots of tiredness out of my neck, setting aside the letters I've been reading. The paper is yellowed with age, but Christophe's scrawling handwriting and Caroline's looping French script are still clear after all these years, their words still communicating the warmth of their love for Ella.

Paris
1 September 1938

Ma Chère Ella,
It's my first day at the bank and I feel I have been put in prison! I'm writing to you, under cover of pretending to take notes on the systems of accounting that we are to use for clients, because I miss you more than ever and it's the only way I will stay sane enough to be able to come back again tomorrow and do it all again. I cannot bear to think that this could be a life sentence. But the thought of you makes me believe anything is possible: that the day will come when we will be together again, somewhere, somehow, and that I WILL find a way of making a living from my art. The knowledge that you understand, that you believe in me, keeps me going.

In my mind I am out on Bijou, sailing far beyond the point to the place where the ocean is the colour of your eyes. My memories of this past summer will get me through the drab days spent incarcerated in this dull office until I see you again. Work hard in Edinburgh and I shall work hard in Paris, knowing all the while that there is another way of life waiting out there beyond the walls that now confine us. These walls can never confine our hearts, and mine beats a little faster when I remember that night in the dunes and I think how wonderful it will be to kiss you again.

Sorry for the smudging – Monsieur Arnaud, my jailer, came by to enquire whether I required any further explanation of the bookkeeping methods and to give me a copy of the bank's regulations in case I would like to read through it at home this evening, so I had to hide this letter beneath the ledger tout de suite! I smiled and nodded, although I wanted to tell him that I have not the slightest intention of doing so, since this evening I shall be working on a sketch of the beautiful girl I met on the Île de Ré this summer, who has entirely captured my heart.

We are being released now, allowed out for good behaviour, so I shall hurry to the Poste to send this to you.

It comes with all my love.

Christophe

A little later as Dan and I make our way along the landing, I pause in the doorway of Finn's bedroom. Christophe's letter, filled with dreams of living a different way of life, has reminded me how trapped we are in our own situation. Could we move out to the country, I wonder? Would life be easier there? But the city is where Dan's work is – or at least will be when he finds a job again – and at the moment my salary is the only way we can pay the bills. And we've established a support system now for Finn here; got him a place at the specialist school where he seems to be managing better. So, we can't afford to risk throwing all of that away. We're keeping our heads above water. Only just, admittedly, but to make any major changes now would be to risk going under. So, for the moment I'll settle for the allotment and the gardening project on a scrap of wasteland, and be happy that today was a good day and that Finn is now safely asleep in his bed.

The night light casts its glow into the darkness, keeping the night terrors at bay. In sleep, Finn's fingers curl open softly, instead of contracting into tight fists as they do for so much of the day when he can't relax for a second in his fear of whatever incomprehensible terror the next moment might bring. His fingernails are ragged and bitten, engrained with earth from his gardening today which the bath could not soak away and which he wouldn't let me clean with the nail brush. But tonight, for now, he is sleeping soundly, his habitual twitches stilled.

The light plays across his face, picking out the faint blush on his cheeks from being out in the fresh air today, but also darkening the bruised-looking half-moons beneath his eyes. I tiptoe across the rug with its design of smiling elephants and stoop down to kiss his forehead, oh so carefully gentle, a touch as light as a summer breeze, so that I don't risk waking him. But I treasure this rare opportunity to express my love for him as I never can do when he's awake, before I creep back out.

Dan, who is watching me from the doorway, takes my hand in his and his strong fingers, calloused these days from digging at the allotment, enfold mine for a fleeting, precious moment before he releases them and walks away down the corridor.

Yes, this has been a good day; we'll settle for that.

3, rue des Arcades
Paris
20 September 1938

Dearest Ella,
We are all missing you terribly! It was good to hear your journey home went smoothly. By now you must have embarked upon the secretarial course, so we look forward to receiving some extremely neat, efficiently typed letters from you in future. I hope your fellow students are all 'sympas' (but not so 'sympas' that you forget your friends in Paris and your promise to come and visit us next year).

I adore working at the Louvre. Apart from the Director of Picture Conservation, who is strict, forbidding and scares me rigid as he hovers nearby watching my every move, the staff are all very congenial and I am learning lots. They haven't let me loose on any actual paintings yet, of course, but I am allowed to pass the blades and brushes during the more involved restoration projects (there are some delicate operations: it is not unlike being a surgeon!), and to tidy up the studio. I can't wait to show you, when you are here, what goes on behind the scenes.

Here are the photographs that Papa *took which I promised to send you. Christophe has stolen one of the ones of you in your ball gown and I know he keeps it beneath his pillow! Of all of us, he misses you the most. Maybe he tells you this in the long letters he writes you – he won't let on what's in them – or maybe he's a typical boy who finds it impossible to communicate the truly important things! Don't tell him I said so: he's touchy enough on the subject of Ella-from-Edinburgh as it is.*

Je t'embrasse, my dear friend.

Bisous, *Caroline xx*

3 rue des Arcades,
Paris
1 January 1939

Dear Ella,

Bonne année! Let us hope that 1939 brings peace and prosperity for all, although Paris is still being flooded with refugees from the east who are worried that Germany is once again getting too big for its boots. Surely, though, no one wants another war and sense will reign before anything serious develops? Christophe is more pessimistic, but then he is constantly in a bad mood these days, as he detests his job at the bank and misses being with the girl he loves.

At least now we have your visit confirmed for August, and that is something we are all looking forward to. And I especially, for three reasons: reason number 1: I will be able to see my darling friend and show her Paris; reason number 2: we will go to the Île de Ré again; reason number 3: my poor brother will stop moping around the house like a lovesick puppy and cheer up at last.

Maman *and* Papa *send you their love, as do I. (I would send you Christophe's too, but I know he does that himself – and anyway, I don't think I could find an envelope big enough to hold it all!)*

Your friend,
Caroline xx

Paris
5 July 1939

Ma Chère *Ella,*
I'm sending you this postcard of the Mona Lisa *to whet your appetite for your visit to Paris, I can't wait to introduce you to her, the Louvre's most famous inhabitant with her enigmatic smile . . . I'm allowed to work on real paintings now (nothing as important as this one yet, of course), and when you come I will show you 'my' cherub in the bottom corner of a work by an unknown renaissance artist: fame at last!*

A bientôt (how happy it makes me to write those words!)
Caroline xx

1939, Paris

Ella felt quite the seasoned traveller as she stepped down from the train on to the platform, carrying her cream leather overnight case once again. She scanned the faces in the crowd that surged past her on all sides, eagerly searching for Christophe and Caroline who had promised they'd be here to meet her.

A porter brought the rest of her luggage and set it down beside her. The early August air was hot and stagnant. She breathed in the smell of Paris – a smell distinctively different from the air of Edinburgh or London, composed of coffee and cigarette smoke mingled with top notes of French perfume and a pungent undercurrent of drains. She shrugged off the cardigan that she'd worn to board the train in Edinburgh and stuffed it into her case.

Seconds passed, each one seeming unbearably long as she stood, a sole still point amidst the milling of the crowd, trying not to listen to the niggling voice of doubt within that murmured, 'What if he doesn't come? What if he's fallen in love with someone else? What if it was only the magic of summer on the island that made him feel that way and it'll all be different in the clear light of a Paris summer's day?'

And then she spotted him, pushing his way up the platform towards her, determinedly swimming up-stream to where she stood.

She ran to him, letting herself be carried in the flow of the crowd, and flung her arms around his neck. All doubts disappeared, dissolving like sea-mist in the sun's warmth, as he kissed her. The months apart fell away and memories of their last night on the Île de Ré flooded back as Ella buried her fingers in his hair and felt the heat of his lips on hers. In that moment she knew with complete certainty that space and time could never keep them apart: no matter whether it was on a wind-swept beach, or a city street, or a hot and grimy station platform surrounded by disapproving fellow-passengers, they belonged together, two halves of a perfect whole. She smiled up at him and saw the same absolute certainty written in his eyes too.

'Where is Caroline?' she asked, as he picked up her luggage in one hand and encircled her waist with the other, drawing her close to his side as they walked slowly towards the exit, the last two figures left on the platform.

'She's waiting for us in a *salon de thé* just across the road. She decided to allow me to meet you on my own, as long as I promised to bring you straight there.' He grinned. 'She told me I could have the first five minutes of your company to myself, but hereafter I have to share you with her for the remainder of your stay.'

They crossed the busy street, making for the windows of the tea room opposite. Ella pushed open the door and was immediately enveloped by two things: the first was the delicious sugar-and-almond smell of fresh-baked *macarons* and the second was Caroline, who flung her arms around her long-awaited friend.

Laughing and chatting, breathless with happiness and the need to catch up with so much news immediately – despite having exchanged what Ella's father referred to as 'the daily despatches from across the Channel' – they ordered fresh tea and a plate of cakes and Ella settled herself happily between her beloved friends.

Caroline poured golden Darjeeling tea into a china cup and passed it to Ella. 'Here, have an *éclair*. They're famous for them here. Now, tell us, did you pass the final tests? Are you officially a fully fledged secretary?'

Ella nodded, cutting into the choux pastry with her cake fork. 'Mmm, you're right. These are delicious. Yes, I passed. In fact I graduated with the fastest typing times in my class. My shorthand leaves a little to be desired though, but I've learnt enough to muddle through. I've told Mother that I'll see about some job applications when I get back from France in the autumn, but I'm also planning on making some enquiries while I'm here, to see whether anything might be available. The British Embassy might have something. My parents don't want me to venture further from Morningside than the New Town, so I thought I'd find out what the options might be for me in Paris before I break the news to them that I'm planning on coming here to live for a while. They're worried enough about everything that's going on in Europe at the moment as it is. Father says Germany makes him nervous, despite the fact that both Britain and France approved the move into Czechoslovakia.'

'We understand their concerns.' Caroline sipped her own tea and then carefully replaced her cup on its saucer. 'Though, of course, you'll have us here to support you. And you can stay with us for as long as you like. *Maman* and *Papa* will be pleased to have you.'

'Tell me about the Louvre,' Ella asked Caroline, and her eyes lit up with interest at the prospect of visiting the museum with all its treasures. Beneath the table, Christophe's hand sought out hers and held it tight.

'I can't wait to show you around,' Caroline replied. 'The galleries themselves are fascinating, but it's even more interesting seeing what goes on behind the scenes. Well, *I* think so, anyway.'

'What are you working on at the moment?'

'A small repair to an Italian Madonna by an unknown renaissance artist. At one point there was great excitement as we thought it might be a Fra Angelico, but now it's merely attributed to his school. It's still beautiful though.'

'And the bank?' Ella turned to Christophe, squeezing his hand beneath the damask tablecloth. 'Has Monsieur Dupont forgiven you yet for spilling your coffee all over the ledger the other week?'

He sighed, forking another morsel of chocolate and cream into his mouth. '*Non*, he's not exactly the forgiving type. What's worse, of course, he told *Papa* so I got another lecture about my sloppiness and lack of application. But how can I apply myself to something I loathe? And, adding injury to insult, something that keeps me from my painting. How I envy you, Caroline.'

His sister nodded, wiping the corner of her mouth with her napkin. 'I know. You tell me so every day,' she sighed. 'But you know *Papa* isn't prepared to fund you as an artist. You need to stick at the bank for the time being, at least until you've saved up enough to be independent and then you can do as you wish. For the time being, try not to antagonise *Papa* even further. You know how worried he is. Let's forget our woes while we have Ella with us and enjoy every moment of her stay.'

They gathered up their belongings, and Christophe picked up Ella's cases and pulled open the door to venture out into the August heat once more.

'Are we going to take a tram?' Ella asked, noticing the iron tracks laid into the cobbles of the street.

'No, they've mostly been decommissioned now. Everyone uses the Metro nowadays anyway. And of course the future is the automobile.' Christophe set her cases down on the pavement and raised an arm to hail one of the round-shouldered cabs from the stream of passing traffic.

'*Numéro trois, rue des Arcades, s'il vous plaît, monsieur.*'

Ella threaded a hand through the arms of each of her two friends and settled back against the smooth leather seat of the taxi, feeling excited, as she peered through the window to try to glimpse passing landmarks, at the prospect of seeing Paris properly for the very first time.

The Martets' home in the rue des Arcades exuded the same air of serene elegance as the house on the Île de Ré, although with a great deal more formality. The building was a tall townhouse made of biscuit-coloured stone and capped with a mansard roof of grey slates. A long sweep of wrought-iron balconies ran the length of the terrace.

Marianne opened the black front door with its gleaming brass fittings and enfolded Ella in a warm embrace. 'Come in, dearest Ella. *Bienvenue*. How was your journey? And how is your dear mamma?' Her dark curls, which were tamed into the same neat *chignon* she'd worn for the Governor's ball, seemed shot through with more fine threads of silver than last summer – or perhaps it was just the Parisian evening light which made them appear so, thought Ella.

In the *salon*, the sash windows were pushed open to allow the evening air in, cooling the high-ceilinged room. Through the windows, which were framed by long drapes in an exotic sienna-yellow silk embroidered with a design of Chinese birds and flowers, the first lights were coming on in neighbouring drawing-rooms as dusk fell over the city. A vase of long-stemmed lilies, sitting on an oval library table at one end of the drawing-room, filled the warm air with a perfume that transported Ella straight back to the Governor's mansion on the island and that perfect evening last summer when she and Christophe had waltzed together.

He sat next to her now and smiled as their eyes met. Was he remembering that same evening, she wondered? Their moonlit flight through the dunes? Dancing on the beach? Their kisses amongst the sea-grass? She longed to be alone with him again, craving his touch.

Monsieur Martet bustled in, rubbing his hands. 'Ah, Ella dear girl, you've arrived. Welcome to Paris. We've all been looking forward to having you with us again, not least Caroline and Christophe as I'm sure you know. Let me pour you a drink. Marianne's favourite is a Negroni – would you care to try one?'

Ella wasn't sure, such a thing being unheard of back in Morningside. What on earth would her parents say if they knew she was drinking cocktails before dinner? But it sounded most sophisticated and, after all, she *was* now in Paris and ready to sample all that the city had to offer, so she accepted the glass her host held out to her and took a tentative sip of the deep red concoction. It was like nothing she had ever tasted before, an intriguing balance of flavours, sweet, but with a bitter edge, refreshing but potent.

'Do you like it?' Monsieur Martet asked, his moustache lifting with the corners of his smile.

'Yes, I do. Very much in fact. Although I think I'd better only drink one or I very much doubt I'll be capable of getting up from this sofa.' He beamed even more broadly at her response, and she sensed the slight tension in the atmosphere, which he had seemed to bring into the room with him, lift slightly. Or perhaps it was just the warmth of the evening, the heady hit of the drink, and her acute awareness of Christophe sitting so close to her that made her limbs relax and her head feel light all of a sudden.

She watched, leaning back against the sofa's soft cushions, as Monsieur Martet stooped to hand his wife her cocktail, the glass suddenly lit with a rich, carmine glow in the final rays of sunlight that glanced through the windows. Marianne reached to take it from him, and, as she did so, she met her husband's gaze, the two of them exchanging a smile of such utter love that Ella blushed, surprised at witnessing this moment of intimacy between them. She'd hardly considered Monsieur Martet – so distant and eternally preoccupied – capable of such depths of emotion. But now she looked at Christophe's parents in a new light, realising there were hidden depths to their relationship. Perhaps their different characters provided the perfect balance: Marianne's gentle, kindly and artistic nature meeting her husband's determinedly pragmatic ambition to form a complex but satisfying marriage, not unlike the contrasting ingredients in the glass which Ella held in her hands, the components blending together and complementing one another in a heady cocktail.

Christophe nudged her. 'Ella, you are lost in thought. Come back to us!'

She smiled at the touch of his hand against the flesh of her arm and replied, 'I think it must be the cocktail, or perhaps it's simply being in Paris; it's going to my head.'

Over dinner, the conversation turned, inevitably, to the latest rumours from Germany. 'Paris is still being flooded with refugees,' Marianne explained to Ella. 'People are so worried that Germany will not respect her new boundaries, even with the latest expansion, and there are rumours of persecution of the Jews in the eastern countries. My cousin, Agnès, has brought her family to Paris, but she's still terrified what might happen if the Nazi dogma spreads. Unlike me, you see, she married a Jew, whereas I dared to marry outside of both my religions.' She smiled at her husband across the table. 'Love has a lot to answer for, *n'est-ce pas, chéri?*'

Ella considered this fact carefully, as she dissected the *turbot à la crème* on the plate before her. She hadn't realised that Marianne had Jewish roots. Didn't the religion pass along the maternal line? Were Christophe and Caroline Jewish too? She felt so foolish for not having known this before, although there had been no churchgoing of any kind on the island last summer, which had only added to the liberty she had felt there.

As if reading her mind, Caroline said, 'As you will have noticed, Ella, we are not a very religious family. *Maman's* father was a Jew, but

Grand-mère was a Catholic. Both *Maman* and *Papa's* families lapsed from adhering to any particular religion a generation or two ago. Given what we see happening in some parts of the world today, perhaps we are all better off without it. Does that shock you?'

Ella thought for a moment. 'No, not really. It seems to me that you all have a deep faith in one another, and in truth and beauty; and perhaps that's the only faith that really matters. My parents have always insisted that we go to church every Sunday, but I have to say that I've never felt it to be a particularly spiritually uplifting experience. In fact, now I come to think of it, I felt closer to whatever God there may be when we were out sailing on *Bijou* last summer than I've ever felt anywhere else.'

Christophe beamed his approval. 'You see, she understands perfectly. God is present in beauty and freedom. That's what counts.'

Monsieur Martet tut-tutted faintly, although when Ella glanced at him down the table, his expression was anything but disapproving. He was smiling at his wife in the candlelight and the look in his eyes told Marianne again, as eloquently as any words could have done, that he loved her, body and soul.

She decided that Paris was a little like one of the *centime* coins that jingled in her purse – far lighter than the heavy threepenny bits and penny pieces back at home. And, like those same coins, the city had two sides. The first was the one she'd anticipated: elegant, cultured, glamorous, a Paris familiar from the photographs and articles she'd pored over in the *Picture Post* and *National Geographic* magazines. She visited shops and galleries with Caroline and Marianne, drinking in the latest Parisian fashions along with the tiny cups of strong black coffee that she learned to order whenever they paused at a café to restore their energies. She also visited Caroline at the Louvre, learning far more about art from a few hours with her friend in the museum's labyrinthine galleries than she'd ever learned in art lessons at school. They met Christophe after work and the three would stroll beside the Seine, watching the boats that ploughed up and down the river, or pausing to admire the work of the artists who'd set up their easels opposite Notre Dame to paint the cathedral's soaring stone traceries and their shifting reflections in the water below. She savoured every moment, but especially those early-evening walks, holding Christophe's hand and laughing as he described the latest scrapes he'd got himself into at the bank. Occasionally, Caroline would make an excuse to leave the two of them alone and then they would find a secluded stretch of the riverbank and kiss beneath the dusty leaves of the plane trees that lined the road above them, to the evident appreciation and encouragement of passing boatmen.

But then there was another side to the city too. In the midst of the gaiety and opulence, groups of bewildered-looking refugees limped along the streets of Paris, their faces blank and grey with the shock of finding themselves in a strange place, washed up like flotsam and jetsam on the Parisian streets, dispossessed of their houses and their belongings. They brought with them, along with their shabby suitcases and bulging carpet-bags, a reminder of the threat that continued to gather strength just beyond France's eastern borders.

It seemed to Ella, as she began to grow accustomed to the nuances of life in Paris, that the city was preoccupied; its citizens were going about their daily lives as they'd always done, but with an air of vague distraction, keeping one ear open for the latest news of German manoeuvring. Normality and an impending sense of turbulence sat alongside each other in Paris that summer: two sides of the same coin.

In the Martets' home, Ella spent a day helping Marianne alter and launder a trunkful of Christophe and Caroline's cast-off clothing.

'Cousin Agnès wasn't able to bring much out with her when they left Austria, so these may come in handy for the children.'

'How old are they?' asked Ella as she took up the hem of an old skirt of Caroline's.

'Albert is twelve and Béatrice is ten. They're darling children. He is rather studious and serious, always with his nose buried in a book. His sister is far more outgoing, a truly sunny little girl, with the same curly hair as Caroline. I think you will like them. You'll meet them one day soon, we'll have them over for lunch one Sunday once you youngsters get back from the island.' She sighed. 'I wish I could come with you, but I won't get to the Île de Ré this summer. There has been too much to do here in Paris. However, I shall take great delight in thinking of the three of you there, even if only for the week.' Pausing, Marianne put down the pair of scissors she was using to snip a thread and placed her hand over Ella's. 'You are like family to us you know, my dear. We are very pleased to have you here with us. You make my son, in particular, very happy indeed and that fills my heart with joy.'

Ella blushed, her gaze fixed on her sewing, then raised her eyes to Marianne's. 'He makes me very happy too.' And she saw that Marianne understood all that there was to understand, and that her hopes were the same as Ella's and Christophe's: that their future would, somehow, some day, be shared.

Marianne nodded, smiling. Then, reaching for a shirt of Christophe's, she said, 'And now, let's see if this collar can be turned to make it as good as new . . .'

Suddenly the front door rattled, the sound of it being flung open with some force which made both of them jump. Marianne put the shirt back into the mending basket and rose hurriedly.

Caroline could be heard calling as she ran upstairs, '*Maman!* Ella! Where are you?' She burst through the drawing-room door, curls escaping from the clasps which held her hair up. 'I have important news! I've been working on a special project – top-secret, I'm afraid, so I can't tell you the specific details. But we are sending some of the artworks from the museum to other locations in France, places where they'll be safe in case the Germans take it into their stupid heads to drop bombs on us or try to invade, or any other crazy plan.'

'Goodness, Caroline, really! I'm sure it's not going to come to that!' exclaimed her mother, although Ella noticed that she raised a hand, involuntarily, to the buttons of her white blouse as if to calm the panicked thump of her heart beneath them. 'You know that Adolf Hitler has changed his tune now; it's all over the newspapers.'

'Sorry, *Maman*, this is just in case *Monsieur* Hitler's words turn out not to be worth the paper they are written on. I know it's a bit extreme, but *Monsieur le Directeur* says it's better to be safe than sorry. He says it's like Noah building the ark – it had to be done *before* it started to rain, even when nobody believed it would be needed. And, hopefully, in this case it really won't.' She turned to Ella. 'But I'm going to need help from you and Christophe. We have to disguise what we're doing, so that only a very few people know where the artworks are concealed. We can't make it obvious that we're moving works of art around the country. I've been helping to pack up some of the items. And then I had a stroke of genius! One of the items is to be delivered to the Château de Chambord, which is on our way to La Pallice to catch the ferry to the island. So we're going to take it with us and drop it off there on Monday, just as if we were stopping off to do a little sightseeing on our way to the coast. A security guard from the museum will be coming with us, of course. They wouldn't just let us set off with a work of art in the trunk of our car on our own. It will look quite natural, as if we are two couples going off on holiday, stopping with the rest of the tourists to visit the château. We'll drop the guard at a station just after Chambord so he can catch a train back to Paris, and then carry on to La Pallice as planned. It's the perfect cover.'

Marianne shook her head. 'Caroline, this plan sounds ridiculous. I think your museum Director is being somewhat alarmist. And what could be so precious as to warrant this bizarre subterfuge? There must be hundreds of works of art that need to be kept safe. Are you going to have teams of young people driving each of them around the country one at a time? Because it doesn't seem a very efficient way of doing it if that is the case.'

'No, *Maman*, most of the works that are going to be moved will go a little later, probably in lorries, when the need arises. But just a very few selected pieces are being spirited away now because they are simply too precious to risk losing. I know it sounds a little bizarre, but you have to admit these are bizarre times in which we live!'

Marianne allowed her hand to fall and rest, once again, on the mending basket in her lap. She smiled at last, although with a trace of sadness, Ella thought. 'Well, who am I to stand in the way of a matter of state importance? Yes, I suppose you must do it. But please drive carefully. And telephone me from the island to let me know you've got there safely, will you?'

Caroline flung her arms around her mother and kissed her. 'Of course! Now come, Ella, I think I can hear Christophe back from work. Let's go and tell him . . .'

They packed on Sunday evening. 'Just take a few things, there won't be much room in the trunk of the car,' Caroline urged. 'The package is quite bulky. We won't need much on the island anyway – Ella, you can borrow some of my summer things, which are already down there.'

Early the next day, before the Monday morning city had begun to awaken fully, Christophe brought the Martets' car – a gleaming

Peugeot, his father's latest prized possession – around to the front of the house. They stowed their bags in the boot, and then drove carefully through the empty streets to pull up by a side entrance of the Louvre. Caroline hurried in, re-emerging a few minutes later with two men who carried between them a bulky wooden crate. Gingerly, they loaded it into the trunk of the car, rearranging the luggage around it so that it was safely wedged in place. Caroline shook hands with one of the men, listening carefully and nodding as he gave her a few final directions, and then came around to the driver's door. 'Sorry, Christophe but, by order of the Director, the museum's security guard will have to drive. This is Grégoire. You don't mind, do you? You can sit in the back, with Ella.'

Christophe climbed out and shook the hand of the guard as they exchanged places. Caroline settled herself beside Grégoire and the car pulled slowly away from the kerb and into the streets of Paris once more, heading south and then west out of the city. Christophe leaned forward and tapped his sister on the shoulder. 'Alright, now you can tell us. What's in the package?'

Caroline shook her head, glancing at Grégoire whose eyes were fixed on the road ahead as he negotiated the way carefully through the increasingly busy traffic. 'You don't need to know that. In fact, it's far better that you don't. Sorry,' she said, looking back over her shoulder with a teasing smile, 'but you two are just here for camouflage. You don't have the appropriate security clearance for that sort of classified information!'

'Oh, come on, Caroline! You can tell us, especially since we've so kindly agreed to help you with your top-secret operation.'

She clamped her lips together and shook her head emphatically. '*Non*. It's more than my job is worth. Now stop asking questions and let Grégoire concentrate on driving. The last thing we want is for someone to crash into us!'

Eventually they left behind the suburbs of Paris and reached the open road towards the Loire.

I am perfectly content, thought Ella, sitting in the back of the car with Christophe at her side and watching the countryside unfurl, as Caroline and Grégoire discussed museum matters in the front. She was looking forward to seeing the Loire Valley, and to delivering the package in the trunk at Chambord which, she hoped, might afford them the opportunity to look round the château. And then, by that evening, they should be on the ferry, crossing to the Île de Ré. She leant her head against the glass of the car window and watched the procession of plane trees file past on the long, straight road, trees planted on the orders of the Emperor Napoleon over a century ago so that their branches would shade his armies as they marched to and from battle. She hoped they would continue to provide their shade for more peaceful travellers, not wanting to contemplate the possibility of any more armies marching through France.

At her side, she sensed Christophe glancing at her every now and then, as though he was committing her profile to memory, watching the alternating sunshine and shade cast shadows across her face, throwing into relief her cheek bones, her lips, her lashes.

Her reverie was interrupted suddenly by a loud clang and a rhythmic banging sound, and the car slowed suddenly, losing power. Grégoire pulled over to the side of the road and they all got out. Opening the bonnet, the guard peered into the engine and swore under his breath. Straightening up, he turned to Caroline. 'It looks like a problem with the gearbox. What a time to break down!'

'*Oh, mon Dieu!*' Ella heard the panic in Caroline's voice. 'What are we to do? If anything happens to the picture . . .'

Grégoire remained calm. 'Don't worry, we'll get it fixed.' He pointed to a milestone at the roadside just ahead of them. 'It's only a kilometre to the next village. We'll ask there, maybe someone will have some tools and be able to help us fix it. I know a little about mechanics myself – my cousin has a garage in Sèvres, and I used to work there before I took up my job at the museum.' He wiped his hands on his handkerchief. 'We'll need to push – Mademoiselle Martet, you can steer. *Allons-y.*'

As he and Christophe shed their jackets, Ella climbed out of the car. 'Mademoiselle Lennox, you can stay inside if you wish.'

'*Non, merci.* I'll help push. I may not be all that strong, but at least I won't be adding to the weight of the car.'

Christophe flashed her a grin of approval before setting his shoulder to the car's rear flank. Grégoire took up his position on the other side and the car slowly moved back out into the road.

'It's a good thing it wasn't all uphill!' panted Grégoire as they reached the village and pulled up in front of an *auberge*, which, apart from a baker's shop, appeared to be the only commerce that the hamlet had to offer. 'I'll go in here and make some enquiries, Mademoiselle Martet, you stay with the car.'

He emerged a few minutes later, accompanied by the innkeeper who carried a toolbox. The two men stooped over the engine and for several minutes muffled thumps, accompanied by the occasional oath, could be heard emanating from beneath the bonnet.

With a shake of his head, Grégoire re-emerged.

'Well, we've located the problem. It's an issue with the gears, as I thought. A part of the fly-wheel has sheared right off, damaging the mechanism. It'll need a replacement part. I'll telephone my cousin, see if by any chance he can get hold of what we need. If so, I can hop on a train back to Paris and come back with it as quickly as possible. Don't worry, Mademoiselle Martet, all is not lost. Where there's a will, there's a way!'

Caroline was pacing up and down the street, distraught. 'I can't believe this is happening. *Oh, mon Dieu!*'

Christophe put a reassuring hand on her arm. 'Calm down, Caroline. It sounds as if Grégoire has got it all in hand. He seems such a capable type. Don't worry, he'll sort out the car. The worst case will be that we only deliver your package to Chambord tomorrow, instead of today, and we miss one day on the Île de Ré. *C'est pas grave!*'

Eventually, Grégoire returned from phoning and he and Caroline stepped across the road to confer in urgent whispers beside the hedgerow. Finally, she nodded and he headed back into the inn to finalise arrangements.

'All sorted out now?' Christophe reached to open the boot and remove the crated package within.

'No!' Caroline grabbed his arm.

'Honestly, why are you so sensitive? It's not like you. Whatever's in here must be something very special indeed.' He stopped short, and then, as an involuntary flash of alarm flickered across Caroline's face, Christophe seemed to come to a realisation and a slow smile of delight spread over his features.

'You're not telling me it's the . . . ?'

Caroline nodded miserably, a barely perceptible movement, and mouthed, 'the *Mona Lisa*'. Ella stepped forward to put an arm around her, the enormity of the situation suddenly overwhelming both girls. Caroline suppressed a sob, and Ella scarcely knew whether to cry herself, or to laugh out loud at their predicament.

Just then, Grégoire re-emerged from the inn, clapping the innkeeper on the back. 'Right then, it's all organised. My cousin can lay his hands on the part we need. This kind gentleman is going to give me a lift to the station at Orléans. I'll be back tomorrow morning with the part – my cousin will drive me down and help fix the car – and then we can continue on our way. Our holiday will only be delayed by half a day.' He shot a warning look at the three of them, signalling that they should keep up the charade. 'Christophe, could you help us push the car round to the back of the inn? That way it'll be off the road for the night.'

'Fortunately, we have rooms for you,' the innkeeper said, beaming. 'There's a nice twin room for the young ladies. I'm afraid the young gentleman will have to make do with the garret, because otherwise we are fully booked. The last week of August is always one of our busiest times, with everyone heading back to Paris from their holidays. But, as it's an emergency and only for one night . . .'

'That will be fine, thank you. We're so grateful to you for your help.' Caroline pulled herself together.

'Shall I give you a hand bringing in your luggage?' The innkeeper took a step towards the boot of the car.

'Thank you, but no, I think we can manage,' Christophe laid a restraining hand on his arm. 'Let's get the car round to the back and then Grégoire and I will unload a few things from there.'

The two men carried the wooden crate carefully upstairs. 'Put it in the attic room,' urged Christophe in a whisper. 'I'll guard it with my life! It'll be safer there, away from the prying eyes of other guests.'

Reluctantly, Caroline agreed that perhaps it would be the safest option, and then they waved Grégoire off as he headed for the railway station.

Caroline only managed to pick at her dinner that evening, toying with the food on the plate in front of her.

'Relax, *ma soeur*,' said Christophe, pouring her another glass of rough *vin de pays* from the glass pitcher the innkeeper had deposited on their table along with their meal. 'Grégoire will be back first thing. The best you can do tonight is to get a good night's sleep so that you are ready for further adventures tomorrow! Now, drink that and then we'll turn in. I think everyone's exhausted after today's excitement.'

Darkness fell, and Ella lay in bed listening to Caroline's breathing grow slower and deeper as sleep finally claimed her. The noises of the inn's other inhabitants fell silent at last, and then rays of soft light poured in through the slats of the shutters as the moon rose. She tossed and turned, unable to sleep.

Eventually, she got up and, on silent feet, crept along the corridor and up the narrow stairs that led to the attic. She tried the door, but it was locked. With her heart pounding, she tapped very gently. Immediately, there came a whisper, 'Ella, is that you?'

'Yes.'

The key turned quietly in the lock and Christophe opened the door, ushering her in and immediately locking the door again behind her. Holding a finger to his lips, he pointed, soundlessly, to the mantelpiece in one corner of the tiny garret room. He'd opened the shutters, and moonlight flooded in, illuminating the painting that sat there.

Ella gasped, scarcely able to believe what she saw.

Christophe held a finger against her lips now, so that she wouldn't say a word. He led her to the single bed, a thin, lumpy mattress on a rusted bedstead. There they sat, side by side, leaning against the over-stuffed bolster, and gazed at the most famous painting in the world, lit by moonshine so that its colours glowed with mysterious depths.

Ella turned and smiled at him, at the wonder of it all, at the sight of such beauty in the poorest and plainest of rooms. She saw, now, that this was all that mattered; that, from here on, there would always be this truth – of finding beauty in the most unlikely places.

Then Christophe took her in his arms and they floated through the night, adrift on a raft in a moonlit ocean, far from the preoccupations of the world beyond, with La Gioconda herself smiling over them in silent benediction.

Ella awoke just as dawn was starting to infuse the little attic room with its soft, grey light. She woke Christophe with a gentle kiss. Still drowsy, he pulled her to him, smiling lazily as he smoothed her hair away from her face. He held her to him in an embrace that she wished would never end.

Returning his smile, she whispered, 'Christophe, I have to go. I must get back before Caroline wakes up. And you need to pack *her* away safely,' she gestured to the painting on the mantel-shelf, 'before anyone finds out exactly where and how she's spent her night.'

He nodded. 'Don't worry, I memorised precisely how she was packed, all those layers of wrappings. And I'll screw the crate back together exactly as it was. But we still have a little time. Stay, just for a few minutes more . . .'

Eventually, she tore herself away and crept, on silent feet, back to the bedroom where Caroline was still sunk in a deep sleep. Ella slipped between the sheets of her own bed and lay there as the sun began to rise, watching dust motes dance as the first long beams slid between the gaps in the shutters and remembering the magical night that had gone before. Her memories felt dreamlike, and she hugged herself, knowing that she and Christophe had shared a gift that was precious beyond words.

Ella looked across at Caroline. She was stirring, sighing as she awoke, lying quietly for a minute and then, realising where she was, she sat bolt upright. Ella smiled. 'Good morning. Did you sleep well?'

'I rather think I did.' Caroline stretched and yawned. 'Though I had the strangest dreams. And you?'

Ella nodded. 'I had a very strange dream too. And now I'm ready for a large breakfast, before Grégoire returns. Come on, let's go and see what's on offer.'

Washed and dressed, they made their way downstairs to the dining-room. 'Do you think we should go and see if Christophe's awake?' Caroline hesitated on the landing, as if to make for the attic stairs.

Ella took her hand. 'No, let him sleep. We can come and find him after breakfast if he's still not appeared.' The last thing she wanted was for Caroline to walk in and find him reassembling the crate.

The innkeeper brought jugs of coffee and warm milk and placed a basket of bread and croissants in front of them. 'Your young man is back already. Must have had a very early start. He and his cousin are outside now, working on the car. They'll be in soon, I shouldn't wonder.'

Caroline smiled with relief and reached for a hunk of golden-crusted baguette.

'I hope you've left me some?' Christophe ruffled his sister's hair as he pulled up a chair. 'Grégoire says they've nearly finished. They've fixed the car so that it'll get us to La Pallice and back, and then it can go into the garage to be checked over thoroughly when we get home to Paris. If we take it to his cousin's garage, he's promised to give us a good deal on the price.'

After breakfast, Grégoire and Christophe carried the crate down from the attic and stowed it carefully in the trunk once again. Then, waved off by the innkeeper, they set off for Chambord.

Two hours later, Ella pressed her face against the car window as they drove up the long, tree-lined *allée* that led to the château. The building rose up before them, its towers and turrets dominating the flat plain stretching alongside the river. Grégoire presented some documents to the guard on the gate and he directed them to drive round to a side door, away from the more public visitors' entrance in the middle of the castle's keep. Another guard awaited them there, and he and Grégoire carried the crate from the car into the château. They shook hands, and the château guard turned to Caroline. 'We'll take good care of this for you, *Mademoiselle*. And please tell *Monsieur le Directeur* that we await with pleasure the other deliveries.'

Grégoire consulted his watch. 'Do you want to spend time visiting the château, or shall we be off? There's a fast train from Tours back to Paris at midday – I might just make it if you're happy to press on.'

Reluctantly, Ella tore herself away from the tantalising glimpse of finely carved stonework and a wall hung with rich artworks that she could see down a corridor leading from the dark, cramped office in which they stood.

'Yes, let's get off,' agreed Christophe. 'We still have a long drive ahead of us and we need to make sure we reach La Pallice before the last ferry departs. We can't risk missing yet another night of our holiday on the Île de Ré!'

They arrived at the house beside the dunes as the sun was slipping beyond the horizon, sinking into the ocean and painting the sky crimson with its last rays. Clambering out of the car, Ella took a deep breath, drinking in the salted scent of the sea and listening for the hush of the waves from the beach.

Caroline set out the supper that Sandrine had left for them on the terrace, ladling bowls of *garbure* – a soup thick with chicken and vegetables from Sandrine's *potager* – into pottery bowls. Christophe poured the wine and Ella smiled, glad that they would have these few precious days on the island.

The three of them sat, late into the night, watching a million stars appear, sipping the last of their wine and breathing in the sweet scents of jasmine and honeysuckle. Ella spoke again of her dream of moving to Paris just as soon as she'd convinced her parents to let her, and of making enquiries about possible work when they returned to the city, before she set off home to Edinburgh. Christophe talked of promotion within the bank which, he hoped, would hasten his ability to save enough money to be independent of his parents. And Ella wondered whether there were other, as yet unspoken plans to be made for a future together, which might include marriage, and children, and holidays on the Île de Ré filled with sunshine and sea air and love.

As though by mutual agreement, none of the three sought out news from the outside world that week, preferring to turn their backs on the turmoil and strife on mainland Europe and, with war looming, hoping that diplomacy would somehow work. Instead, they spent each day doing the things they loved best: cycling across the island for picnics on their favourite beaches; luxuriating in the golden haze of the late August afternoons, the girls reading on the terrace while Christophe worked at his sketch-book; picking sun-ripe fruit in the orchard – soft figs and the last perfumed white peaches – while Anaïs cropped the bleached grass contentedly nearby; sitting out late into the warm nights, talking of their plans and reminiscing, the twins making Ella laugh at their stories of holidays they'd spent on the island when they were young; and, of course, sailing *Bijou* out across the aquamarine expanse of the ocean, the boat dancing joyfully before the wind as she heeled to, her hull lifting from the water as though, encouraged by the sea-birds calling above her, she too might spread her wings and fly.

It was Sunday, September had just begun, and even in the space of just a week the light was noticeably softer, lending a golden haze to the mown cornfields where hay-bales sat, neatly stacked, amidst a foaming froth of Queen Anne's lace, which had sprung up opportunistically after the mowers had passed. The pyramids of salt, raked from the shallow pans on the island's north-west shore, dazzled the eye with their sun-bleached whiteness, like drifts of fresh-fallen snow come early. Ella, Christophe and Caroline had returned from a cycle ride, pedalling back through the deserted, late-afternoon lanes of Sainte Marie de Ré, where the low rays of the sun shone through the tissue paper petals of the hollyhocks, setting their colours aglow.

Sitting on the terrace with glasses of cool water, Christophe glanced lazily at his wristwatch as the church bell began to sound. 'This is an odd time for them to sound Evensong,' he remarked. 'It's only just gone five.' They sipped their drinks. But then, one by one, they set their glasses back on the table as the bell continued to toll, on and on as though it would never end.

Caroline's eyes grew wide with alarm. 'Christophe . . . ?'

As one, the three of them rose and moved quickly to the drawing-room to switch on the radiogram. They caught the end of the announcement, scarcely able to take in the words that filled the peaceful room, resonating from walls hung with watercolour scenes of summers gone by.

'*This morning, with our ally Great Britain, France issued an ultimatum to the German leader, demanding the withdrawal of his troops from Poland. The deadline has passed and therefore, with deep regret, both France and Britain are now at war with Germany . . .*'

Numb with disbelief, Ella gazed through the open window, framed by its billowing curtains of white muslin, out across the vineyards to where the spire of the church in Sainte Marie rose from the marshlands to point heavenwards as the news tolled out from village to village across the island. A flock of doves, disturbed by the alarm call of the bells, soared skywards as one and then scattered, falling back to earth again as though attempting to take shelter from a storm.

No one had any appetite for supper that evening, and Caroline excused herself early to go and finish packing up the house. There had been no need for discussion. They had all simply made their way upstairs from the drawing-room to pack their things and prepare for the journey back to Paris the next morning. Instinctively, they each knew that they needed to be back there, to plan what to do next. Ella felt a heavy sickness in the pit of her stomach, along with a sudden, childlike longing to see her parents, wishing she could hear the sound of their voices telling her not to worry, that everything would be alright.

Christophe took her hand and, snatching up a rug from where it hung over the back of one of the chairs on the terrace, he led her, wordlessly, through the sand-dunes to the beach. They sat there together, as the sun set far out over the ocean and darkness fell. He drew her to him, draping the blanket around their shoulders as a faint chill crept into the air.

They watched as, one by one, the stars came out, their light reflecting in the ink-black sea, and listening to the waves, which, tonight, brought little comfort as they whispered warnings of hidden menace – of warships and U-boats – in a sighing lament.

Ella turned and kissed Christophe, tasting salt on his lips. 'We will be together you know, no matter what,' she told him.

She glimpsed the expression in his starlit eyes, a sadness as deep as the ocean itself. 'I will not ask you to stay in Paris now, my beautiful Ella. Please, for my sake, go back to Scotland as quickly as you can. Your parents will wish it, in any case. And there you will surely be safer. That is my heartfelt wish. That you will keep yourself safe, so that when this war is over you will come back to me.'

'But . . .'

'Shhh.' He pressed a finger to her lips, stopping her protestations. 'Please, Ella.'

He kissed her again, and she pressed close to him, longing to give him anything that he asked of her and more.

And, afterwards, they fell asleep in each other's arms, their breath quietening and becoming one with the soft sighing of the sea.

The journey home was a blur. Everything had been rearranged in such haste that Ella felt a little shell-shocked to find herself standing on the platform in London, waiting to board the sleeper to Edinburgh. On the boat, she'd felt almost like an exile herself, pushed northwards ahead of the tide of refugees and troops that was flooding into Paris now.

When they'd arrived back at the Martets' home in Paris, a telegram from Edinburgh was already awaiting her arrival. '*Come home. Wiring money for ticket. Await confirmation.*'

And so a telegram had been sent back to her parents to let them know that Ella would be on the train the next day, connecting through London and arriving at Waverley Station the following morning.

She was distraught that her plans to stay in Paris had been dashed so brutally. And she was heartbroken to be leaving Christophe. Their parting had felt like a physical wrench. He'd held her tightly to him at the *Gare du Nord* and whispered that he didn't want to let her go.

'I'll come back,' she'd promised. 'Like you said. When this war is over, I'll come to find you. We will be together in the end.'

He'd smiled down at her and smoothed her hair back from her forehead so that he could place a kiss there. 'Ella, I want to tell you something. Without asking for any commitment from you, because the future is so uncertain now . . . I know I am undeserving, and until I am more financially independent I can't expect . . .' He tailed off, tongue-tied for once.

She reached up then and kissed him. 'Shhh. There's no need to say anything. If your heart knows what my heart knows, then it's all understood anyway. Am I right?'

He'd looked deep into her eyes, reading what was written there for him alone, and then nodded.

'That's fine then. I'm glad we've got that sorted out.' She took his hand and squeezed it in hers, as the conductor blew his whistle. 'I'll write. I love you.'

'*Je t'aime*, Ella Lennox,' he'd whispered back. And then he'd stood, looking utterly wretched as she walked away to board the train, and watched as it pulled away from the platform.

And she'd pressed her hand against the glass of the carriage window, as if still reaching for him across the distance that was tearing them apart.

2014, Edinburgh

Getting Granny Ella to the allotment has involved a week's worth of military-style planning.

'Why not wait until spring, when there'll be more things growing?' Dan asked when I suggested it to him. 'October's hardly the best time of year to see it.'

'Because she might not be capable of it by then,' I replied, pushing the thought that she might not be here at all by then to the back of my mind. 'This half-term break might be the last chance.'

'Bring her here to the flat instead then, for a cup of tea.'

I shook my head. 'She'd never manage the stairs. And anyway, the main point of the exercise is to see Finn. He'll hide in his room if we're here at home, but at the allotment you and he can potter as normal and she can sit and watch. She loves being out in the fresh air too. Two birds, one stone.'

To my amazement, for once it all seems to be working out just as I've planned. I dropped Dan and Finn off, along with the bags containing the picnic lunch and the camping stove, and left them to set up the rusty deck-chairs on the more sheltered side of the shed while I went to collect Ella.

She picks her way along the path between the plots, placing her stick carefully amongst the bark chips for balance as she pauses to admire the blaze of mop-headed chrysanthemums on the plot next door to ours. Dan comes to greet us, leaving Finn digging up potatoes and counting them into a basket at his side.

Ella sinks thankfully on to one of the chairs and then takes a deep breath of the autumn air which smells of earth and fallen leaves, but also – faintly – of the last late blooms of the honeysuckle that has tucked itself into the sheltered corner by the shed.

'Oh!' she exclaims, turning her face towards the sweetness of the yellow stamens, 'It does my old heart good to smell that.'

Finn glances up to see what she's talking about and then returns to his potato harvesting with renewed concentration.

'Well, it's not quite Marianne Martet's garden on the Île de Ré,' I say with a smile, 'but at least the weather's behaved itself for our picnic.'

I tuck a rug over her knees and then busy myself getting the stove going to warm the soup.

'Quite an adventure.' Ella surveys our plot with its neat rows of vegetables that are Dan and Finn's pride and joy. 'Now, tell me what you've planted here.'

Dan points out the onions, kale and Brussels sprouts – 'for our Christmas dinner' – and the potatoes.

'Looks like a good crop,' Ella comments. To my relief she seems to know, instinctively, not to push Finn by addressing him directly.

'Fifty-seven,' Finn says, not looking up. 'And there's a pumpkin too. Only one. We took the other flowers off to make one big one grow. I'm going to measure it later.'

Dan and I exchange a glance. He seems to have accepted Ella with none of the anxiety he usually displays when meeting new people. Working outside in the fresh air, with his hands in the earth, really does seem to help calm him.

I set out the lunch – steaming mugs of soup and a plate of sandwiches I'd made at home with an assortment of fillings, plumping for this as the simplest option to satisfy the varying dietary requirements of this gathering. Finn selects a Marmite one that I've cut into a perfect square with the crusts removed, which is one of the few configurations he will tolerate; Ella nibbles at a dainty egg mayonnaise triangle; and Dan devours a cheese and pickle doorstop as he tells Ella about the gardening project that he and Finn are now working on two afternoons a week after school. Finn, chewing his sandwich, hums tunelessly to himself and swings his feet in their wellington boots, watching the silver filaments of thistle-down that dance in the watercolour sunshine.

An hour later, I'm packing the picnic things away, preparing to take Ella back to the nursing home in time for her afternoon nap, and Dan is cleaning the tools and putting them back in the shed, when Finn suddenly comes to stand in front of his great-grandmother. He's holding a green-leafed sprig of honeysuckle with a single, sweet-scented bloom at the end. He lays it on the tartan travelling rug that covers her lap.

'Take this home with you,' he says. 'To do your old heart good there too.'

As Ella reaches to take it, my throat catches at the sight of the unexpected gesture as well as the juxtaposition of his smooth, if slightly grubby, fingers so close to her age-blotched skin. And as she smiles, his eyes meet hers for a fleeting moment, with that exact same green-and-gold gaze.

'I think my old heart is very well indeed after spending time in such good company today,' she says. 'Thank you, Finn.'

1940, Edinburgh

'Come away from the window, Ella, you're spoiling the blackout,' her mother chided her gently. 'There's nothing to see this hogmanay anyway, what with everyone staying indoors and no lights allowed. There'll be no first footing this year.'

It was bitterly cold outside and a sharp frost had dusted the cobble-stones like icing sugar, glinting defiantly in the moonlight which, unlike the city's street lamps, couldn't be extinguished. Ella sighed, longing suddenly for a slice of thickly iced Christmas cake; but there'd be none next year now that people were saying that everything was to be rationed.

'I doubt Mr Hitler is going to bomb Morningside just because I peeped out to see whether anyone anywhere was going to dare to celebrate the end of 1939 . . .' But then the first air raid on Great Britain, back in October, had been on warships moored in the Firth of Forth, so she knew that nowhere was safe. She sighed, pulling the heavy velvet curtains closed and came away from the window to join her parents beside the fire.

Her mother was reading a pamphlet issued by the local Scottish Women's Rural Institute on jam-making. 'Well, my New Year's resolution to help the war effort is going to be this.' She brandished the paper at her husband and daughter. 'We're being given extra supplies of sugar and as many jars as we can fill. Though Lord knows what we'll find to make it with in January. There's a recipe here for carrot marmalade, if we can get a few oranges – apparently it's good for night-blindness.' She glanced at Ella over the top of her spectacles. Letters from France were few and far between now that they were at war, and Ella was worrying herself away to a mere shadow of the glowing girl who'd returned after her two summers there.

Her father set aside the copy of *The Scotsman* he'd been reading and banked up the fire with another shovelful of coal to see them through to midnight. Thick, brown-grey smoke streamed up the chimney for a few moments until the coal dust caught and blazed with renewed vigour.

Ella picked up the newspaper and leafed through it distractedly.

'You can come along and help us if you like.' Her mother handed her the smudgy leaflet. 'Mrs Macpherson says it's all hands to the pump at a time like this. Maybe if you do something practical to help with the war effort it'll help to take your mind off things a wee bit. Even if it is only making jam. We'll be running sessions at the weekends too, when you're not at work.'

She suspected that Ella's job at her father's insurance office, answering the phones and doing the typing, wasn't helping matters. Mr Lennox had insisted that his daughter's secretarial skills were urgently needed when his former secretary, the redoubtable Miss McIntyre, had handed in her notice the day after war was declared and gone off to work in a munitions factory.

Absent-mindedly, Ella put aside the sheet of paper her mother had handed her, absorbed by an article she was reading in the newspaper. Suddenly, her eyes had recovered a little of their old sparkle in the firelight.

'You know what, Mother? I think you're right. I *do* need to do something practical. Father, I'm sorry, and I know that insurance is a vital cog in the machinery of this country as you're always saying, but I just can't sit in that office any more. Look at this article: women are enlisting for the armed services. Not to fight, of course, but to work in support roles. They're calling here for more recruits. I'm going to join the WAAF! Oh, Father, please, may I?'

He took the paper back from her and scanned it, although he'd already read it all from cover to cover and knew exactly the article to which she was referring: beneath it was an image of a recruitment poster, with the bold invitation to '*Serve in the WAAF with the men who fly*'.

He set the newspaper aside at last and turned to meet his daughter's beseeching gaze. Her face was thin and pale, but her expression was more animated than he'd seen it in several months.

'If you are serious about this, Ella, then we will consider it' – he held up a hand to stop her excited interjection – 'but on one condition. You may explore the possibility of working for the Women's Auxiliary Air Force which, I believe, is a useful and necessary institution from what I've read, but only if work can be found for you here in Scotland. I will not countenance you moving so far from home, at your young age, that we cannot see you from time to time to reassure ourselves of your well-being.'

She flung her arms around him and planted a resounding kiss on his cheek. 'Thank you, Father, thank you!'

The carriage clock on the mantelpiece began to chime midnight.

'Well.' Her father rose to his feet seemingly about to pour three small glasses of sweet sherry from the decanter on the sideboard, but he pulled his handkerchief from his trouser pocket and wiped his eyes very thoroughly before he did so. He filled them just halfway and then picked up two of the crystal sherry glasses and handed them to Ella and her mother. 'I propose a toast. To 1940. To us all, may we be kept safe and may there be a swift end to this wretched war.' He paused and cleared his throat. 'And to absent friends.'

'Absent friends,' echoed Ella, and she sipped down her sherry as quickly as she could, then kissed her parents goodnight and ran upstairs to write a letter to Caroline and Christophe telling them that she would be sending them all her love and protection shortly, courtesy of the Royal Air Force.

Ella knocked on the door of the austerely furnished office at RAF Gulford, her dark blonde hair pinned back in a tidy roll, clutching her handbag which contained her certificate and references from Buchanan's Secretarial College. A voice barked, 'Come in!' and she found herself standing before Squadron Officer Macpherson, the equally redoubtable sister-in-law of the Mrs Macpherson who chaired the branch of the Scottish Rural Women's Institute where Ella's mother had been assisting with jam-making for the war effort.

'So, Eleanor, you wish to join the Women's Auxiliary Air Force.' Squadron Officer Macpherson squared up the papers on the desk in front of her and fixed Ella with a steely eyed glance. 'We have a number of roles to fill at this juncture, and I should say that your secretarial skills would be a welcome addition to the office here at Gulford. Yes, thank you, Victoria, you may leave the tray here.' She broke off to glare at the girl in the air-force blue uniform who'd just brought in two cups of tea, as ordered, and was dawdling to grin at Ella instead of returning smartly to her post at the filing cabinets in the outer office.

Accepting the cup that was handed to her, Ella looked past Squadron Officer Macpherson to the window behind the desk, beyond which the deserted East Lothian airfield could be seen, comprising little more than a couple of Nissen huts and a makeshift hangar at one end of a landing strip surrounded by potato fields. The winter sky was a cold, flat grey and the wind, which blew straight in off the North Sea, snatched at the wind sock, causing it to spin wildly and strain at its fixings like a hunting dog eager for the off. A herring gull, which had been huddling on the scrubby grass alongside the runway, flapped its wings clumsily and then took off, suddenly graceful as it returned to its natural element, banking with outspread wings before disappearing seawards.

'We shall also be requiring communications operators, a vital role, if that would be of interest. I'm sure you'd soon pick it up.'

Ella swallowed a sip of the tea, which was scarcely more than luke-warm and as weak as pond water, and plucked up her courage.

'Thank you, I shall be pleased to accept whatever position you are able to offer me. I am absolutely committed to joining the WAAF and I very much appreciate you giving me this opportunity.' She was aware that her mother's formidable network of Edinburgh connections had already got her this far this quickly, and she didn't want to push her luck.

'But . . .' Ella hesitated.

'Yes, my dear?'

'Well, it's just that I should really like a role that's a bit more practical. With the planes, I mean. I read that there's someone called a rigger, who gets the aircraft ready to go and sees them back in and so on. And I know I don't have any mechanical skills, but I promise you I'm a fast learner. And I should so like to be outside in the open air.'

Squadron Officer Macpherson pressed her lips together firmly. 'Hmm, I see.' She smiled, a little grimly. 'Very well, Eleanor, you may have your wish. Let's see what you're made of. But I won't be surprised if, within a couple of weeks, you are sitting here begging me to transfer you to a nice clean administrative role in a nice warm office.'

Ella beamed. 'Oh, I won't, Squadron Officer Macpherson. I prom-ise. Thank you so much for giving me this chance.'

Her commanding officer stood, straightening the hem of her serge jacket, and extended a hand. 'In that case, welcome to RAF Gulford, Eleanor. Now, let's sort you out with your uniform and see if we can find you a billet.'

As the two girls took off their damp overcoats and hung them on the hooks in the narrow hallway of their digs, Jeanie Cochrane, their landlady, hailed them from the kitchen. 'There's a letter come for you, Ella.' She handed her a flimsy envelope, addressed in Christophe's distinctive handwriting, then turned back to stir the pot of mince – which was mostly onions and diced carrots, in fact, to pad out the fatty scraps of grey meat that the ration allowed. 'That'll be from your young man in France then?'

'Aha, how is the gorgeous Christophe?' Vicky pulled off her peaked cap and ran her fingers through her dark curls in a vague attempt to tidy the tangle the April wind had made of them on the bike ride home from the airfield. She sighed. 'It's so romantic, having a foreign boyfriend. I bet French boys treat their girls a lot better than British ones do. I'm going to have to find myself a foreign fella too. There's a rumour that we're going to get some Polish airmen stationed at the base, though I doubt the Poles are as romantic as the French.' Vicky had progressed from her job amongst the filing cabinets to being a communications operator, which gave her access to all sorts of interesting and useful information.

'Supper'll be twenty minutes. I've just put the tatties on to boil.' Jeanie turned to her young son, Dougie, who had come in from playing with his friends in the close now that they had been called in for their tea by their own mothers. 'Not so fast. You can wash your hands and get that table set. Leave the girls in peace for five minutes, why don't you?'

With his father in the army now and off to a training camp somewhere in the Highlands, Dougie was enjoying the leeway that being 'At War' entailed in the Cochrane household. Ella was aware that his status amongst his peers in the village of Gulford had shot up with the arrival of the two glamorous WAAFs. She'd overheard him telling them that *he* wasn't interested in girls, but that Archie's big brother, Tam, reckoned they were 'right bonny ones, they lassies'. Ella and Vicky spoiled Dougie and sometimes gave him sweets from their rations, if there were any.

Ella knew that, as she worked on the planes, Dougie was secretly hoping that one day she might be able to cadge him a ride in one.

Ella ran upstairs clutching her letter, while Vicky tactfully remained in the kitchen with Jeanie and Dougie to give her a little privacy in their shared bedroom whilst she read it.

'Supper's on the table. Time to tear yourself away from your French lover-boy.' Vicky tapped on the bedroom door before sticking her head around it. 'Oh Ella, sweetheart, what is it?'

Ella lay curled on her side on her bed, with the letter crumpled in her hand, her cheeks wet with tears that were soaking her pillow. Vicky sat down beside her and gave her shoulder a comforting squeeze.

Fumbling in the pocket of her jump-suit, Ella pulled out an oil-smudged handkerchief and blew her nose. 'He's joined up,' she said, miserably, carefully smoothing out the sheets of Christophe's letter and folding them so that they'd fit into the cigar box that she kept on the chest of drawers that separated the two beds in their sparsely furnished room. She reached up now and opened the box, its faint smell reminding her of the Martets' Paris home, of Monsieur Martet's after-dinner cigars, and French furniture polish and white lilies. She gently touched the shells that sat in the box on top of Christophe's letters and the postcard of the *Mona Lisa* that Caroline had sent her: a razor shell, a sun-bleached oyster shell and Neptune's locket, the hinged clamshell Christophe had given her that first night in the dunes.

She wiped her eyes and turned to her friend. 'I knew he would, but I'd been hoping against hope that something would happen to stop it – some vital war work at the bank. Or flat feet. Anything that would keep him safely behind a desk in Paris.'

Vicky nodded sympathetically. 'Yes, but Ella, you know the French need every able-bodied man they have now that Mr Hitler is knocking at their front door.'

Ella knew that as well as anyone. Lately, the two squadrons currently based at RAF Gulford had begun a new pattern of training sorties.

Previously, the Hurricane aircraft had been practising torpedo bombing in the Firth of Forth, with a view to deployment to protect the British fleet, rumoured to be concealed in Scapa Flow, if Vicky's gleanings of information were correct. But these past ten days the planes she'd been sending up had been practising air combat manoeuvres, and Sandy, the flight sergeant who worked in the hangar fixing the planes when they needed more than just routine maintenance, said it was a sign that the boys were about to be deployed elsewhere. 'Aye, it'll be Holland or France right enough. Now, young Ella, hand me up that wrench so we can get things fixed up good and well to keep our boys safe while they're giving that Adolf Hitler a right royal boot up his Nazi backside.'

Vicky passed Ella her hairbrush. 'Come on, make yourself present-able. Jeanie's mince and tatties will be getting cold. Christophe will be alright and we're going to make sure our boys are there to help. One concerted effort from all the Allies together and the Germans will be put back in their box. It'll all be over by the summer and then you and your Christophe can get married and live happily ever after in Paris with your six children. And don't forget, bags I chief bridesmaid.'

Ella smiled wanly, then obediently ran the brush through her hair, unpinning and untangling the plaited knot in which she wore it for work to keep it safely out of the way, and smoothing out the wavy tresses which were still damp from the rain.

'Come an' get it before Dougie eats yours too!' Jeanie shouted up the stairs, and the two girls trooped down for their supper.

Next morning, Ella propped her bike against the side of the hangar, reporting for duty as usual and going to find Sandy to get her orders. It was still chilly, even though Easter was past and the first lambs were shivering on uncertain legs in the fields. But at least the mornings were starting to get a little lighter now. In January and February, she'd cycled to the airfield in pitch-darkness, through air so sharp with winter's bitter frost that her hands would freeze around the handlebars, even in the woollen gloves that her mother had knitted her, and her nose and cheeks were nipped red with cold. She had chilblains on her fingers and toes where she'd warmed them too fast on the rubber hot-water bottle that Jeanie gave her to put into her bed at night to take the damp chill off the sheets. Even with the extra blankets that Mother had given her from home, it was hard to get warm enough to drop off to sleep at night. But she soon warmed up when she got to work, kept busy with her tasks carrying out daily inspections on the aircraft stationed at the base, refuelling the planes and, on freezing cold mornings, plugging in the batteries to start the Hurricanes' engines. Sometimes, the planes had to have their engines revved during checks and Sandy would make Ella and one of the other WAAF flight mechanics sit on the tail fins, one on each side, to weight the aircraft down and prevent it from taking off. 'Hold on tight girls,' he'd yell, climbing into the cockpit, 'if one of you falls off the other will be flying out over the Bass Rock before you know where you are!'

'Morning, Ella,' Sandy nodded to her now as she entered the hangar. 'Are the other girls here yet? Can you go and round them up please? We've an important briefing this morning.'

It was as he'd predicted. The two squadrons were being deployed, it was rumoured, to airbases in Europe. 'So let's get everything done perfect this morning and give the boys a good send off, eh?'

By lunchtime, the Hurricanes were lined up and ready for the off. As she finished refuelling the last one, Ella kissed her gasoline-scented fingers and patted the aircraft. The pilot, waiting to climb into the cockpit, grinned at her. 'How about one of those for me as well? No point kissing Gertie here, she can't kiss you back as well as I can.'

Sandy shook his head. 'Sorry pal, that kiss is no' for you. She's sending it to her boy in France. So make sure you take good care and deliver it for her. And then go and give those Germans what for, for the rest of us.'

The noise of engines split the air, reverberating off the corrugated tin huts, then climbing to a roar as the aircraft began to taxi. Ella and the other ground staff waved them off, and even Squadron Officer Macpherson came out to salute before turning to herd her chattering WAAFs back into the office.

As the last plane climbed into the sky, the pilot looped back low over the airfield one final time before climbing and setting his course south and east. Ella stood, watching as the Hurricane dwindled to the size of a tiny toy and then disappeared into the clouds. 'Keep him safe,' she whispered, her chapped fingers knotted together as if in prayer. 'Keep them all safe.'

3 rue des Arcades,
Paris
10 April 1940

Ma Chère *Ella,*
How I miss you, and all our carefree times both here and on the island. They seem very long ago and far away now, although in my mind they are more real than the nightmare that goes on all around us.

I'm writing in haste as I have just one day of leave and have come home to say 'au revoir' to Maman, Papa and Caroline (who all send you their love). I've now completed what passes for basic training and am being deployed to join the French 2nd Army.

Caroline's work at the museum continues, despite all the upheavals, and you will be pleased to know that several more packages, similar to the one that we delivered together last summer, have found their way to safe homes. It seems strange that people still come and visit the museum when all around life is in disarray, but I suppose it gives them a sense of stability in a turbulent world, to come and lose themselves amongst the art that remains in our peaceful galleries.

Papa has tried to persuade Maman to go the Île de Ré where she will be safer, but she refuses to leave when he and Caroline must remain here for their work, and she says she wants to stay as close to me as she can, even if it is only here in Paris.

We are all trying to put a brave face on things. But the truth – which I can admit only to you – is that we are frightened. France never wanted this, with memories of the last Great War still fresh in the minds of our fathers. We lost so many men then, the country has scarcely had a chance to recover. The army that we have scrabbled together is padded out with old men and boys. But now we have no choice. And so I pray to any and all the gods that we will all be kept safe and that I will see my family again very soon.

And I pray the same thing for you too, my darling Ella. Thank you for sending us your brave pilots. I will look up into the sky and know you are there helping to protect us. With your help, and our determination, surely the Maginot Line will hold fast and freedom will triumph for all who have suffered through this cruel and insane oppression.

Je t'embrasse très fort, ma chère Ella, as do Papa, Maman and Caroline.

With all my love, always,
Christophe

'It's started.' Vicky had snatched a moment away from her radio to pass on the news. 'I've just had word from London. They're sending up our boys from the bases on the Continent. The Germans are attacking on all fronts. Aircraft and tanks, apparently. There's fierce fighting in Belgium, that's where it seems to be concentrated as far as I can make out, but there's a lot of activity in northern France too.'

'Have you heard anything about the Ardennes?' Ella's throat constricted with fear and the words came out as scarcely more than a whisper. She knew, from what little she'd been able to glean from the news reports, that the French 2nd Army had joined the other battalions holding the Maginot Line in that region.

'Nothing specifically from there, no. Just Belgium in general at the moment. Sorry, got to get back before Miss Macpherson notices I'm not actually on a lav break after all. I'll send word the minute I manage to hear any more.'

'Right lass,' Sandy said gruffly, eyeing Ella from beneath his craggy eyebrows. He'd noticed the colour drain from her cheeks. 'Give me a hand with fixing yon prop, will you?'

May had brought kinder weather and today there was some warmth in the Scottish sunshine. A few cowslips were showing their shy faces in the grass alongside the runway and, whilst the breeze off the sea still had a keen edge, it blew more gently than usual between the grey-green flanks of the latest squadron of aircraft lined up at RAF Gulford.

'Come on, Ella, and bring those tools with you. Let's get this old lady ready to fly again.'

Ella was desperate for news, but there was none. Or, at least, there was none directly from Christophe, no word from Caroline either, no note, no letter.

There was plenty of news in the papers and the newsreels at the cinema. It had happened so fast in the end: the Battle of France had lasted about six weeks, which were filled with panic and chaos and reports of intense fighting.

Ella and her parents huddled around the radiogram when she came home for the day on the last Sunday in May. The King was attending a special service at Westminster Abbey and a national day of prayer had been declared for 'our soldiers in dire peril in France', desperate measures which said as much about what was happening across the Channel as any news bulletin's sketchy reporting could.

Afterwards, the Lennox family sat around the dining table and tried to apply themselves to their Sunday meal, although Ella could scarcely choke down the lunch her mother had made.

'The newspapers say our Allied troops in the north of France have been cut off. The panzer divisions managed to smash right through the defences on the Somme. Thousands are stranded there, backed up against the Channel,' Mr Lennox remarked, setting down his knife and fork and giving up the struggle with the gristly piece of boiled beef on his plate.

'Those poor souls. Surely there's something more that can be done to save them?' Ella's mother folded her napkin and placed it beside her plate with a sigh.

'They're doing their best, Mother. But the fighting goes on day and night, and we've lost so many aircraft that it's hard to know where to send the ones that are left.'

Her mother hugged her tight as Ella left to catch the bus back to Gulford later that afternoon. 'Here,' she handed her a parcel wrapped in brown paper and tied up with string. 'It's a tea loaf for you to share with Vicky and Jeanie. Make sure you eat properly, won't you? Keeping your strength up so that you can do your job well is your patriotic duty these days.'

When Ella and Vicky arrived at the base next morning, Squadron Officer Macpherson met them at the office door. 'It's some good news at last, girls!' Their commanding officer was positively beaming. 'Mr Churchill announced last night that Operation Dynamo is underway. Every seaworthy vessel along the south coast has gone to help. They've begun evacuating troops from Dunkirk. Thousands are out already. They're bringing our boys home.'

As the news broke of the ships that went to help snatch back British, French and Belgian troops on those desperate days at the end of May, Ella thought often of *Bijou*, picturing tiny boats just like her sailing to the rescue, and she hoped, against hope, that somehow Christophe had made it to the Pas de Calais and been saved. She prayed for a miracle, feeling guilty that she couldn't be more pleased for the hundreds of thousands of men who were rescued that week, when all she wanted was news of just one. But still no news came.

And then, two weeks later, there came another bulletin that made her heart stand still. Paris had fallen: France was now in German hands.

'Come on, Ella. Come with us.' Vicky was pinning up her hair in front of the mirror in their bedroom. 'You don't have to dance if you don't want to – although goodness knows there are more pilots queuing up to ask you than any of the rest of us. Just come along for one evening for some fun and some company of your own age, instead of sitting here with Jeanie and Dougie listening to the news and fretting.'

Vicky sat down on the bed beside Ella, brushing out her unruly curls. 'Look, I know it's hard being apart from Christophe and you miss him terribly. But he wouldn't expect you to sit at home letting life pass you by. After all, it's your patriotic duty to keep up the spirits of our own boys – that's how I look at it. Go on. Come to the dance.'

You'll enjoy it. And, Lord only knows, you need to have a bit of fun sometimes.'

'Sorry, Vicky, I just can't.'

'Well, I'm very disappointed in you Miss Lennox' – Vicky could do a mean impersonation of Squadron Officer Macpherson's strident tones – 'I expect my gels to show a bit more fighting spirit.'

'My fighting spirit is all reserved for the job these days,' Ella sighed. 'I know I'm being a bit pathetic. I just feel so flat. I saw a glimpse of what my life really could be when I was in France. There was so much promise; it was all just beginning. And now the war has slammed the door shut in my face. I know that sounds awfully selfish when people are suffering so. But I'm terrified that, when all of this is over, it'll be gone. I can't imagine what my life will be like if I can't go back to be with Christophe.'

Vicky patted her hand. 'Don't worry, Ella. Life goes on – come what may. Even if this bloody awful war changes everything, we'll win through in the end. The world might be different when it's all over, but you'll be alright. Christophe too, I'm sure.' She stood up, pulling down her pencil skirt where it had rucked up a little around her hips. 'Now, are my seams straight?' She turned so that Ella could check the backs of her stockings. 'Last chance to change your mind and come with us. No? Alright then, have fun mouldering beside the wireless!'

Ella smiled and shook her head. 'Actually, I've got another contact at the Red Cross to write to, so I think I'll get the letter done tonight.'

As the months had gone by with no word of the Martets, she had continued to pursue every means she could think of to try to find out what had happened to them all. She listened obsessively to the official news bulletins on the wireless and in the cinema, desperate for any mention of Paris or the Free French, the depleted remnants of France's army who were now fighting for their country where they could under the direction of General de Gaulle from his headquarters in England. She pestered Vicky and the other radio operators on the base for any snippets of news that they could glean over the air waves; and she wrote letters to anyone she could think of who might be able to get word through to France or back from France.

Mostly, though, her petitioning was met with annoyed impatience. 'Miss Lennox, our priority is to communicate – where we are able to do so – with the families of British servicemen. I'm sorry, we simply do not have the resources, let alone the capabilities, to track down missing French soldiers too.'

She knew she was searching for a needle in a very large and very chaotic haystack, but since there was nothing else she could do except carry on searching that was what she did.

Yet, all around her the war swept onwards, gathering momentum as the Germans focused their fearsome firepower on Britain. On the first day of July, the Luftwaffe announced their presence over British skies by bombing Wick, one of the most northerly airbases in Scotland. Lives were lost that day, despite the brave defence put up by the Hurricane pilots who Ella saw off from their East Lothian base.

All through that summer, and into the autumn, the Battle of Britain raged. All leave was cancelled, and the crews at RAF Gulford were busier than ever. Each time she waved the squadron off on another sortie, the bone-shaking roar of the Hurricanes' engines seemed to Ella to represent the desperation she felt, her longing for an end to the war. It was unbearable to count the aircraft back in and realise some of their number were missing.

Ella tried to stay focused on the job, methodically ticking off each task on her check-lists. They all knew that the Hawker Hurricanes were workhorses, less glamorous than the Spitfires which were gaining a reputation as the thoroughbred racehorses of the skies. But, as Sandy told Ella, 'Our 'uns are getting the job done too. When it comes to downing a German bomber, give me a Hurricane any day. They're a damn sight more sturdy and just look how many we've managed to get back down safely even when they've been shot to buggery.'

But they all knew, as well, that the aircraft's Achilles heel was fire: the pilot sat just behind the aircraft's gravity fuel tank and more than a few of the boys they'd sent off from Gulford had been horrifically badly burned by a jet of flame shooting through the instrument panel in front of them. This war was a random, casually cruel lucky dip. Young lives curtailed so abruptly: '*Assumed missing*' written on the reports. Families left in a harrowing limbo of loss and grief, without the closure of a body to bury, a coffin to mourn over; husbands, sons and brothers disappearing into thin air.

Ella immersed herself in her job, working such long hours that summer that she scarcely had time to notice that autumn had arrived. Then, all of a sudden, it was time to harvest the potatoes in the fields surrounding the base and the wind from the sea regained its bitter edge, numbing her fingers as she tightened engine bolts and mended worn tyres. And she realised that the nights were drawing in as September rolled into October. At last, the bombing raids on British cities began to tail off thanks, in part, to the Luftwaffe's Stukas being savaged in the skies by the Hurricane pilots sent up from RAF Gulford and a hundred other airfields across the country. But, whilst she gave thanks that fewer pilots were being lost, Ella longed to stay busy, to be kept running from plane to plane from dawn to dusk so that she wouldn't have a minute to think. Because when she did think, images of Christophe, injured or dead, flooded, unbidden, into her mind, and the terror that the Martets' must surely be feeling, living their lives in occupied France, tormented her dreams through the long, dark winter nights.

And then the seasons turned again and it was spring. In March, Scotland reeled as Clydebank was bombed and more civilian lives were lost. Ella had run out of contacts to write to in order to try and find out what had happened to Christophe, so she began all over again, pestering the organisations she had already tried, even wangling an introduction to a female SOE agent (through his contact with the pilots on the base, Sandy knew people who knew people), who was rumoured to be about to be deployed into France, and begging the girl to try to find out news of the Martet family of 3, rue des Arcades, should she make it to Paris. But still no word came.

One summer's day, when even the blue sky and scudding white clouds above RAF Gulford couldn't dispel the gloom of the war grinding on interminably with Germany's recent invasion of Russia, Ella packed away her tools as usual and cycled back to her digs. When she walked into the kitchen, her parents were sitting at the table nursing cups of tea which Jeanie had brewed for them. And her heart stood still. Because they wouldn't have come all this way, unannounced, unless there was news.

Her mother embraced her, with a careful gentleness that made Ella's heart break into a thousand pieces. And then she handed Ella an envelope, addressed to the house in Morningside and franked with a Spanish postmark, which contained a note and another, longer letter.

The note was from Monsieur Martet to Mr and Mrs Lennox, asking them to read the enclosed letter from Caroline and to make sure that they were with Ella when she read it.

With trembling hands, scarcely able to breathe, Ella unfolded the letter. She hesitated, realising that even though it was the definite news for which she'd been longing for over a year, she didn't want to begin to read. Because once she did, it would make the truth real. And maybe, after all, it was better to go on without knowing the truth, to be able to go on hoping, instead of knowing and giving up.

14 July 1941

Dearest Ella,
I write this letter not knowing whether it will ever reach you, like the others I have written over the past year. Maybe you have received them, but when there can be no reply we have no way of knowing. And so I must keep on

trying, because I know you will be thinking about us and wondering and worrying. In any case, I hold out a little more hope that this one will get through because now we are on the island and Benoît will take this when he goes out to tend to his lobster pots. Like a message in a bottle, it will be borne by the waters of the Atlantic, bobbing from fishing-boat to fishing-boat on a secret tide which allows such messages to wash up in Spain, from where they can be sent onwards by more conventional means. I cast it out on these stormy and uncertain waters in the hope that, this time, it will finally reach you.

If you have had any of my other letters, then you will know the news of Christophe. I do not wish to re-open those wounds, which I know cannot possibly have healed, although I pray that time will work its magic on us all in the end so that we can get through each day without having to bear the searing pain of loss. But if they have not reached you then I must tell you again. He was killed on one of the first days of the Battle of France, in May last year. All we have of him is a scrap of paper with the Paris address scribbled on it in his handwriting, sent back with the letter from the Croix Rouge *confirming that he died, without regaining consciousness, after being caught in machine-gun fire just outside Sedan when the German forces attacked in the Ardennes. The piece of paper was in the pocket of his jacket, which had his name clearly marked so that they were able to identify him. His body is buried, with the bodies of others who died that day, in a field far away on the other side of the country, so we cannot visit him and lay flowers on his grave. But one day we will do so, and he will smile down on us and know how much we all still love him even though he is gone from us for ever.*

We stayed on in Paris, even after hearing the news. Maman was inconsolable, but refused to leave Papa and me, who still had our work there, even though we begged her to go to the island. The Nazis reopened the Louvre at the end of last summer, as a propaganda exercise to show how civilised the conquering force really was – a hollow charade of a public relations exercise as they had shut off many of the galleries and, I am convinced, have been stealing works of art right, left and centre to send back to their Fatherland.

But now, dear Ella, I must write of our further trag-edy. In May, they came and took Maman away. We have been frantic, trying to find out where she has been sent. They are deporting anyone of Jewish descent, and we fear she is now in a deportation camp in Drancy. She was visiting Cousin Agnès at the time: they took her and the children too, so we can only hope that they are all together still, so that, wherever she may be, she is with those who love her, just as she will surely be supporting them through whatever they may be suffering.

Papa and I have fled to the island: we cannot stay in Paris any longer in these dreadful times, so filled with fear and the terrible, terrible pain of loss. We are still in the occupied part of France, and the Île de Ré is a strategic part of the Germans' defences so the island is littered with hideous cement boxes and barbed wire. But you know that this place has always had its own spirit of wildness and indomitability, and this still prevails even today. If it weren't for the curfew and a few restricted areas, you would scarcely know there was a war on here. We live very quietly and very simply, clinging to each other to get through the days until there is an end to this living nightmare in which we find ourselves.

Pray for us, dear Ella, as we pray for you. Please pray that Maman *will be returned to us safely in the end. I know your heart will be broken, as ours are. Maybe that is the only comfort we can find now, in the knowledge that we are not alone in our pain and suffering, along with so many others who have lost so much in this terrible war.*

May these words find their way to you, and may you be surrounded by those who love you best when you read them. I cannot bear to think of your suffering. And I know that Christophe too would not want you to suffer. He would want you to live your life, a life filled with as much beauty and joy and love as you can possibly cram into it. Do so, please, for his sake, and for ours.

Je t'embrasse très fort, ma chère *Ella*.

With all my love,

Caroline xxx

2014, Edinburgh

Ella is lying in her bed today, propped up on snowy pillows, too tired
to get up and sit in her chair. The nurse had warned me that she might
not be able to stay awake for long, that she's been drifting this past week
on the sea of memory that is beginning to carry her from us. But I have
so many questions for her and, though I try to rein them in, I'm also
conscious that time is running out and so I must ask them if I'm to get
her story down before it's too late. Her voice is a little weaker today,
wavering, as she remembers.

'The war changed everything, in ways we could never have imagined. From the most mundane aspects of our daily lives to the broadest
principles of the world as a whole – everything we had once known,
everything we'd taken for granted, was altered by that terrible war.
You find that suddenly there are no certainties any more, you're in
unchartered territory, so much is destroyed . . . But there's a freedom
in destruction too. Who's to say what's right and what's wrong when
life can end at any moment? When that fact is brought home to you so
brutally? Reading that letter of Caroline's, I thought of the thousands of
families across the world who had read letters like that and who would
be reading more letters like that the next day and the day after that . . . I
thought of Monsieur Martet and Caroline having had to read that awful
news, and then to have Marianne taken from them, and I wondered
how life could possibly go on for any of us . . .'

I rummage in my bag for a tissue, wiping my eyes and wondering why I seem to cry so often and so easily these days. I do so, silently, in the night when I lie awake listening to Dan's gentle breathing, which serves only to magnify the widening gulf between us as we drift further apart. I grieve for our marriage, which has somehow become lost amongst the heaps of ironing, the clutter of Finn's toys and the weight of our worries that have piled up, like flotsam on a flood-tide, in what used to feel like our family home.

And I've been grieving for Christophe too, ever since I read Caroline's letter last night. As I'd transcribed her words on to the computer screen the tears had poured down my face.

Ella reaches for my hand. 'But you see, Kendra dear, you have a choice. You can either let the pain overwhelm you, defining your life from that point on – perhaps even ending it or, at best, consigning you to a living death – or you can find a way to bear it, to carry it with you and still go on living. As you well know yourself, you can't always choose what life throws at you. But you always have a choice in how you deal with it. Caroline's words gave me that choice; they were my lifeline when I read that letter: "*He would want you to live your life, a life filled with as much beauty and joy and love as you can possibly cram into it. Do so, please, for his sake, and for ours.*" I realised that I had to do as she asked, for her sake and for her father's. That if I could do it then maybe she could too. That was our pact. And it was one that would bind us even more tightly together, as the sisters we had so hoped we would become.'

Her eyes close and her complexion looks waxen against the white of the pillows.

'Granny?' Her eyelids flicker open again briefly, although I can see that she's drifting as the flood of memories carries her back to another time and place. Then, as her eyes close once more, she smiles. I have to lean in close to hear the words she whispers.

'Rhona? My darling girl. Thank you for coming . . .'

PART 2

1942, Scotland

Not long after she'd received Caroline's letter, Ella was approached one day by Wing Commander Johnstone, the senior officer on the base at Gulford. She was fitting a battery into one of the aircraft outside the hangar when she saw him sauntering over to her. Ella stood to attention and he saluted her back, then came to look more closely at her work.

'You enjoy working on the planes, don't you, Aircraftwoman Lennox?'

'Yes, sir, very much.'

'And I know you do an excellent job. Your superior officers have high praise for your attitude and the standard of your work. They say you put your heart into it.'

Ella nodded, dropping her gaze for a moment. Since learning of Christophe's death, she had been so broken that sometimes she felt that all she had left to give to this job was her heart – or what was left of it. Some days it was hard to summon up the energy to continue.

The wind swirled across the airfield carrying with it the faint cries of the sea-gulls. Tucking a loose strand of hair back under her cap, Ella's hand shook as she was ambushed yet again by the image of Christophe's face close to hers that night in the dunes, the love in his eyes shining like moonlight on water. She couldn't yet bring herself to believe his shattered body lay lonely in a makeshift grave in an unknown part of France.

She blinked the image away, trying to stay focused on the officer who stood before her now.

'I'm also told that you speak French?' Wing Commander Johnstone continued.

'Yes, sir.'

'How would you feel about transferring to a slightly different role?' His tone was nonchalant, although she sensed that he was choosing his words carefully. 'A colleague of mine is looking for a French speaker to help out with a special project.'

Ella looked him in the eye, her interest piqued. 'Well, that would depend, sir. You see, I like my job because I feel I'm making a real difference on the Continent. Every aircraft I send off is a direct connection with the war. I'd like to help, but only if it means still being able to make a difference over there.'

The lines around her superior officer's eyes crinkled deeply as he smiled a broad smile of amusement. 'Oh, don't worry, Aircraftwoman Lennox. I think it's safe to say you'd still be making a difference alright. And, in fact, I believe it would be a role that could give you even more of a direct link to France.'

'In that case, sir, I'd like to know more.'

'Very good. I'll make the necessary telephone call. Squadron Officer Macpherson will give you your orders shortly.' He saluted her smartly. 'And in the meantime . . .'

'Yes, sir?'

He patted the undercarriage of the Hurricane. 'Keep up the good work.'

It was not without regret that Ella handed over her mechanic's blue serge jump suit in return for the smartly tailored skirt and jacket worn by most WAAFs. Before she left RAF Gulford she'd been put down for some basic wireless training in preparation for her new role. When she walked into the office at RAF Gulford on the first day of the training, a couple of pilots who were lounging outside the door looked her up and down. One removed his cigarette from between his lips and gave a long, low whistle. But the appearance of Squadron Officer Macpherson, who gave him one of her iciest glares, made him jump to attention and salute her respectfully.

'Right, Ella, we're going to give you your wireless operator's training here before you leave us.' She was brisk and efficient, but Ella felt that Squadron Officer Macpherson might miss her when she was gone, and she knew that she would miss her too.

Vicky was horribly torn about Ella's going as well. 'There, I knew you'd look like a knock-out in the proper uniform.' She'd beamed when they were dressing that morning. 'I'm going to show you how the radio kit works. But I really, really don't want you to go. I'm going to miss you awfully.' She'd hugged Ella tightly, to hide the tears that were pooling in her eyes.

Sandy was silent when she took her leave of the airfield. 'I'll keep in touch,' Ella promised, as she hugged him goodbye. He still said nothing, seemingly unable to speak, but cleared his throat gruffly and patted her on the back.

Then he held her at arm's length and smiled at her, finding his voice. 'Any time you get fed up sitting behind a desk, just you come straight back here. I'll keep your tool-kit at the ready for you, lass.'

The army truck jolted along the interminable, twisting single-track road that hugged the rugged contours of the land, swerving every now and then to avoid stray sheep and making Ella's stomach lurch and churn with a mixture of nerves and nausea. It had been a long day's drive from Edinburgh to the wilderness of Scotland's west coast, and it was growing dark as they turned off the tiny road to bump along the drive of Arisaig House. The grey stone building, glimpsed between a phalanx of tall pines, with its blacked-out windows, and the dark hills rising steeply behind it, looked somewhat forbidding to Ella as she peered out through the window. She craned her neck to look up at the clock tower that stood sentry on one side of the courtyard, its gilded hands pointing towards eleven o'clock. As the truck drew to a halt, silence fell, broken only by the ticking of the cooling engine and the faint, plaintive cry of a nightbird from the seashore somewhere below them. A door opened, throwing a rectangle of light across the gravel, and Ella stepped out of the car and made her way towards it.

'Welcome to Arisaig, Miss Lennox.' The officer, in army uniform, glanced at her appraisingly. 'You must be tired and hungry after your long drive. Let's get you something to eat. Then, as it's late, we'll sign you in and get a driver to take you straight to your billet. You'll be staying at Back of Keppoch, it's not far at all.'

Ella discovered she was ravenously hungry as she perched on a bench at one end of a long table in a cavernous kitchen. The churning in her stomach had settled now that she was no longer in the car and, although she was still feeling a little nervous, she tucked into the bread and ham that an orderly in a khaki army sweater had placed in front of her.

She was still not entirely sure what she was doing here: the briefing in Edinburgh had been vague, to say the least. As instructed, she'd met a Mr Brown at the North British Hotel. He'd stood as she'd walked into the Palm Court, his professional manner not quite concealing the light of appreciation in his eyes as he'd shaken her hand. He was wearing civvies, but had the bearing of a military man, tall and well-built under his suit and with the air of someone more at home out of doors than sitting at a little round table in a smart hotel. As she'd taken off her peaked cap and smoothed a strand of hair back into its neat bun,

Ella had noticed how handsome he was, his classically regular features creasing as he'd smiled at her reassuringly.

Over a pot of tea, he'd told her, 'It's a special project. We're developing some new radio technology for use in the field. We'll be needing a fluent French speaker, who understands how things work, to help train operatives and put together instructions that can be communicated to our contacts at the other end. I'm afraid I can't tell you more than that for the time being, Miss Lennox. I think you understand that there are many different aspects to the fight against the Axis powers in this war. Some of our methods are required, by their very nature, to remain confidential. In undertaking this project, your discretion will need to be ensured. You will be briefed further, on a need-to-know basis, when you reach your destination on the west coast. Would you be able to work under these conditions, do you think?'

She'd nodded. 'Mr Brown, as long as what I am doing will help our efforts in France, I'm eager to be of help in any way possible.'

'Very well then. I shall be in touch once I've arranged transport for you. Please be packed and ready to leave by Monday.' He'd stood and shaken her hand. 'Thank you for your assistance, Miss Lennox.'

And then she'd left, but she had noticed that he watched from the steps of the hotel as she'd walked away along Princes Street, her back straight in the air-force blue jacket and her hair tucked neatly under her peaked WAAF cap, to catch the bus for home.

In the kitchen at Arisaig House, the officer nodded approvingly at her clean plate. 'You made short work of that! You really must have been hungry. Would you like some more? No? A cup of tea then? – for both of us please, Sergeant McKay,' he asked the orderly.

As she sipped from her steaming mug, Ella glanced over its rim to take in her surroundings. She felt completely disoriented, suddenly finding herself in this new and strange place, away from the familiarity of Edinburgh and Gulford.

'Is there anything you'd like to ask me about what you're doing here?' The officer set his own mug down on the table and reached for a biscuit from the plate the orderly had put in front of them.

Ella laughed. 'Am I allowed to?'

'Now that you're safely here in Arisaig, yes.'

'Alright. What *am* I doing here? All I know is it's a top-secret project, something to do with wirelesses, and you need things translated into French.'

He nodded. 'Let me start at the beginning. Have you heard of the SOE?'

'The Special Operations Executive? Yes, vaguely, it's rumoured to exist and I did once speak to a girl who might have been an agent, though I never really knew if she was.'

The orderly, who was topping up her mug with more tea, guffawed. 'Oh, it exists alright. Some say it stands for the "Stately 'Omes of England" – or in this case Scotland – 'cos they've taken them all over. Otherwise fondly known as the Baker Street Irregulars.'

'Yes, thank you, Sergeant McKay, that will do.' The officer dismissed the orderly's interjection. 'Well, that's who we are, whatever you choose to call us. Arisaig is one of the SOE's commando training centres, where we prepare our agents for deployment in the field. The remoteness of this place makes it easier to keep it a secret and the rugged terrain is perfect for our purposes too. And so, where do you come in? Well, the organisation has been developing some new technology. We're calling it the S-Phone. It's a UHF radio-telephone, a kind of wireless, and it will enable our agents to communicate with incoming pilots and help them to locate unmarked drop zones in France far more accurately so that we can coordinate landings or the dropping of agents and supplies. Your linguistic skills will be helpful in training up our agents here and in preparing instructions for our colleagues in France, who will need to learn to use the ground transceivers that will be delivered to them. You come highly recommended, Miss Lennox. We've done our homework on you, you see.'

Ella felt slightly dizzy, her tired mind struggling to take in so much information at the end of such a long day. Perhaps it was the emotional strain catching up with her as well.

'But anyway, that's enough for tonight. You'll be properly briefed in the morning. Sergeant McKay here will drive you to your billet now and someone will be back to pick you up tomorrow morning at nine o'clock sharp. Make sure you have a good breakfast,' he added with a grin. 'You're going to need it!'

'We meet again, Miss Lennox.' The man standing outside the croft house where she'd spent the night held out his hand.

'Mr Brown. I wasn't expecting to see you here.'

He smiled, the lines on his face creasing into an attractive grin that extended to his amused eyes: they were a candid blue, she realised, and his skin was tanned, hinting at days spent outdoors – reinforcing the impression that she'd gained of him in the Palm Court at the hotel.

'Actually, it's Angus Dalrymple.'

She laughed. 'I should have known. Are all you undercover agents called Mr Brown?'

'No,' he replied, mock serious, 'some of us are called Mr Jones. And I believe there are one or two Mr Smiths as well.'

'Pleased to meet you – properly – Angus Dalrymple.' As Ella shook his hand, she noted his firm grip and wondered whether he'd noticed the calluses on her palms from her work at the airfield.

'Jump in,' he gestured to the car, a utility vehicle fondly known as a 'Tilly'. It was a glorious morning and, as she climbed into the cab, Ella paused for a moment to look around and get her bearings. To the east, the sun had risen through the hills which were tinted purple with summer heather above the dark evergreen woodlands in which their lower slopes were clad; in the opposite direction, a bay of golden sand could be glimpsed below them, and beyond it a series of jagged, blue-grey islands, which seemed to float upon the breath-taking clarity of the sea. The breeze carried to them the faint scent of seaweed which mingled with the peat smoke that was issuing from the chimney of the croft. A kittiwake mewled above her, reminding her of times spent sailing out over this same ocean from another island a thousand miles to the south. She took a deep breath, drinking in the pure, clear air, noticing how fresh it was after the coal-smoke smog of Edinburgh and the faint perfume of gasoline fumes that had always pervaded the air at Gulford, in spite of the constant blustering of the North Sea wind.

They rattled up the road, away from the beach, back to Arisaig House. In the light of a glorious west-coast day, the building looked a good deal less forbidding than it had last night, its square-paned windows glinting in the sunshine. 'Come in,' said Angus, 'and I'll introduce you to the team.'

The house was elegant and welcoming, with the morning sunlight streaming in on to polished oak floors and a grand staircase leading to the upper floors. He led her into the drawing-room, where a group of people were clustered around a mahogany table on which sat piles of papers and a piece of apparatus consisting of a curved metal box, an aerial, several small battery packs held together by canvas straps, a set of headphones and a small microphone. Ella recognised the components as a radio, although it was a good deal more compact than the ones she'd learned to operate at RAF Gulford.

'Harry, Dougal, Anja, George, Stefan – this is Ella.' She noted that surnames were not used, presumably a policy of the centre. They were all dressed in casual clothes and she suddenly felt out of place in her WAAF uniform.

In fact, as she discovered over the next few days, after the disciplined, orderly routine of RAF Gulford, here at Arisaig she felt as if she'd fallen down a rabbit hole and ended up in a wonderland where odd groups of people seemed to be doing bizarre things at strange times of the day and night. No one batted an eyelid when sudden explosions were heard from the other side of the hill behind the house; at lunch, she sat next to a man whose face was blacked out with camouflage as he drank the hearty broth Sergeant McKay had served up. It was not unusual, when they were ensconced in the drawing-room, learning how the components of the S-Phone worked, to glance up and see a group of commandos stealthily creeping towards the window with lethal-looking knives held in their fists; and one day when two local women came to the kitchen door with a basket of herring to sell, Sergeant McKay suddenly guffawed with laughter half-way through their negotiations and said, 'Very good, Alf! Charlie! You bloody nearly had me there!'

She quickly learned that one never asked questions: there was no point as no one ever gave a straight answer about what they were doing. Perhaps some of them weren't sure themselves. The situation seemed to be fluid and pretty chaotic at times, with comings and goings day and night. The S-Phone project hit an occasional set-back, but through it all Angus Dalrymple retained his air of amused assurance, so Ella assumed it was all part of some overall plan over which someone, somewhere must have been in control.

Opportunities to socialise were rare and Ella would usually return to her billet in the croft house down by the shore at Back of Keppoch in the evenings to read or write letters to her parents, reassuring them that she was employed in mundane technical training to do with being a wireless operator. But one evening, after a supper of venison steaks (one of the commando training exercises involved stalking and killing a deer armed only with a knife, which meant that the kitchen at Arisaig House was kept well-supplied), Angus pushed back his chair and said, 'Right then, we made good progress today. I think we've all earned a drink at the inn.'

The others agreed with alacrity, and they piled into two Tillys, which bounced along the long, rutted driveway and down the hill to where a cluster of white buildings nestled along the darkened shore. There were no lights showing, so Ella blinked as Angus pushed open the door of the inn and they stepped into the warmth and light concealed within. The hubbub of raised voices – she made out at least three different languages as well as the lilting local accent – and laughter enveloped them.

Sitting at a table in the corner, which a group of khaki-uniformed officers had chivalrously vacated when Ella and Anja appeared, they sipped half-pints of dark, bitter-tasting beer, which was the only drink on offer apart from whisky. It felt good to enjoy normality for once, a welcome break from the surreal wonderland of their daily training and from the constant reminders of the war. As she tilted her glass to take another sip, Ella met Angus's glance from the other side of the table. When he smiled, his blue eyes and strong, weather-tanned features reminded her of the bracken-clad hills and the crystal-clear sea that surrounded and protected the settlement of Arisaig, as if he were chiselled from the craggy landscape that enfolded them and kept them safe here.

She returned his smile and then turned back to ask Anja about her family back in Poland. Her parents were still there, she said, but she and her brother had fled when the Germans invaded. 'And now we are trying to fight to get our country back. My brother is with the Air Force. Last time I had contact with him he was stationed in England, in Norfolk. Do you know where it is?'

Ella nodded, enjoying listening to Anja's rich, rolling accent. 'And your parents?'

'My mother is a teacher; my father an engineer. He is foreman in a factory which the Germans have commandeered. They are making specialist equipment for the war effort. Every chance he gets, my father ensures that the machinery breaks down. I recently learned your British expression – to put a spanner in the works.' She grinned. 'There are many different ways to fight, as we know.' Then her expression grew serious again. 'I heard news from a friend of my brother's, who is in an underground group back home. My father has to manage the workers who are sent from prison camps each day to work in the factory. They say they are like living skeletons. Conditions in the camps are rumoured to be terrible. All the more reason to finish my training here and get back so that I can put some spanners in the works too.'

Ella clinked her glass against Anja's. 'Here's luck to you. To all of your family. And to spanners in the works.'

When the evening drew to a close, they stepped out into the quiet darkness and Angus pulled the door shut behind them, shutting in the light and noise of the inn. 'Jump in, Ella, I'll run you over the hill.'

'I can easily walk. There's enough light to see the road.' The moon was almost full, hanging in a black silk sky besequinned with a thousand stars.

'It's no bother,' he insisted. 'It's only a few minutes' drive.'

Outside the croft house, he switched off the engine and they sat for a moment, listening to the hush of the waves on the beach beyond the cropped grass of the machair. The water was calm in the bay and the moon lit a path to the islands beyond.

Ella sensed Angus turning to watch her profile as she gazed towards the sea, lost in her thoughts. A single tear painted a fine thread of silver on her cheek before she brushed it away. He reached across, his strong, capable fingers enfolding hers. And as he held her hand, she felt his vital warmth and strength permeate her skin, like the first rays of spring sunshine thawing the frozen ground of winter.

She leant towards him and brushed her lips, fleetingly, against his cheek. And then, without a word, she opened the door and got out of the car. He sat there, watching as she paused in the doorway of the white cottage and turned to smile back at him. His eyes were unfathomable in the shadows as he raised a hand in salute. Only after she had stepped into the kitchen, where the range muttered quietly to itself, and closed the door behind her, did she hear the ignition turn over and the car drive away, the sound of the engine fading as she climbed the stairs to bed.

Finally, the day came when they were ready to test the S-Phone in the field. The entire group assembled down on the shore. It was approaching midsummer's day and, that far north, the daylight lasted long into the evening, the sun only setting well after ten o'clock. Anja wore the apparatus, the battery packs cinched around her waist and the transceiver itself strapped on to her chest. She fitted the headphones in position and slotted the aerial into the front of the S-Phone, then glanced at her wrist-watch. It was approaching eight thirty, the time they'd been given by the RAF who'd allocated a plane to fly over the area so that they could take it in turns to practise talking the pilot in to various selected drop zones.

'Okay.' Angus gave Anja the thumbs-up. 'Start transmitting.'

They knew the plane would be approaching from the west, out over the sea, so she turned to face the evening sun which bathed them all in its clear golden light. She turned the knob on top of the transceiver and spoke the call sign into her microphone. There was a crackle of static and then the pilot's response, from the air transceiver, came through her headphones loud and clear. Using the coded coordinates she'd been given, Anja directed the pilot and then, suddenly, the plane swooped in low over Eilan Bàn and Loch nan Ceall to buzz the group assembled on the beach. They cheered and waved, then Anja handed the set over to Stefan so that he could take his turn.

Angus insisted that Ella have a go with the kit as well. 'It'll help you understand exactly how it works in practice so that you can make sure your translated instructions are absolutely accurate.' Ella had already drawn up a first draft of the French version of the instruction manual, but she jotted down a couple of additional notes, based on the experience of using the S-Phone in earnest. Once the details had been finalised, she would be responsible for coding the French instructions using an SOE cipher system. Angus had explained that the final version would be printed on silk as it was a material that was easier to conceal within the lining of an item of clothing, one which wouldn't give itself away with the telltale rustle of paper if the courier was stopped and subjected to a search.

The tests were successful, thankfully for them all. Once completed, the pilot swooped low over the beach one final time, saluted them with a tilt of his wings and then soared off above the hills, heading back to base for the night.

Harry packed the kit away and the others trooped back up to the house as Ella scribbled a final point in her notebook before gathering her belongings back into her rucksack. She'd stopped wearing her WAAF uniform after the first day and followed the lead of the others in more casual attire, which offered a greater degree of freedom and practicality when covering the rugged terrain. It felt good to be back in slacks again, which reminded her of the jump suit she'd worn at RAF Gulford.

A faint chill crept into the evening air now as the sun sank low beyond the islands of Eigg and Rum, far out beyond the bay, so she pulled a soft woollen cardigan from her pack. Angus had waited behind when the others left and he took the garment from her without a word and held it for her to slip her arms into the sleeves.

'Thank you.' She smiled at him.

'My pleasure.'

They both stood, silent for a minute, watching as the setting sun began to paint the western sky in shades of crimson and rose.

'The tests went well,' Ella remarked, feeling awkward suddenly in the silence.

'They did.' Angus nodded, never taking his eyes off the far horizon.

Ella pulled the edges of her cardigan across her chest and turned back to watch the sunset again, her arms wrapped around herself. The waves shushed softly on to the shore as the fading light turned the hills of Rum purple and then grey, and Ella thought of Caroline on another very different island, far to the south in these same waters. Was she watching this same sunset from the white house with the shutters of sea-mist blue? And where was Marianne? Was there a sunset at all, wherever she was?

'Penny for them?' Angus asked gently.

She turned to meet his gaze with a barely perceptible shake of her head. 'I was thinking of friends in France. Wondering what life is like for them now. It all seems so very far away and so very long ago.' She looked back out across the water where the reflections were fading, as if in a darkening mirror.

'You must miss him very much indeed.' He said it quietly, watching her profile.

Ella was silent for a moment.

He knew.

Of course, he knew: as the officer said on her first night here, they'd done their homework before they'd recruited her. And in a way it was a relief not to have to speak to Angus about Christophe, not to have to try to explain how he'd made her feel and how she felt now that she'd lost him. Not that she could ever have found the words to do so anyway.

She nodded, feeling glad that Angus understood. And feeling, too, that here was someone who was strong enough to be able to handle that knowledge, perhaps even strong enough to be able to help her bear it.

She turned her face away from the last rays of the sun as it slid beyond the far horizon and met his gaze again. It was the first time in more than two years that she'd looked at another man properly, as anything other than a colleague. And the man she saw beside her now was one who was brave enough to stand there alongside her in her grief and her pain, bearing witness to it and keeping her company in the midst of it.

And that, she realised suddenly, was something very great indeed.

His eyes met hers and she felt something stir deep in her heart. It was a sensation she'd thought she'd never feel again. She stood on tiptoes as she reached to bring her lips to his, the toes of her boots making half-moon dents in the damp sand. He wrapped an arm around her waist and pulled her close to him and she let herself lean in to the safe haven of his embrace.

The storms out at sea beyond the dusk-misted islands couldn't reach her here: she took refuge in his arms and felt, at last, the faint pulse of her heart as it began to beat again.

2014, Edinburgh

'Grandad was a secret agent? And you too! I can't believe we never knew! Does Mum know? And Robbie?'

Ella shakes her head. 'A lot of this remained classified until quite recently. We got into the habit of not mentioning it and so it became easier just to let things lie. Rhona and Robbie knew their father had been in the army in the war, and that I'd been in the WAAF. But, to children, life before they were born is ancient history, so they were never really that interested in knowing more.'

'Amazing.' I look at my frail old granny in a whole new light now. She's up again today, a little stronger than the last time I visited. Sitting in her chair in her pastel-coloured cardigan and tweed skirt, her white hair as light as thistle-down and her hands folded quietly in her lap, you would never imagine that she had once fixed planes and handled top-secret radio technology. 'And I bet Grandad was very handsome. No wonder you fell for him, even though you were still grieving for Christophe.'

Ella's eyes mist over, and she seems far away suddenly, perhaps seeing people and places that beckon her back to a time long gone. But I take her hand, as if drawing her back to the present, and her gaze focuses on my face again.

'Angus had a good heart. I saw that straight away. And he offered strength and solidity; someone I could trust at a time when the world seemed such a treacherous place to be. He was so alive too. That was another thing we had in common, that energy, the drive to get on with life. But he had something else as well: a quietly assured determination to fight for what was right in that war, to put an end to the darkness and destruction, to save lives.' She pauses. 'And he saved my life too, in many different ways. He brought back the light. He gave me so much to live for.'

She lets go of my hand and reaches for the hand-held tape recorder which sits on her bedside cabinet. 'But more of that anon . . . here's the next tape. I do hope you're not bored yet?'

I laugh. 'Bored is the last thing I am, Granny! I can't wait to hear the next instalment.' I slip the tape into my bag and begin to pull on my coat.

'Give my love to Dan and Finn. And please tell Finn that his honeysuckle has lasted well.' The sprig is in a bud vase beside her bed, where she can smell its faint perfume. But the last delicate flower filament hangs from the stem now and the leaves are beginning to drop, scattering themselves beside the blue bowl of shells, shot through with its lightning bolt of gold.

1942, Scotland

It was the only time she'd seen Angus rattled. They were in a briefing session, running through the final instructions with the group of
SOE agents who were about to deliver the first S-Phone transceivers
to Resistance groups in occupied territories, when an officer in army
fatigues knocked on the door. He handed Angus a note. As he read it,
the colour drained from his face and he turned away, momentarily, from
the others who were watching him expectantly. When he turned back,
he'd regained his composure, although the expression in his eyes was
one of deep pain and sadness.

'I'm sorry to have to tell you that the French drop into the Loire
valley will have to be postponed. There's been an incident. We've lost
our key agent there and she was the one who was going to receive the
first transceiver and pass it on to her contacts in a Resistance cell in
that area.'

They all knew that this part of France was an especially important
drop zone. The plan had been to land a plane in Vichy France, the
unoccupied part of the country, and rendezvous with the female SOE
agent so that she could cross back into occupied territory with the transceiver. The French *Résistance* was playing a key role in the Allies' struggle
to regain a foothold in France and the S-Phones were a vital part of the
plan to ensure landings of agents and supplies of munitions could be
coordinated without the Nazis intercepting the communications.

'How was she lost?' asked Anja.

'Someone denounced members of the Resistance cell to the Gestapo. She was with them when they were raided. They executed everyone who was there.' Angus's response was terse and matter-of-fact, although the strain in his expression belied his anguish.

'It's a total bloody tragedy.' Harry pressed his fingertips against his eyes, saddened by the loss of one of their colleagues, but frustrated too, at this major set-back to all their meticulous planning.

'I'll do it instead.' There was no hesitation in Ella's voice. She spoke calmly, with absolute determination.

'No, Ella. That's impossible. We'll have to liaise with other agents in France, see if there's anyone else we can deploy. Or perhaps I should go myself?' said Angus, turning to Harry.

'You know that's not going to work,' Harry said. 'It has to be a female, otherwise the crossing guards will smell a rat.'

'I'll do it,' Ella repeated. 'I know the kit. I speak French fluently. I can go in, hand over the phone and be out again before anyone knows what's happened. It makes sense. If they think they've wiped out a Resistance cell in that area then they won't be looking for anyone else so soon afterwards. We need to stick to the original timescale; you know how vital our support is in France.'

'Ella, it takes months to train an agent,' said Angus. 'What you've learnt in your few weeks here is nothing more than the tip of the iceberg. It wouldn't be safe. The last thing we want is for the S-Phone to fall into enemy hands before we've even begun to use it.'

'Yes, but it's a trade-off, isn't it? There'll always be that risk. I'll do it.'

Angus shook his head, and Harry chipped in again, 'The thing is, Ella, it takes a certain mentality, a certain background to be selected to be an agent. You have to be able to take the really tough decisions when the chips are down. Would you have what it takes to destroy the kit and take a suicide pill if you were caught? I'm sorry to be so blunt, but it could come to that. Agents have to be prepared to put the greater aims before their own lives sometimes. I've always admired you and thought you'd make an excellent agent, but there has to be a reason they've not asked you to take on that role or they would have done so already: you must have strong family ties, or something else in your make-up that means they doubt you'd be capable of taking the right decisions under pressure if push came to shove.'

Banishing thoughts of her parents' faces – they would have been aghast if they'd known what she was suggesting – Ella shook her head. 'Look, I know how this works. I'm not stupid and I've spent enough time here to know what the job might entail. But I am the obvious choice for this drop; we all know that. There are two days left, so give me the extra bits of training I'm going to need and let's get the job done.'

Harry looked at Angus. 'She's right, you know. D'you think it could work?'

Angus started to protest again, but Ella stood and put a hand on his arm to stop him. 'Angus.' She looked him straight in the eye, a look of steely determination in her green-gold gaze. 'Please. I'll do it.'

The plane bumped and lurched, hidden in the turbulent cover of the clouds as the pilot circled, trying to locate the drop zone and make sure it was safe to land. The original plan, to parachute the kit in, had been altered as Ella hadn't had time to complete the necessary training. Even though landing the aircraft – albeit briefly and in the unoccupied zone – would increase the riskiness of the operation, Angus had decided it was the only option.

The plane lurched violently again. *This is exactly what the kit will help to avoid*, thought Ella as she crouched in the fuselage, her stomach doing its own series of loop-the-loops and her heart thrumming as loudly as the aircraft's engines, as a powerful mixture of airsickness and nerves surged through her again. She placed a hand over the S-Phone radio transceiver that was strapped beneath her overcoat. In doing so, her fingers brushed the coat button that concealed the suicide pill. Angus hadn't been able to look her in the eye when he'd briefed her on it.

'I'm sorry, Ella, but I have to give you this. We can't take the risk of you being captured and tortured. You know too much about the project. But, I assure you, it's just a precaution. You aren't going to be caught. You'll be out again the next night, just as soon as you've handed over the phone in the safe house. The coded instruction manual is sewn into the lining here, see? And here's your knife. Again, hopefully, you won't have to use it. But, just in case . . .' She'd slid the commando knife back into its sheath and fastened it to her belt.

He'd come to see her off. As the pilot was running through his final checks, Angus pulled her to him, slipping his hands beneath the bulk of her overcoat so that he could encircle her slim waist and feel the vital warmth of her one more time. 'Come back safely, Ella. Don't take any risks.'

They both smiled at his words: risks were exactly what they were all taking with this venture, and well they knew it.

As the plane swooped down out of the cloud cover, she replaced her hand on the harness that strapped her in, trepidation making her clutch it tightly as she tried not to think about those risks now, nor the pill concealed in the third button of her coat. She needed to keep a clear head, to remain completely focused on her instructions. Any mistakes could put other lives at risk too, not just her own.

The pilot made his steep and bumpy landing on to a tiny airstrip concealed within woodland somewhere to the south of the Loire River. Ella remembered the château at Chambord, where they'd dropped off another item of precious cargo a few years ago. Where was the painting now? Kept safe somewhere, she hoped.

She clambered out of the plane and the pilot whispered, 'Good luck.' She nodded, gave him the thumbs-up and then stooped and ran towards the trees, where a dimmed torch was circling, beckoning her. The plane turned, taxied, then raced along the short runway and took off, the nose lifting sharply to clear the trees again. Forcing down the panic that rose in her throat as the aircraft lifted into the air, she continued running towards the dim light.

The man was young, scarcely more than a boy really. He held a finger to his lips and motioned to her to follow. She stayed close to him, her eyes straining to make out the path in the darkness of the forest. They were moving as quickly as possible, but the terrain underfoot was rough, criss-crossed by tree-roots, and there were loose stones that made her stumble, going over on her ankle sharply at one point, making her gasp with the sudden shooting pain. She tried to take more care: she couldn't afford to risk an injury that could jeopardise the whole plan. She walked it off, willing her limbs to move smoothly, relieved that the sprain hadn't been worse.

Eventually, they came to a point where the darkness of the trees opened out before them, softly illuminated, and then she saw that the eerie glow came from the moon reflecting off a river that flowed quietly past. Her guide turned to her and whispered, '*Le Cher.*' He held a finger to his lips again.

She nodded, thankful for the extra light, but recognising at the same time that it made them more vulnerable. This tributary of the Loire was the demarcation line between the occupied and unoccupied zones here, so there were likely to be Nazi patrols just over on the other bank.

They ducked back into the shadows and continued to follow a narrow path through the trees on the south bank. Finally, they reached an area where the ancient woodland had been newly felled, the massive trunks lying haphazardly amongst piles of fresh-smelling sawdust. '*Les Boches.*' The boy gesticulated, telling her that the Nazis had been responsible for this. She surmised that they must, therefore, be approaching the crossing point if the Germans suspected there to be activity in this area that was worth clearing the forest for. They rounded a corner and, lit by the moon as it shone through a break in the clouds, the white turrets of a fine château rose up on the far bank. She looked more closely. In fact, the château didn't only occupy the northern bank; it sat squarely in the middle of the stream, linked to a tower on the far side, and with a long covered gallery, three storeys high, borne on a series of stone arches that bridged the whole span of the river, linking it to the southern bank as well.

'Chenonceau,' her guide whispered. He scanned the far side of the river, searching for something. Then he shook his head and put a finger to his lips once again. 'It's not yet safe.' He gestured to her to follow his lead and sit down, huddling against one of the huge felled trunks. He explained, 'There will be a sign once the German patrols have gone. We will see a quilt hanging from one of the windows, as if being aired. Then you can go.'

It was slightly damp on the mossy ground and a phrase came into her head: *The darkest hour is just before the dawn. Where did that proverb come from?* she wondered, shivering slightly, thankful for her thick overcoat, which she rearranged to insulate herself from the chill that rose up from the earth and seeped into her bones. She checked her watch, tilting its face so that she could read it in the moonlight. There was still a while to go before sunrise. She was thankful for the cover of darkness, but knew that it would soon be gone, as the new day began to brush a barely perceptible opalescence across the sky beyond the pale traceries of Chenonceau's turrets.

She ran through her instructions in her head again, mentally rehearsing each step of the operation. She needed to enter the château and cross the covered bridge. She would be met by a contact inside who would hand her a headscarf and a basket. The two of them would walk out into the village, once morning came, to make it look as if they were going to the shops. She would be taken to the safe house where a member of the *Résistance* would be waiting and she would hand over the transceiver and instructions, giving as much of a briefing as possible. Then the contact from the château would come back for her and they would walk back together, carrying their shopping baskets. She would be concealed inside Chenonceau until dusk, at which point she'd return here to the forest. Another guide – or perhaps this same boy – would be waiting to lead her back to the pick-up point, and the plane would return for her under cover of darkness once again.

'Straight in and out, no fancy stuff. We've simplified the plan as much as possible,' Angus had explained. 'Once our Resistance contact has the first transceiver operational, we'll be able to do a bigger drop, with more units that they can distribute through their network.'

All she had to do was execute this series of simple steps; yet each one was fraught with potential risks. She felt her heartbeat pick up and took a couple of slow, deep breaths to calm it. She needed to keep a clear head and not panic, no matter what happened. Being able to think straight, to make the right decisions under pressure, was what was going to get her back to the safety of Scotland. Back to her parents. Back to Angus.

No distractions, she admonished herself. She concentrated on thinking of Caroline, wishing she could tell her friend that she was here, on French soil, bringing help, doing her bit to hasten the end of this awful war.

She kept her breath slow, calming the jangle of her nerves so that she could keep her senses about her.

She pressed her fingertips into the moss-covered ground, shivering again and swallowing the lump that blocked her throat as she thought of Christophe's beautiful, war-battered body buried all those miles away beneath this same chill soil. A cold anger flickered within her suddenly, helping to crystallise her emotions into a clear resolution to see this mission through.

Periodically, her guide peered round from behind the shelter of the tree trunk and eventually he stood, gesturing to her to do the same. She scrambled to her feet, easing the stiffness out of the tense, cold muscles of her legs. In the first faint light of dawn, a quilt had been hung from one of the upper windows of the château. He pointed to the door at the end of the covered bridge and mimed that she should knock on it four times.

She nodded and then set off, darting across the open ground. She felt completely exposed, suddenly aware that she was being watched, and not only by the guide. She sent up a brief prayer that the only other eyes that were following her progress at this moment were friendly ones from within the château.

With a thudding heart, she reached a wooden drawbridge and crossed it to the heavy door at the end of the bridge where she knocked four times, as instructed. There was a silence, filled only with the first tentative trill of bird-song from the woods behind her and the pounding of her blood in her ears. And then, almost weeping with relief, she heard the sound of footsteps approaching the door. Bolts slid back, a key turned and the door swung open a crack. She slipped through it and found herself standing in a long corridor. The windows were covered with thick blackout material and, once the door had been closed safely behind her, a lantern was lit, causing her to blink as her eyes adjusted to the sudden light.

She took a long breath, to calm the racing of her pulse, and then blinked again, in surprise this time. If at Arisaig she'd felt a little like Alice in Wonderland, here, she realised, she had most definitely stepped through the Looking Glass. Because she found herself standing in a long, elegant gallery, paved with black and white tiles whose diamond pattern seemed to swim and shift as it drew the eye to the far end. The hall's white stonewalls were bare, lined with a series of tall, rounded niches. They were big enough for a person to conceal themselves in and, as she followed the lantern-bearer, she couldn't help casting nervous glances into the shadows on either side. At the far end was a massive carved stone fireplace with a small wooden door on each side of it. They went through one of the doors, along a corridor, which twisted and turned, and she realised she must now have crossed the river and be in the main body of the château.

They descended a staircase and pushed open another door. Ella found herself standing in a cavernous kitchen, whose arched ceiling formed part of the stone piers supporting the château. A fire blazed in the hearth and a vast cast-iron range was giving out a steady heat, as well, warming the room. The lantern-light made the brass pots and pans hanging on one wall gleam invitingly and Ella suddenly realised she was ravenously hungry.

'Welcome to Chenonceau.' The woman who'd led her here extended a hand. 'We do not introduce ourselves by name, I think it's better that way, n'est-ce pas? Sit down here and warm yourself. I'll get you something to eat while we wait.'

Having eaten a hunk of hard bread ('We have to make it from chestnuts these days as the Germans take all the wheat. And the coffee is made with chicory. They have reduced us to eating like animals,' lamented the woman), spread with jam made from yellow plums to make it palatable, Ella felt her energy levels rise again. When the sun came up, the woman opened the blind that covered the kitchen's small window and the room was flooded with the light that reflected off the river. She wished she could explore the château – it seemed a beautiful and intriguing place – but Ella knew that was impossible. She needed to remain concealed so that as few people as possible were aware of the presence of an extra person amongst the staff. The warmth of the range made her feel drowsy after her sleepless night and she felt safe enough in this friendly stronghold to close her eyes for a few minutes and doze.

Eventually, she was woken by the sound of the door opening and a pair of sturdy boots crossing the stone flags. Another woman stood before her and solemnly offered her hand for Ella to shake. Wordlessly, she passed her a headscarf in a distinctive, bright-red paisley fabric and Ella drew it over her hair and knotted it under her chin. She picked up the wicker basket that the woman had set on the floor and nodded that she was ready. The woman led her back up the stairs and through the castle's elegant rooms to the main door which was the château's northern entrance. They walked briskly, but not fast enough to draw attention to themselves – just two women setting off to shop in the village. Despite the temptation to look around at the château's formal gardens and statuary, she was careful to keep her gaze lowered, as if she were accustomed to the setting. Ella had been warned to expect a Nazi presence since there were troops occupying some of the buildings in the grounds of Chenonceau and, as they crossed the final narrow bridge to the river's north bank, she spotted the distinctive uniforms. But this morning expedition was clearly part of the normal routine at the château because the guards scarcely glanced at the women as they passed and one even raised a hand in acknowledgement.

The woman led her into the village and they turned off the main road, down a small side street. She pointed to a house with a blue door and then whispered, 'I'll be back for you in one hour.' Ella checked her watch and nodded.

The door of the house was opened as she approached it by a woman who must have been watching out for her from behind the heavy lace curtains that hung in the window. She was ushered into a small parlour at the back of the house, which gave on to a courtyard hemmed in by high walls, affording complete privacy. A man stood up as she entered the room and shook her hand, his own broad palm as hard and leathery as a glove. Again, they didn't exchange names and there were no pleasantries. She slipped off her overcoat and began unbuckling the S-Phone concealed beneath it. He inspected the component parts with interest, nodding his approval and understanding. Quickly and quietly, conscious that she needed to make every minute count, she showed him how it worked, explaining how to connect the aerial and point it directly at the receiving transceiver. She used the tip of her commando knife to unpick the stitching of the lining of her coat and handed him the silk squares on which the coded instruction manual was printed. He nodded again, smiling broadly, then kissed her hard on either cheek. 'Mademoiselle, we know you have been most courageous in bringing us this. Your friends in France are grateful and we salute you.'

'Use it well,' she said with a smile. 'I hope it will save many lives.' She paused, imagining the friends and colleagues this man must have lost so very recently in the Gestapo's raid. 'And I pray for an end to this war very soon.'

The woman, who had been keeping watch from her station behind the lace curtains, beckoned that it was time to go. Ella pulled on her coat, fastening the buttons again to conceal the fact that a part of the lining now hung loose, and tied the distinctive, bright scarf over her head. The woman from the château was on the doorstep and she quickly slipped a couple of the paper-wrapped parcels of shopping from her basket into Ella's.

As they reached the castle grounds, a pair of German guards stopped them. 'What have you managed to glean in the shops today?' one asked in broken French.

Ella proffered her basket and he picked up one of the packages and sniffed it. He wrinkled his nose. 'I don't know how you French can bear to eat such stinking cheeses.' He tossed it back into the basket.

Ella smiled, keeping her eyes downcast. 'It's good with *soupe à l'oignon*,' she said, surprised to hear the tone of her own voice was light and steady, not betraying the terror that made her heart thud in her chest behind the buttons of her coat. She nodded towards the other woman's basket, which contained several large brown onions.

The Germans waved them on and they crossed back into the château. It was only once she was safely back in the warm stronghold of the kitchen that Ella drew in a deep gulp of air, realising she'd scarcely dared breathe since she left the house.

She'd done it! The first S-Phone was now safely delivered into the hands of the *Résistance*. She felt a rush of joy at the thought, then immediately gathered her wits about her. Angus had warned her: 'Don't relax your guard for a moment until you are safely back in the plane and out of enemy territory. Remember, the job's not done until you are home.'

She sat quietly in a corner of the kitchen, watching the two women go about their daily chores, saying little, eating the food they offered her to keep her strength up and trying to stay focused on the evening to come.

Dusk fell and they retraced their steps through the darkened château and along the length of the gallery across the river. The woman covered her lantern before drawing back the bolts on the door and opening it a crack. Ella slipped out into the darkness, feeling a pang of longing, for a split second, to stay in the warm safety of the castle under the protection of these people who were risking their lives for her; but she forced herself to walk forwards, her heart thumping again beneath her heavy overcoat as she stepped across the drawbridge and out into the area of felled trees. She ducked down and hurried across the clearing to the cover of the forest, then paused to get her bearings and check her watch. Her guide was supposed to have been here by now. She scanned the woods, her eyes straining to catch a glimpse of dimmed torchlight. But all she saw was darkness and shadows. There was no sound, other than the quietly flowing river behind her.

And suddenly she felt very, very alone. She made her breathing as quiet as possible, calming the sense of panic that was welling up in her chest. Her guide was just late, that was all, she reassured herself. There was still plenty of time to get back to the tiny airstrip before the plane arrived to pick her up. She stood, leaning against the reassuring bulk of an ancient oak. A few acorns lay at her feet, and she stooped and picked one up, rubbing her thumb against its rough cap as she tried to stay calm.

The minutes ticked by. After almost an hour, she realised that it was now time to go if she was to make it to the rendezvous point in time. Desperately, she scanned the woods and the clearing one last time. Across the river, the white fairy-tale castle glinted in a ray of moonlight, a mythical place of safety that she could no longer get to.

She needed to stay focused, not to allow herself to be distracted by panicked thoughts of what might be lurking in the pitch-black shadows between the trees.

She had no option. She had to go.

Taking her bearings from the moon and the river, she set off in what she hoped was the right direction, trying to spot waymarks as she went, in case she got lost and needed to retrace her steps. But it was difficult in the dark woods and, once she'd turned away from the faint, moonlit glow of the river, she felt disorientated amongst the trees that pressed in all around her. She followed the narrow path – she thought it was the one they'd been on the night before – but the forest was criss-crossed by an intricate network of such trails, some made by human footsteps, others by animals. Every now and then she paused, straining to hear the sound of a breaking twig or to glimpse a dimmed torch between the trees, but there was nothing.

A ray of moonshine penetrated the canopy of leaves above her and she tilted her wrist towards it to read her watch. Ten more minutes until the plane would land. She needed to find the clearing, fast. She jumped as an owl hooted on a branch somewhere above her. Was it really an owl? Or was it a signal? She hesitated for a few precious moments, listening, hoping; but then she glimpsed the bird, swooping silently away on pale wings into the darkness. Which way now? She'd lost her bearings completely and the moon had disappeared again. She set off, almost blindly, panic thumping against the tight drum of her chest.

And then she heard it. The distinct thrum of the plane's engine. She turned towards it. She'd gone off course, she needed to get there fast.

Angus had warned her: 'The pilot can't wait, it's just too dangerous. In and out fast, remember. If you're not there . . .' he'd tailed off.

Then he'd said, quietly, 'Just be there, Ella.'

She was running now, stumbling over tree-roots, her breath coming in gasps, burning her throat. The engine noise grew to a roar as the plane flew directly over her, dropping towards the airstrip. 'I'm here,' she screamed, but the words were only in her head.

Desperately, she ran in the direction of the noise, which had descended to ground level somewhere ahead of her. Then the roar quietened suddenly as the plane drew to a halt, its engine idling. Running headlong now, she tripped and fell, sprawling on to the earth, scraping her hands on stones. She scrambled to her feet, no time to check the damage, and ran onwards.

And then the sound of the engine changed, picking up again as the plane turned and taxied. 'No! I'm here! Come back!' But again the screaming was only in her head.

She blundered onwards through the trees towards the noise, but the pitch changed and she knew the pilot was revving for take-off. She reached the edge of the clearing just as the plane left the ground at the far end of the runway and climbed steeply into the night sky.

Then she slumped down, her back against the trunk of a tree, trying to draw breath, but her inhalation took the form of a single, involuntary sob of despair.

Her palms stung and throbbed and she realised there was blood oozing from a deep cut just above the ball of her thumb. She reached into her coat pocket for a handkerchief to tie around it and then stood stock still because, off to her right, through the trees, she could see a bright light, weaving to and fro. She froze, shrinking back into the shadows, listening with every fibre in her body.

And then she heard the voices. Two of them. Speaking German.

They'd spotted the plane. Thank God it had got away in time. But the drop site was compromised. And she was in dire danger.

All of a sudden, a deathly calm descended over Ella. The panic she'd felt before evaporated. She waited, watching as the light drew closer. Silently, she slipped the knife from its sheath at her waist. And then she quickly unscrewed the button on her overcoat and felt for the hard capsule contained within it. She held the pill between her fingers, not wavering for a second. She knew what she would have to do. She waited.

In that moment, which seemed to stretch to a small infinity, she realised that she didn't fear death; because it meant she would be where Christophe was.

She closed her eyes for a second, trying to summon his face but, to her surprise, the face that she saw was Marianne's, smiling at her gently, comforting her, reassuring her that she wasn't quite so alone after all.

The German soldiers reached the far side of the clearing and swept the ground with their searchlight, illuminating the runway. The light flooded the corner where Ella stood and she pressed herself closer to the far side of the tree, praying they hadn't seen her. She gripped the pill between her fingers a little more tightly.

One of the men stepped out into the clearing, backlit by his colleague's torch, and began to walk in her direction. Ella raised the pill to her lips, still feeling ice-calm.

And then something very strange happened.

The light of the torch described a sweeping arc, up into the air above the trees, then fell again as the Nazi soldier sank silently to the ground. His colleague turned, shouting a question, and in the same split second, a single shot rang out.

Stunned, Ella lowered the hand holding the pill to her side. And then someone picked up the Germans' torch and stepped out into the clearing, calling her name.

'Angus,' she sobbed, and stumbled into the open, sinking to her knees as he reached out an arm and caught her.

He knelt, holding her, calming her, speaking words of reassurance. 'You're alright, Ella. You're alright.'

She wept then, clinging to him, this man who'd snatched her back from the edge of the precipice, sobbing, 'You came to find me. I was lost and you came to find me.'

He half carried her back into the shadows next to the trees and took both her hands in his. 'Ella, stay here. Just sit tight.' He uncurled the fingers of her right hand and found the suicide pill that was clutched there. He took it and put it in his pocket. 'You won't be needing this now.'

Then he sprinted back to where the second Nazi's body lay huddled beside the runway and dragged it into the trees, where he'd ended the life of the first with a silent swipe of his knife. He covered them with branches and leaves and then stepped back into the clearing. As Ella watched, he stood and faced the direction from which the plane had left and opened his coat. He fitted an aerial into the S-Phone strapped to his chest and called the pilot back in.

'I've got her. The area is secured. Safe to return. I repeat, safe to return.'

2014, Edinburgh

The honeysuckle has been cleared away from Ella's bedside cabinet, but I busy myself arranging the bunch of white lilies that I've brought her, hoping they'll remind her of the night she danced with Christophe back when they were together, happily oblivious to the horrors that were gathering just beyond the horizon.

She glances at me sharply, her eyes bright and clear today, as I set the vase down. Despite a layer of carefully applied concealer, I sense her taking in the dark half-moons beneath my eyes and am conscious, suddenly, that my hair could do with a wash. My hands are shaking slightly, as they do on the days when the exhaustion and anxiety are overwhelming, and a little water slops on to the bedside cabinet. She continues to watch me closely as I reach for a handful of tissues to mop up the spill.

Self-conscious all of a sudden, I reach into my bag, grateful for the distraction. 'Look, Granny, I've brought one of the photo albums with me today.'

It's dated 1945. Afterwards.

Apart from the snaps of her at RAF Gulford in her mechanic's overalls, grinning towards Vicky's camera as she wields a large oil can beside a Hurricane, and a more formal one of her in her WAAF uniform, there are no photos of Ella during the war.

'What did you do afterwards, Granny? After the S-Phone operation in France? Did you learn how to do a parachute jump? And did you go back again on any more missions?'

She laughs, shaking her head. 'No, my dear. I'm afraid the remainder of my Air Force career was far more mundane. I wanted to do more, but it was decided by the powers-that-be that I was still "not suitable for Field Operations" and that my French-speaking skills were needed elsewhere. I was sent back to East Lothian, to a prep school which had been commandeered as a specialist training centre for SOE wireless operators. I spent the rest of the war intercepting the Nazis' French propaganda broadcasts and translating them. We used to transmit rude songs by Spike Jones in return sometimes, to get our own back, and other times we'd broadcast nonsense to make the Germans think it was coded information – I always used to enjoy thinking of them wasting precious resources trying to decode it – as cover for the real messages we were transmitting to French *Résistance* cells. And then I became one of the trainers at Belhaven Hill, teaching other SOE operatives how to use some of the specialist wireless equipment. I came across many women far more courageous than I. But, no, I never went back on any other missions.'

'And Grandad?'

'Oh yes, he carried on his work. I didn't know what he was up to a lot of the time; it was too highly classified. He stayed on at Arisaig, but he'd come through to Edinburgh whenever he could and we'd meet up for tea dances at the North British Hotel. When I introduced him to my parents, of course they thought he was just marvellous too. We courted. We had fun. Life went on, despite the war. In some ways it was more concentrated, more intensely lived because of the risks and the threats that were always there in the background. I loved him very much. And not just because he'd saved my life. I loved him for the handsome, brave, funny man he was.' She pats my hand. 'And a jolly good thing it was too. Your mother and Robbie wouldn't be here otherwise, nor you, nor Finn. A very good thing all round.'

I open the pages of the photo album on my lap, to their wedding photo. Ella turns to stroke the leaves of the lilies in the vase beside her. 'I had these in my bouquet on that day too, see? Oh, how the scent takes me back . . .'

1945, Edinburgh

Angus and Ella were married in the church that her family had always attended, at Holy Corner, on a bright Saturday morning in late May, just a couple of weeks after VE Day. It still felt as if the whole country were celebrating, as if their wedding were part of the joy that continued to resonate around the world at Nazi Germany's unconditional surrender. They emerged from the church into a cloud of confetti thrown by friends and family, which settled like wind-blown petals on the folds of Ella's lace dress and veil.

In the car that was taking them to the wedding breakfast, she brushed a leaf of confetti from Angus's khaki uniform and kissed him on the lips. He took her hand in his.

'Alright, Mrs Dalrymple?'

'Very alright.' She smiled, giving his hand a squeeze.

'You look so beautiful, my Ella. Thank you for making me the happiest man alive. The proudest one too.'

The car pulled up in front of the North British Hotel and he stepped out, then offered her his hand. There was a smattering of applause from the small group of passers-by who'd paused to enjoy the happy spectacle of a couple of newly-weds in the May sunshine.

She took his arm and the hotel doorman stood to attention as they crossed the threshold.

'So, here we are again, Mr Brown. Little did you imagine on that day when you interviewed me that you'd end up saving my life and then marrying me,' she teased him.

'Actually, I did,' he smiled down at her. 'The marrying you bit, at least. I have to admit, it crossed my mind.'

'Well that's very impressive forward planning! But then that always has been one of your strengths.'

'Ready?' he asked her, inclining his head towards the Palm Court, where the wedding party awaited them.

'Ready,' she replied. And together they stepped into the room full of cheering friends.

They honeymooned at Arisaig, staying in one of the croft houses that was empty, temporarily, now that the commando training unit was being disbanded.

Those two weeks were some of the happiest days of Ella's life. They walked along white-sand beaches with the sweeping backdrop of Hebridean islands; they took a boat out to explore quiet bays beneath Rum's soaring peaks, watching stags roam across the hillside and eagles glide against a cerulean sky, sailing back with the setting sun behind them, accompanied once by a school of porpoises. Angus caught mackerel, which Ella cooked on the peat-fired range in the cottage, and they sat together, late into the evenings, talking and reading. And at night, they lay in each other's arms, luxuriating in the miracle of a future filled with love and hope now that the war in Europe was over at last.

'I think I'd like us to have two children,' Ella whispered to him in the darkness, her head nestled into the perfect dip between his shoulder and his chest. 'A boy and a girl.'

She felt him nod. 'And they'll both be as intelligent and as beautiful as their mother,' he whispered back, turning to her again.

On the final day, they wandered down to the shore, stopping at the red postbox by the side of the road so that Ella could post the card she was sending to Caroline on the Île de Ré. It was a postcard showing the beach at Arisaig, and she'd scrawled on the back of it '*On honeymoon! Here's our new address . . . Hoping to hear from you soon. Much love, Ella (Dalrymple!)*'

'One of the best things about the war being over is having the post running properly again,' Ella remarked. She'd written a long letter to Caroline on VE Day, and it had felt such a luxury to be able to tell her friend all her news from the past years and to feel confident that, this time, it would reach her, eventually, on the Île de Ré. She hadn't had a reply yet, but maybe there would be a letter waiting for her when they got back to Edinburgh, and she hoped it would bring the good news that Marianne had returned to them and that the three Martets were together on the island; the news that the family could, at last, travel together to visit Christophe's grave, so far away from the island on the other side of France, to lay flowers on it and to grieve there. She tried to shut out the doubts – the memory of Marianne's face appearing to her when she'd been lost in the woods that night in France; the horrendous stories of what the Allies had found when they entered Poland and liberated the so-called work camps there. Surely gentle, beautiful Marianne could never have ended up in one of those terrible places?

Continuing down to the beach, Ella was lost in thought as they wandered along the shore-line, stepping over gleaming ribbons of kelp that had washed up here and there on the high tide.

Angus paused, stooping to pick something up. 'Here you go. A memento of two perfect weeks.' He placed a double white clamshell, still hinged in the centre, into her open palm.

'Ella? Are you alright?'

She shook her head, smiling through the sudden tears, which she blinked away, letting the westerly wind dry them. 'Sorry. It reminded me of something.' She stroked the shell, turning it over to admire the perfect smoothness held within its curves. 'Someone I once knew told me that these are called Neptune's lockets.'

He examined her face minutely, reading the faint contraction of pain in her green eyes and the sadness that lay just beneath the surface of her smile as she remembered.

After a long moment's silence, he cleared his throat. 'Do you want to talk about him?'

She hesitated, torn. Then took his hand in hers. She was still holding the shell he'd given her in the other hand as they began to walk again. And as they walked, she told him about her first love, awakened on an island moored in a sea of light, where she'd discovered freedom and beauty and a whole new sense of what really mattered in this world.

When she'd finished, he turned to face her, still holding her hand in his. With the other, he drew back a wind-blown strand of her hair and gently kissed her forehead.

'I see. I'm sorry. And now I understand it all a little better.' He touched the shell which she still held. 'So . . . Neptune's locket.'

He put a finger under her chin, raising her face to his, and looked deep into her eyes, as though searching for a truth there.

'Do you think there could be a space for me in the other half of it? Because that is what I want, Ella, more than anything. I don't want to try to replace him – how could I compete, in any case, with the man who gave you the *Mona Lisa?*' His eyes creased in a smile, then grew serious again. 'But do you think, perhaps, that there can be room for me too in your heart? Alongside your memories of him?'

She stood on tiptoes and kissed his lips. 'Of course, Angus. You're there already.'

And yet, as they turned and walked back towards the little white cottage, she realised that as she'd spoken those words her gaze had dropped and then she'd looked away, to the south, towards an island that lay a thousand miles distant.

House-proud and anxious at the same time, Ella ran her duster over the mantelshelf, giving one last glance around the room to make sure everything was neat and tidy for her parents' first formal visit to the apartment that Angus and she had moved into on their return to Edinburgh. Her father had helped them to buy it, a flat in Marchmont looking over the Meadows, and they'd spent the summer evenings once Angus returned from work renovating it, removing faded and peeling wallpaper and replacing it with a more modern print, and painting the stained old woodwork a bright white gloss. After months of work, it was now ready for her parents' inspection and Ella was a little nervous, not sure whether they'd approve of the modern look they'd chosen.

But she had no such fears where Angus was concerned. Both her parents adored him, the son they'd never had. 'And that's without knowing that you saved my life!' Ella laughed. They never talked about the details of what had happened to anyone. Ella knew that there were other things that Angus couldn't discuss, even with her, and she accepted that it went with the territory. If anyone asked how they'd met, they simply said, 'We worked together during the war.'

Angus was peeling potatoes in the kitchen. She kissed him on the cheek and he reached out a dripping hand and pulled her to him, caressing the slight roundness of her belly through her apron. 'Is the sproglet going to behave itself for its grandparents' visit do you think?'

'I sincerely hope so. The sickness has been much better for two whole days now and I'm looking forward to a big Sunday lunch for once!'

'There you go, spuds duly peeled and ready for roasting, ma'am.'

'Thank you. In that case you may stand down now. I think I've got the rest of the meal under control. I just need to get these in the oven once they've come to the boil . . . Oh! That'll be them.'

'I'll get the door. You finish up here. Don't worry, Mrs Dalrymple, they're going to approve wholeheartedly of what you've done to your new home.'

Ella took off her apron and hung it on a hook behind the scullery door, smoothing her hair into place as she hurried through to the sitting-room. Her parents hugged her and then went back to admiring the way they'd arranged the room with the sleek new furniture they'd bought. Angus poured glasses of sherry for the Lennoxes and a lemonade for Ella and they raised them in a toast. 'To your future in your new home, and to your growing family,' said Mr Lennox.

'Oh, here you go, Ella, I almost forgot in all this excitement,' Mrs Lennox delved into her handbag. 'There's a letter for you from Caroline at long last. She can't have received your new address when she sent it.' She squinted at the smudged postmark. 'It looks as though it was posted back in May. It's taken months to get here! I suppose it's taking France a while to get things back to normal . . .'

'Finally!' Ella's eyes lit up. This was the first news she'd had from her old friend and she felt relief flood her veins. Having heard nothing for so many months, despite the war being over and the postal service slowly getting back to normal, she'd begun to fear the worst for the entire Martet family. She'd tried telephoning the house in Paris once, but the operator had said that the number was disconnected, so she'd just had to hope that the letters she'd sent to the house on the Île de Ré would eventually find their way to Caroline, wherever she might be now.

'Go ahead and open it. I know you can't wait to read it. I'll show your parents the rest of the flat while we leave you to it.' Ella shot Angus a grateful look, and he ruffled her hair as he led her parents out of the room.

They came back into the sitting-room a little while later to find Ella sitting bolt upright, gazing, unseeing, out of the bay window at the trees whose leaves were showing the first golden flecks here and there amongst the green, hinting that the end of the summer was near. The letter was folded on the table in front of her.

'Ella? Are you alright?' her mother asked, concerned.

She turned to face them, looking dazed, and Angus came over and knelt in front of her, taking her hands in his. 'What is it?'

Her eyes focused on his face slowly, as if she was coming back to the Edinburgh sitting-room from a very long way away. She nodded numbly, her expression a strange, unreadable mixture of emotions. She took a deep breath.

'Marianne is dead. She was sent to one of the camps. She never came back.'

'Oh, Ella, I'm so sorry. That was the worst of our fears. My poor, dear Marianne. And poor Caroline, her poor father. To have lost so much . . .'

Ella nodded, numbly.

'But there's more news too. Better news for them. Christophe is alive. He wasn't killed, but injured and kept as a prisoner-of-war in a German camp. He's coming home to them.'

Then she burst into heart-wrenching sobs, swept away by the tidal wave of conflicting emotions that the letter had brought.

Ste Marie de Ré
26 May 1945

Dearest Ella,
At last the grim nightmare of the war is over and I can write to you with our news. And what news there is to catch up on . . . I scarcely know where to begin. Papa

and I are still in deep shock with all that we have had to come to terms with in the past weeks, and we still don't know all the facts quite yet. There is such pain. But in the midst of our terrible sadness there is joy too. Our quiet life here on the island has been overturned by a maelstrom of conflicting emotions, at the facts that we have scarcely had time to absorb. So, please forgive the fact that this letter will be a confused jumble of darkness and light, but that is how our lives are now; perversely, they have become even more turbulent in the aftermath of the war, when peace has brought us such news . . .

First of all, I have to tell you of our terrible sadness. Maman *is gone. I can still hardly believe it, even as I write those words and I look at them on the page, in black and white, in disbelief. The* Croix Rouge *has published a list of names of those deported from Drancy to the camps in Poland and on it is the name Marianne Martet. She was taken to Auschwitz in one of the first convoys that summer, not long after she arrived in Drancy, as were Agnès, Albert and Béatrice. None of them survived. We can only imagine the horrors that they suffered and hope that they managed to stay together and to support one another until the end came. I feel such anger and such despair as I think of it – my gentle, beautiful mother, taken, imprisoned like an animal and executed, simply because of who her forefathers were. Thank God, the forces of such inhuman evil have been defeated now, because I do not think I could carry on living in a world where they held sway.*

You will understand, I know, what this news has done to us. My father is a broken man and it is truly awful to see. I fear for his heart. It was never strong and now there are days when I look at him and I wonder how much longer he will be able to carry on, bearing the unbearable for the days he has left in this world. I know he would rather be where she is.

And I thought he was on the brink of leaving this world, when the other news reached us and gave him something to live for, after all. A letter arrived from a hospital in Alsace. The handwriting was so familiar to us and yet, for a moment, we could not place it. And then we realised. Christophe. He is alive, dearest Ella, can you believe it? For I cannot quite, even now! He was not killed on that day in May five years ago. He was badly injured by shrapnel from a bombing raid in the Ardennes as the panzer divisions were advancing on the Maginot Line. His legs were shattered. His comrades knew the tanks were coming and so one of the officers exchanged his jacket and his identity documents for Christophe's, knowing that they had to leave him to be taken prisoner and that he would stand a far greater chance of better treatment at the hands of the Nazis if they thought he was an officer. Christophe scribbled our address in Paris on a piece of paper torn from his sketch-book and asked the man to contact us, to let us know what had happened to him. But his colleague never made it – it was he who was killed at Sedan that day, his death reported to us as that of Christophe.

So, for all these years, Christophe has been incarcerated in Germany, in a prisoner-of-war camp. He had to maintain the charade of being an officer, but they were reasonably well looked-after there, he says. His injuries were treated, although there are still problems, which he is now having operations for at the hospital in Alsace.

As soon as he can, he will come back home here, to the island. We are about to leave, to go and find him. We long to see him, to hold him in our arms and to help him regain his strength. To bring him home. We haven't told him about Maman yet, fearing that he may not be strong enough to bear that news: it must wait until we are with him. But he has asked after you. And I hope that one day soon, when you have received my letter, you will write back to us with your news.

And, although I know I have no right to hope this, after all this time with no news of you, perhaps you will come back to France, as we had all dreamt, and our lives will pick up again together, as they were meant to be before Fate intervened and took our dreams from us for so long.

I must finish now as I will run to the post office to send this to you before we leave for Alsace this afternoon. We have a long journey ahead of us, in every sense, but there is light in the darkness now. Write to us soon, dearest Ella.

With my love,
Caroline xxx

2014, Edinburgh

I hold the letter closer to the lamp to make out one or two of the words which are slightly smudged. I found it at the bottom of the shoe-box full of letters, most of which are from Caroline. But this one, like a few of the others, is from Christophe. I brush my fingers across the page, imagining his hand holding the pen, writing the words, folding the sheets of paper, sealing them into an envelope. How heavy his heart must have been; and how mixed Ella's emotions when she opened it with trembling fingers and read this letter from a ghost whose memory she thought she'd finally laid to rest.

Ste Marie de Ré
31 October 1945

Dear Ella,
I've come to the beach to write this letter, sitting with my back against the dunes and the sun on my face, which feels so good after all those months incarcerated in a hospital bed. As I struggle to find the words to write, the wind is trying to snatch the paper away, further hindering me in my task.

I have begun so many letters to you and then torn them up because it seems impossible to set down on paper all that I want to say. But at the same time, I feel I must write to you because, even if my letter causes us both some pain, the silence between us is unbearable.

I must start, though, by sending my congratulations on your marriage and on the news that you are to be a mother. And please believe me when I say that my good wishes are heartfelt. Angus is a very lucky man. You deserve much joy and much love.

As I watch the waves wash on to the sand, memories of you flood back. These memories are some of my most treasured possessions. They've kept me going when all has seemed lost. They are the things I am most thankful for. So, you should know, dear Ella, that you helped me to survive the terror and the horror of war and that, even in the darkest moments, I knew that truth and beauty would ultimately triumph because I carried them with me, untouchable and unbreakable, in my heart. You were with me, helping me face each ordeal . . .

The day it happened – the day life changed forever – I was at my post, but it was a sunny May morning and, from the canopy of fresh green leaves above my head I remember that a concerto of bird-song filled the air. So I put aside my rifle and pulled out my sketch-book. I would capture the beauty of this place and send it to you in my next letter . . . and you would smile when you opened it, understanding that I was still the same old Christophe, finding beauty in the most ordinary surroundings. I wanted to draw the way the sunlight dappled through the leaves on to the moss-covered stones beside that stream . . .

'That's funny,' I thought, only half noticing as I sketched. 'The birds have stopped singing.'

I glanced up the track that led through the woods, up the hill where the sun had risen that morning. And then I heard it. The reason why there was no more bird-song in the sunlit leaves above my head.

After the noise of the tanks crashing their way through the undergrowth, I don't remember much. The captain of my battalion came to find me where I lay in the crater left by the shell. My legs were badly shattered and he knew I would stand more of a chance of survival if the Germans captured me. But he also knew I would be treated far better if I were taken prisoner as an officer and so he exchanged my jacket for his and swapped our overcoats and our identity papers. And so I became Captain Fabien Dumas for the remainder of the war, held in prisoner-of-war camp Stalag Luft VIII-A with other captured officers, once it was decided that I would survive and my injuries had been patched up in a German field hospital.

You were with me there, Ella, in the sketches I drew from memory which reminded me that there was a freedom in my heart that no prison could ever confine.

Each day now I feel a bit more of my strength returning, thanks to the sea air, good home-cooking and Caroline's unstinting care. My legs are mending well after the operations. I have much to be thankful for, even if so much has been lost too.

And all that we have been through has brought me much closer to my father. Losing my mother has destroyed him, Ella – your heart would break to see him. But he *has his two children beside him again now and so I pray that he can grow stronger too. The most worrying thing is that he no longer disapproves of my art! I never thought I would miss the days when he was so discouraging, but I do. It amazes me how time can make us look upon things so differently.*

As I must look upon you differently too now.

Ella-from-Edinburgh, I wish you much happiness and much love. May your family flourish.

Christophe

1955, Edinburgh

'Come on, Robbie, you don't want to be late!' Ella swept her six-year-old son into her arms and cuddled him to her as she tied the laces on his school shoes. They'd been brand new at the start of the week, the black leather gleaming, but already the toes were scuffed and she expected the laces would soon be frayed and knotted. She buried her nose in the soft warmth at the back of his neck, giving him the kiss that she knew he'd be too embarrassed to receive in public before he was much older.

Rhona, three years his elder, looked on from the doorway, with her coat already buttoned and her school satchel slung across one shoulder. She was a neat, organised child and she disapproved of her little brother's tendencies towards chaos and mess, especially in the mornings. She sighed with impatience as he wriggled down from his mother's lap and began to search for one of his plimsolls which had, inexplicably, removed itself from its rightful place in his gym bag. But then, distracted from the search, he picked up a Dinky car transporter and began pushing it towards the garage Daddy had made for him, making vrooming noises as he did so.

'Come *on*, Robbie, you're going to make us all late.' Rhona's annoyance spilled over and she marched across to him and pulled the toy from his hand, deliberately placing it on a bookshelf that she knew he couldn't reach.

'Hey!' he protested. 'Give it back! Mummy,' he wailed, 'she's being horrible to me.'

Ella was lying on the floor, stretching an arm as far under Robbie's bed as she could reach. She re-emerged, triumphantly, with the missing gym shoe and patted her stiffly lacquered hairstyle back into place. 'Right, Robbie, put your coat on and, Rhona, don't be a meanie. Here' – she took the toy down from the shelf and put it beside the garage – 'it'll be waiting for you when you get home today. Now, let's get going, we don't want to miss the tram.'

She held both her children's hands as they walked to the tram stop. They'd moved out of the flat in Marchmont when Robbie was born and bought their first family home at Fairmilehead, one of the last houses on the southern edge of the city, recently built and with a garden big enough for the children to play in and views out towards the Pentland Hills. It meant a lengthy tram ride to get to school and back, but Ella enjoyed every minute spent with her children, so she didn't begrudge the time. Angus occasionally took them in the morning, although usually he left earlier to get into the office. He'd joined Ella's father's insurance business and, now that Mr Lennox had retired, he was running it and had ambitious plans for future expansion.

Their lifestyle was comfortable and secure. And if Ella was occasionally bored with her role as a housewife, being a mother made up for it. With memories of the horrors of the recent past still fresh in their minds, Angus and Ella both knew the value of the safety and freedom that they now enjoyed. They had a comfortable home and were able to afford a car and all the latest gadgets – a television set; a globe-shaped Hoover vacuum cleaner, which made cleaning their new fitted carpets so much easier; and a gleaming electric cooker for Ella to use in the kitchen. They were the envy of their many friends. There were members of their extended family who were close by to offer help and advice, whether it was looked-for or not. They were the perfect couple, with the perfect lives. And they both adored their children.

But there was something else too. Something not visible to anyone else. Something just below the surface which made them both tread carefully within their marriage.

Ever since that day when Caroline's letter had arrived, things had been different. It was hard to pinpoint exactly how their relationship had changed – although the reason why it had done so was crystal clear. Christophe, alive in France, was a phantom whose presence haunted them both. He was there when Ella paused as she was hanging out the washing on the line to look south, to the distance beyond the gorse-clad hills, seeing, in her mind's eye, a far-off island bathed in a clearer, warmer light; he was there when she dusted the jar of shells which sat on the windowsill in the bathroom, which Angus and the children had collected on west-coast beaches during their family holidays; and he was still there despite the fact that she'd taken some of his love letters from the cigar box hidden at the back of her wardrobe and fed them into the fire as part of her silent promise to her husband that she would be the very best wife to him that she could be.

The foundations of their relationship had been rocked and they had cracked. The family that they were building together upon those same foundations could easily topple and fall if she didn't do all that she could to reinforce them again. So, Ella lived in a constant state of anxiety, treading carefully, looking ahead the whole time to try to spot anything that might further undermine Angus's trust in her and taking steps to skirt around those potential pitfalls. How could she make him believe her love for him ever measured up when he knew what had gone before?

Most of all, she worried for Angus himself. There had been a subtle, seismic shift that day when she'd read Caroline's letter and, although on the surface her husband appeared as strong and capable as ever, Ella sensed an almost imperceptible hesitation when he put his arms around her and, every now and then, she caught a glimpse of the doubt in his candid blue eyes.

Caroline still wrote from time to time and Ella was always careful to pass the letters to Angus for him to read, so that he'd know she wasn't keeping anything to do with Christophe from him. Caroline only mentioned her brother very fleetingly every now and then in any case, as if she, too, realised how delicate the situation must be from Ella and Angus's point of view.

Monsieur Martet had died in 1946, a few months after Christophe had returned to the Île de Ré. Caroline had written that she was just thankful that he'd known his son was still alive and had been able to bring him home; but his heart hadn't been able to bear the sadness of losing Marianne and one night he had closed his eyes and gone to join her, death bringing the peace, at last, that he'd been denied towards the end of his life.

Caroline was alone now in the white house with the pale blue shutters, having decided to stay on the island rather than return to the house in Paris. She wrote that she'd opened a small art gallery in Sainte Marie where she displayed the work of some of the colony of artists who lived on the island, and she'd begun to have a degree of success in selling them to the summer visitors who wanted to take home with them a reminder of the glimpse of freedom and peace that they'd found there. Christophe, she wrote, had moved back to Paris where he was painting. And his work was beginning to gain recognition in the city and beyond.

But all of that was so far removed from Ella's day-to-day existence that it felt as if she was reading a novel when she read the letters from Caroline, a story of people and places that couldn't exist in reality.

And, so here she was, living her life with her husband and her children who anchored her in that reality every day.

She rumpled Robbie's hair and he ran through the school gate to the boys' entrance without a backward glance, dragging his gym bag along the playground floor in his wake, having spotted a group of his friends.

'Remember to hand in the note about the trip to the Botanical Gardens today, won't you?' she said to Rhona, hugging her tightly, knowing that it was acceptable to do so as it was different for girls.

'I will, Mummy. See you this afternoon.' Ella stood at the gates, watching. Rhona turned back, as Ella had known she would, and she waved a little wave of encouragement and solidarity, then blew her daughter one last kiss before turning away to go and do the day's food shop before she returned to the security and predictability of their home.

'Did you have a good day?' Ella asked Rhona.

'It was alright. I got an alpha plus in mathematics. And my painting of the seaside has been put up on the wall.'

'Well done, Rhona. And how about you, Robbie? How was your day?'

He shrugged, trailing behind them as they walked to the tram stop. 'Alright.' He was unforthcoming, and Ella thought he looked a little pale.

'You must be tired after your first week back. Never mind, it's the weekend now and I've got your favourite sausages for supper, with mashed potatoes. You'd better have an early night tonight.'

Thank goodness the first week back of term was a short one, she thought. The energy levels they seemed to require at the school were daunting, especially when they were readjusting after the long summer break.

That night, as she tucked Robbie in and bent to kiss him good-night, Ella said, 'There you go. Feeling better now?' He'd eaten most of his supper and then spent the evening happily lying on the floor of his bedroom playing with his cars. He nodded. 'Good. You can have a long lie-in the morning and then you'll be full of beans!' She smiled at him, knowing that he'd be up early, as usual, as it was Saturday and he wouldn't want to waste a second of his weekend. The luxury of long lie-ins was long gone these days in the Dalrymple household.

Later that evening, she turned to Angus in bed and drew his arm around her, trying to ignore the tiny pang of sadness she felt at his not gathering her into his arms automatically, the way he used to do before . . . He kissed her on the forehead, slightly absent-mindedly.

'Is everything alright?' she asked him, trying to keep her tone light.

He smiled at her, as if suddenly seeing her at last. 'Oh, yes, fine, just got a lot on at work at the moment. You alright?'

'Yes, fine. Glad it's the end of the week. It always seems harder getting back into the routine after the holidays.'

He reached over and switched out the lamp on the bedside cabinet and then turned back to her. 'Never mind. The weekend starts here . . .' He began to kiss her properly, more seriously, with intent, and she relaxed into his arms, reassured, losing herself in the moment.

They were awoken the next morning by a hesitant tap on the bedroom door. 'Daddy? Mummy? I've made you a cup of tea.' Rhona pushed the door open, carefully carrying two cups and saucers on a tray. The china rattled as she made her way across the carpet, concentrating hard on not spilling a drop.

'Why, thank you, sweetheart.' Angus took his cup from her and put it on the bedside table then gathered her into a bear hug. 'That's my girl.'

'That's a lovely treat, clever you, Rhona. Thank you. Is Robbie behaving himself?'

'Well, yes, but only because he's not awake yet.' Rhona tucked her already-neat hair, which was the same dark honey colour as her mother's (although her eyes were as blue as her father's), behind her ears, relishing the approval of her parents and the rare opportunity to have them to herself for once.

'I thought it was very peaceful.' Angus consulted his watch. 'It's nearly nine! Miraculous.' He yawned and stretched, exchanging a smile with Ella over his daughter's head and then reaching his arm across to include her in the family hug too. 'A cup of tea and my two best girls, what more could a man want?'

A faint wail interrupted their moment of peace. 'I knew it was too good to last! No, don't worry, you two stay there, I'll go.' Ella got out of bed and pulled her dressing-gown on over her nightie. 'It's alright, Robbie, I'm coming . . .' she called, tying the cord around her waist.

His bedroom was still half dark, the curtains drawn across the windows blocking out the light of a grey Saturday morning. The air in the room smelled stale, of sleep and a night full of troubled dreams. Ella wrinkled her nose at the slightly sweet and fetid edge.

She crossed to the bed where Robbie lay, unmoving beneath his rumpled blankets. She put a cool hand to his forehead as she bent to kiss him, saying, 'What is it my darling, are you not feeling well? Why Robbie, I think you have a temperature . . .'

He gave a feeble wail, his eyes glassy as though his gaze was turned inwards to something inside: something that was consuming him alive, steadily and inexorably.

A wave of panic surged, suddenly, through Ella and she seized hold of his shoulders to bring him to a sitting position. But his hot limbs were heavy and unresponsive between her hands and he fell forwards against her where she held him. She hugged his body desperately against hers, as if she could absorb whatever was wrong with him and draw it out into her own self.

'Mummy,' he murmured, scarcely finding the breath to speak, 'my legs don't work.'

Angus was there in two strides when he heard Ella's scream.

'Call an ambulance! Fast! Oh, Robbie, Robbie! My baby boy!' She was rocking to and fro, her son's small, fragile body held tight in her arms.

'Ella, what is it?' Angus's voice was taut with fear.

She turned to look up at him, tears streaming down her face. And then she whispered the words that parents at that time dreaded the most, 'He's paralysed.'

The polio ward at the children's hospital is the most terrifying place on Earth, Ella thought. She would rather have faced another night lost in a dark, foreign forest than be standing outside the locked door of the ward, pressing her face against the square pane of glass cross-hatched with a grid of wires, trying to catch a glimpse of her son on the other side of it. Nurses moved briskly around the clinical, brightly lit ward, attending to the rows of iron lungs that were arranged in ranks there, each of the large, white cylinders containing one small child. Through the door, she could hear the mechanical push and pull of the machines as air was forced in and out of them, causing their occupants' lungs to rise and fall, cheating the paralysis which would otherwise have made those tiny chests fall still.

The nurses ignored Ella. They were used to desperate parents standing there on the other side of the door, forbidden from entering, unable to touch or hold their children as their small bodies struggled against the silent killer that had invaded them. Ella had begged the Ward Sister to allow her in, just for a few moments, so that she could reassure Robbie that she was there with him. 'I'm very sorry, Mrs Dalrymple, but it's not allowed under any circumstances. We appreciate that this is hard for you, but if we make an exception for one parent then we'll have to allow everyone in. Imagine how it could upset the other children, and how it would increase the risk of carrying contamination home with you. Think of your daughter. You need to protect her, don't you?'

And so Ella had to make do with standing and gazing at Robbie from the other side of the door while she felt as if her heart was being wrenched from her breast. She would smile and wave, hoping he could see her, careful to choke back her anguish until she was walking away down the corridor and safely out of his sight.

For several weeks, Ella made a daily pilgrimage to stand at the door that separated her from her son, braving the stony looks from the hospital staff who disapproved of these troublesome parents who had no regard for the official visiting hours.

At home in the evenings, while Rhona did her homework or sat quietly reading her favourite *Malory Towers* books, Ella would scour books and magazines for any new information about the treatment of polio sufferers or compose notes, which she would press on any nurse who emerged from the ward, to be read to Robbie.

After what felt like several eternities, Robbie was finally pronounced out of danger by the doctor and moved out of the iron lung. Ella was overjoyed when the day came that she could visit him and hold him and give him the hugs and kisses she'd yearned to for so long. His legs were still paralysed and she'd had to turn away, that first day, when she saw him lying on his bed; his muscles were so wasted that his legs looked like fragile twigs, thin enough to snap in a stiff breeze, strapped into metal callipers that ended in a heavy pair of boots. His face was white and drawn, and he lived with the constant anxiety that the disease might return and take him off for good this time. The nurses told her that he was having nightmares, waking screaming and gasping for air, dreaming that his breathing had stopped without the machine to keep it going.

Ella demanded a consultation with the doctor – to the new Ward Sister's intense disapproval – and asked that Robbie be given hot compresses and extra exercises to help rebuild the muscles that hadn't wasted away entirely after his weeks of immobility in the iron lung. She waved an article from a magazine under the doctor's nose. 'Yes, Mrs Dalrymple, I am fully aware of the work of Sister Elizabeth Kenny and we do, in fact, employ some of her techniques. But we simply do not have the resources to dedicate to each individual patient.'

'Let me do it then,' Ella pleaded. 'I can come in and work on his legs every day. Just show me how he needs to do the exercises.'

'That would be entirely against hospital regulations, I'm afraid. I cannot sanction it. My nurses will be up in arms if we have parents running amok in the wards at all hours of the day. However . . .' he held up a hand to forestall Ella's objections, 'should you wish to assist Robbie with his exercises during visiting hours then I think that could be an acceptable compromise. I must insist though, only during official visiting hours.'

And so, Ella would hold Robbie's wasted legs in her strong, capable hands and manipulate them back and forth, flexing and straightening the knobbly joints with their pitiful, protruding bones, trying to encourage the muscles to regenerate. At the same time, she would sing to him and tell him stories to make him laugh and forget, for a few precious minutes, that he was stuck in hospital and might never be able to walk again.

The whole family longed for the day when Robbie could leave the hospital, and Ella was determined that Robbie should come home the second they allowed him out, so that she could embark upon a more intensive programme of rehabilitation and therapy to get his legs moving of their own accord once again. Dedicated though the staff at the hospital were, she knew that he would thrive better at home, where there would be more fresh air and good cooking and where, through sheer determination and will-power, she believed she would get him back on his feet.

But it was a long, slow process and the last of the autumn leaves had been torn from the trees on the Meadows by a snatching, easterly wind the day that they finally wheeled him out of the hospital and drove him back to Fairmilehead.

Gazing out of the car window, Robbie was amazed at the world he had finally re-entered. 'It's already winter,' he said, shaking his head in disbelief. 'I missed the whole of autumn, Mummy.'

Ella, who couldn't stop turning round to look at him, still hardly able to believe he was really coming home at last, felt stunned too as she noticed the bare branches in the suburban gardens that they were passing; she'd been so preoccupied over the past months that she'd scarcely registered the changing seasons either and it was as though, for the first time since the ambulance had whisked her son away from her, she was finally able to see the wider world around them once again. 'I know my darling, but never mind, you're home in time for Christmas and that's all that matters. This one's going to be the best one ever! We'll have to start making some decorations. Do you think you can make the longest paper chain in the whole wide world? I bet you can!'

Angus took a hand from the steering wheel and squeezed Ella's fingers for a second. She knew he was hoping that things would get better now. Both her children needed her – Rhona as well as Robbie. And so did Angus. She'd felt they were drifting apart, the polio infecting their marriage and paralysing the entire family as it devoured their energy and demanded all of their attention.

If anything, though, Ella was even more preoccupied once they got Robbie home. She was determined to devote every available moment of each day to trying to help him to walk again. She administered hot compresses to his legs to try to stimulate the circulation and spent hours doing the therapeutic exercises to keep the limbs moving. They visited the outpatient's ward at the children's hospital regularly and Ella cheered Robbie on as he struggled to walk a few yards between two parallel handrails, his feet dragging in the heavy boots and his unwieldy callipers clicking and jangling. He still couldn't stand without support, but she insisted that he use his legs as often as possible rather than relying on the wheelchair. This meant that going anywhere took ages, and often Angus and Rhona would go to the shops or on outings at the weekends on their own, leaving Ella at home to carry on with Robbie's therapy. The one activity they could still enjoy as a family was a trip to the swimming baths, where Ella would support Robbie in the water as she encouraged him to try to kick whilst Rhona splashed out on her own, practising swimming widths and perfecting her strokes.

As winter turned to spring and then the yellow gorse burst into bloom on the hills surrounding the city, the Dalrymple family settled into its new form, articulated by Robbie one day as his mother flexed and straightened his legs for the millionth time. 'I'm your boy, aren't I, Mummy? And Rhona is Daddy's girl.'

Ella tried to ignore the flush of guilt she felt as she recognised the truth in what he'd said. She was doing the best she could, and, after all, Rhona was far more resilient than her little brother. Whilst Robbie needed her, she had no choice but to devote her time and energy to him. She gathered him in her arms and began to strap the callipers to his legs. 'Well, aren't we lucky to have one each? Now let's see if you can hold my hands and walk to the garden. It's a lovely day, so we can carry on with *The Wind in the Willows* outside in the sunshine this morning.'

Slowly, almost imperceptibly, Robbie grew stronger. And then came the day when Angus got back from work to be greeted at the front door by Rhona, flushed with excitement. 'Guess what, Daddy? Robbie did it! He walked all by himself!'

Watching his son take a few clumsy steps, his legs still confined in the heavy callipers, Ella saw Angus's eyes filled with tears born of the same mix of overwhelming emotion she was experiencing: relief and pain, joy and sadness, love and sheer exhaustion. He pulled her to him and hugged her tight. 'Well done,' he whispered as he kissed her. 'He wouldn't be here if it weren't for you.'

That summer, they holidayed in Arisaig again and the two weeks of sea air and days spent on the white-sand beaches were a tonic for them all. 'I do believe this is the very best medicine there is,' Ella commented as she and Angus sat on a picnic rug watching Rhona and Robbie splashing at the water's edge, filling buckets with wet sand to build a sandcastle, watched by a curious seal out in the bay. 'He'll be strong enough to go back to school in the autumn.'

That night in the white cottage, as the children slept, Angus turned to his wife and drew her to him. But Ella took his hand in hers, wordlessly forestalling its descent over her body, and turned away from him, too tired, too preoccupied.

Gradually, her breath settled into the soft rhythm of sleep, while he lay awake staring, alone, into the darkness.

2014, Edinburgh

Ella's lying in her bed again today when I drop by the nursing home. She's sleeping when I creep in, her hair fanned out across the pillow and her face turned towards the bowl of shells; but then a nurse bustles in, saying she needs to wake her up anyway, to administer her medications.

I don't want to tire her out, but there are questions I need to ask her. About her marriage, about how she got through those times. And whether she and my grandfather were ever able to recapture the love again. It seems absolutely vital that I know this because then I might be able to hope that my own marriage can survive; that there's a chance Dan and I can make it, despite the struggle it all seems to be right now.

She frowns, as if remembering is an effort, but then her eyes seem to focus on the painting of the sailing boat and she nods, licking her lips before she speaks, her voice so quiet that I have to lean in close to hear her. 'Whilst we believed Christophe was dead, it was easier for Angus. But with Christophe alive, suddenly the two loves overlapped, in his mind at least. I knew it might destroy the fragile balance of our marriage. It had been damaged . . . weakened. It was hard for both of us.'

'And then there was Robbie's polio,' I prompt, 'which dealt your marriage another blow?'

She nods. 'You know, probably better than I do, that life can sometimes deal you a difficult hand. You do your best. But it's hard. Although I do think having children is one of the most terrifying, overwhelming, frustrating and fulfilling challenges that life has to offer.' She shoots me an appraising glance. 'But it was easier back then: we had so many opportunities and so few expectations, whereas now I think it's the opposite. It seems to me that your generation probably has the worst of both worlds – expectations too high and opportunities far more limited, suddenly. It's a toxic combination. But you and Dan will find a way to make it work.'

'We have no choice.' I'm a little stung by her remark about our expectations being too high. Dan and I have lost so much. It's hard coming to terms with that, but we're both doing our best in our different ways.

'Perhaps not. But perhaps you do have the choice of acceptance. That's a choice that's always available to us.'

I glance around her room, her world shrunk now to these four magnolia-painted walls, this overheated, chemical-scented air. Does she long for the freedom of her youth? The sweeping white sands and an infinite ocean stretching before her? The possibilities of love and a life to be lived? Or is it enough to hold all of that as a distant memory? The contentment of a life well-lived? Perhaps that's the inevitable parabola of life – a trajectory of hope and desire which rises to a crescendo and then tails off into the wistful acceptance of old age.

'Do you wish you'd done anything differently?' I ask.

'Of course. With hindsight we always see things so much more clearly. But at the time we muddle through, trying to make the best decisions we can, but making all sorts of mistakes along the way. I think the biggest mistake I made was not realising that there are so many different kinds of love. And that there is room for them all. No one excludes the others.'

I wait, watching her expression soften as she thinks back, remembering.

She fixes me suddenly, with that clear-eyed gaze of hers that seems to see right to the heart of matters. 'You see, Kendra, I thought there was a finite amount of love to go round. And that I only had the energy to love my children. And I thought that Robbie needed the lion's share. Those were my biggest mistakes. Whereas now I know better. With the benefit of hindsight.'

She reaches for the glass of water that the nurse has left for her and takes a sip.

'The love that you have for your children, that is the only pure and simple kind. It's overwhelming, instinctive, absolute. But it sits alongside the love that you have for your partner, which is another kind of love entirely. That's anything but simple; it's far more complicated; and yet it's the love that we choose, so it should really be the easiest one of all.' She smiles to herself, her memory drifting backwards into the past again. 'I remember Rhona asking Angus one day what "infinity" was. And he said to her, "Think of the biggest number you can. Then add one to it. And one more. And one more . . ." Her face lit up as she got it, the fact that you can go on forever, adding one more. That's how love is. You can keep adding to it. For infinity.'

I think of Dan. Of the distance that's opened up between us, of how we rarely talk these days. Let alone touch one another. But then I think too of how we chose each other – Ella's words hitting home – and of how that choice was so easy because it felt so right. I think of how Dan loves Finn and cares for him with such patience and understanding. He's seemed happier recently, his involvement in the gardening project and at the allotment giving him a sense of purpose, doing him good as well as Finn. Just as writing Ella's story has given me a sense of purpose too. Supposedly, I'm writing it down for my mother's benefit, so why do I feel it's really for my own? She's a wise old bird, my Granny Ella.

I can see she's tiring again, so I stand and get ready to go, but she reaches out a hand to stop me. 'It's never too late, Kendra. Remember that too.'

She points towards the blue bowl beside her bed.

'It's never too late to try to mend what's been broken.'

1957, Edinburgh

Robbie battled at school. Having missed an entire year, he'd been kept back, so his friends were now one class ahead of him and his sister four; he was jeered at for being too old for his year group, teased about the calliper that he still wore on his right leg and his awkward, jerking gait. During PE lessons he sat on the sidelines, watching his classmates run and jump and play, knowing that he had gone from being one of the most popular boys in his class, and one of the best at football, to a crippled nobody. Each day, when she met him at the school gates, Ella's heart ached a little bit more as she watched him limp across the playground, trailing well behind his stronger, faster, noisier and more confident peers, an awkward, wounded shadow of the child he'd been a year ago.

And so she continued to try everything she could think of to find ways of helping him to rebuild his strength, to minimise his limp, to regain his confidence and his sense of who, she knew, he truly was: a clever, talented, loving and courageous boy who should not be defined by the legacy of his illness.

The summer was threatening to be one of those unremittingly grey ones, where the east coast sea-mist rolled in to blot out the sun on the few days that the flat, dour cloud-cover parted long enough to allow it to shine. It had rained every day for the past week, despite the fact that it was already mid-June, and the gorse flowers on the hills were bruised and bedraggled. *A bit like I am*, thought Ella, as she paused in hanging sheets on the line, trying to make the most of the break in the weather and get a long-overdue wash done. She sat down on the garden bench for a few moments, lifting her face to the tentative gleam of sunshine that had broken through a gap in the clouds. She pushed a strand of hair back into the elastic band that half-heartedly bound her loose ponytail. She was vaguely conscious that she really ought to book an appointment at the hairdresser's, but somehow the days slipped by and she just couldn't seem to get on top of things. It should have been easier with Robbie back at school this year, but she seemed to have sunk all her energy into getting him back on his feet and now there was very little left over to get herself through the days.

She heard the letterbox clatter and, with a sigh, roused herself to go and pick up the post from the doormat. Amongst the mundane brown envelopes was a crisp, cream-coloured one bearing a row of French stamps and Ella felt her spirits rise a little. She made herself a cup of tea and went back outside to settle herself on the bench and read Caroline's letter. As she unfolded the sheet of writing paper, a rectangle of white card fell into her lap . . .

Sainte Marie de Ré
5 June 1957

Ma Chère Ella,
How is Robbie getting on? I think of you every day and
hope that his strength continues to improve. You sounded
so sad the last time you wrote and I know it cannot be
easy for you, watching one of your children struggling.
So I am writing to you today with two propositions . . .
The first is a little escapism to try to cheer you up.
Several of Christophe's paintings will be coming to
Edinburgh shortly. They were first displayed in my little

gallery here on the island, and have gone on a journey from here to Paris and then to London. Can you imagine?! And now they are coming to the Royal Scottish Academy to be included in a summer exhibition. So, I am sending you this invitation to the private view and hope that you and Angus can attend. I want you to write back to me afterwards and tell me what you think of the works and how they are received in Scotland. Please go. You see, I am relying on you to be my eyes and ears and help me out in this way.

And now for the second proposition, which requires a little more travelling than simply a jaunt into town: it is that you come and stay with me here on the Île de Ré this summer. Bring Angus and the children and come for as long as you can – the whole of the school holidays, if you like. Imagine how beneficial it will be for Robbie to be in the sun and the sea air (remember those children we used to see lined up on their beds outside the préventorium*? You know how healthy this climate is). It will do him – and you – the world of good. And I want to meet your family at long, long last! Christophe spends most of his time in Paris now that he is an artist of some renown, so I will be on my own in this big house with bedrooms that are just begging to be filled with my dearest friend and her children. Please say you'll come, dear Ella.*

I will await your reply with impatience.

With my love to you all,

Caroline xxxx

Ella read the letter through and then examined the invitation. The private view was this Friday. She gazed out towards the hills. The clouds seemed to be clearing and the sun shone a little more strongly, suddenly painting the landscape with a thousand nuances of light and shade instead of the drab greys and flat greens of the past wet week.

She closed her eyes and lifted her face to the warmth for a moment. Then she pushed the letter back into its envelope and got to her feet, going back inside to phone and make an appointment at the hairdresser's for Friday morning.

'You look very nice dear,' said Ella's mother, nodding approvingly as her daughter came downstairs wearing a pale blue shift dress which skimmed the curves of her body, still slender even after two children. 'I like your hair in that style. Now don't you worry about a thing and there's no need to hurry back. The children and I will be just fine, won't we Rhona?'

'Thank you.' Ella pulled on the jacket that matched her dress and stooped to kiss Rhona on the cheek. 'But I won't be late. Without Angus, I'm not going to linger. I'll just look at the paintings and come home again. I doubt I'll know anyone there in any case.'

'It's a great pity that Angus couldn't accompany you tonight,' said Mrs Lennox. 'The two of you scarcely ever seem to have the chance to go out together and, if you ask me, it would do you both good to work at it a little harder.'

Ella sighed. The one night that she'd made an effort with her appearance at last, and Angus had some work commitment that was keeping him late at the office. Mind you, perhaps it was just an excuse – he probably felt a little ambivalent about going to look at Christophe's paintings and was staying on at work to get out of it. Still, at least she'd had the sense to turn down Caroline's invitation to spend the summer in France: that clearly would have been asking too much of Angus, even if Christophe wasn't around. It was a shame though, in a way; it probably would have done the whole family good. But perhaps the better

Scottish weather would last until their family fortnight in Arisaig and that would have to do instead.

Ella turned to wave to Rhona and Robbie who were watching her from the doorstep and then hurried along the road to catch the tram into town, her stiletto heels clicking briskly on the pavement.

Princes Street was still busy in the early evening light, the castle sailing high above the gardens where many of the city's inhabitants were making the most of a rare warm Friday evening to walk or sit, or wander to one of the city's bars for an end-of-week drink before making their way home. Ella tugged at the lapels of her jacket a little nervously before joining the small throng who were entering a side door of the RSA beneath a banner that proclaimed the exhibition's title, *Island Landscapes*. She showed her invitation to the gallery guard and was waved inside.

And then she forgot to feel nervous or self-conscious about being there alone because the first picture she saw was a familiar scene. She consulted the programme she'd picked up at the door. '*The Beach at Sainte Marie* (1953). Christophe Martet's landscapes capture the elusive qualities of the Atlantic light around his home on the Île de Ré. Equally renowned for his portraits, the artist now exhibits extensively in Paris and London.'

She moved eagerly from painting to painting, recognising scenes from her summers on the island so many lifetimes ago: a church spire rising from the surrounding marshlands; salt-pans bleached white in the sunlight; beach grasses blowing in the summer's breeze and, beyond the dunes, the colours of the ocean, its blues and greens an infinite play of colour and shade. She bent nearer to this last picture to look more closely at the colour he'd chosen for the deep sea out along the far horizon: viridian. She smiled, remembering.

'Marvellous, isn't it?' Ella was brought back to the room by a voice beside her. 'You're Robbie Dalrymple's mother, aren't you?' She turned to find a smiling couple looking at her expectantly. 'John and Heather Wilcox. We're Hamish's parents. From school?'

'Why, yes, of course. I'm sorry, I was miles away.' Ella shook their hands, recognising them.

'It's these paintings. Isn't it a beautiful exhibition? I love them all, but especially this artist. There's something about the way he captures the feeling of the place. You can almost believe you're on holiday there, smelling the sea!'

Ella nodded. 'I've not really looked at the other pictures, yet. But yes, I think these are wonderful.'

'There appear to be some glasses of sherry over there,' John pointed to a linen-draped table in one corner of the gallery. 'Can I bring you each one?'

Clutching her drink, Ella found herself relaxing and even enjoying the evening as they discussed the paintings and chatted about their children.

'Hamish has been asking if we can invite Robbie round to play one day in the holidays,' said Heather. 'Where is it, exactly, that you live? . . . Why, that's just around the corner from us!'

John looked at his watch and then put his half-drunk glass of sherry down. 'Our car's parked nearby, so why don't we give you a lift home? In fact, why don't we have a quick drink in the Café Royal before we head back?'

Ella glanced at her watch too. It was still early and the thought of a lift home later was very tempting: the pointed toes of her shoes were beginning to pinch. 'Alright, thank you. That would be lovely.'

The bar was busy, but Heather and Ella managed to find a space on one of the leather banquettes while John pushed his way through the throng to buy drinks. It was ages since Ella had been in the Café Royal – or anywhere else much, come to that – and she gazed about happily, taking in the Victorian splendour. They had to shout to make themselves heard above the hubbub of noise that reverberated all around them, rising towards the elaborate ceiling and the mahogany balustrade of the mezzanine above, where diners were enjoying their meals at damask-draped tables.

A sudden crescendo of laughter and applause from the balcony made Ella glance up. It was somebody's birthday and a waiter had brought a dessert lit by a candle to one of the tables.

And then Ella froze, her glass halfway to her lips. The light of the candle briefly illuminated the faces of the couple it was intended for. Her husband's features were thrown into relief. And then, as she watched, Angus leant forward to kiss the hand of the woman sitting across from him.

Ella lowered her glass slowly on to the table before her, stunned. The noise of the bar faded and, for a moment, all she could hear was the sound of the pain that roared in her ears like the crashing of waves.

'Ella? Are you alright?' Heather's touch on her arm brought her back. 'You've gone as white as a sheet all of a sudden.'

With an enormous effort, she pulled herself together. 'Er, yes, I'm sorry. It's just a bit hot in here. And perhaps I'm not used to being out so late,' she joked feebly, grateful for the numbness that was replacing the sensation of shock, allowing her to function. She tried to sip her drink, choking it down, nausea rising in her throat, longing to get out of there and back to the safety of her own home. Only it wasn't safe any more, she realised. It wasn't what she'd thought it was at all. Her home, her marriage, her family: they were all a sham. Her hand shook so violently that she spilled her drink down the front of her dress, the liquid spreading dark as a blood stain over her breast.

John Wilcox downed his pint. 'I agree. It is a bit crowded in here. I'll go and get the car. Bring it round to the door, shall I?'

Ella gathered up her jacket and her handbag. She was desperate to get out of the bar before Angus saw her. 'Why don't we all go? A breath of fresh air would be nice.'

But, as she stood, she saw him glance down and then stiffen as he recognised her. She turned her back on him, struggling to find the sleeve of her jacket, dropping her bag on the floor in her agitation.

John bent to pick it up. 'Come on, Ella. I don't think you're very well. Let's get you home.' And Heather took her arm, solicitous, and led her out into the night, away from the cacophony of laughter and the sight of Angus's horror-struck face.

He tried to tell her it was nothing, that the woman meant nothing at all to him, that he'd succumbed to a moment of madness as he'd felt so lonely, so rejected by Ella. But all she could do was shake her head, distraught, her arms braced across her body, her hands clutching her elbows as she tried to contain the anguish that was threatening to tear her apart.

When she could finally speak, all she'd been able to say was, 'I have to get away. I'm taking the children. I have to get away . . .'

'Please, don't do this, Ella.'

She'd snapped at him then, lashing out in pain. 'You have no right to ask anything of me, Angus Dalrymple. I need to get away, to take some time away from you. I can't think straight. Perhaps the distance will give me some perspective. And it will give you time to decide what you really want.'

'I don't need any time. I know what I want. I have always known what I wanted, Ella, and it's you. And our children. The affair is over. I promise. It's over and nothing like that will ever happen again. But I need you to be present, Ella. You haven't really been here, in our marriage, for a long, long time now. We both need to make an effort.'

Her wounded expression had cut him to the very core. 'I've tried so hard,' she whispered. 'I don't have anything left over any more.'

The silence that followed was a terrible one, filled with the voiceless scream of recrimination and blame.

He'd lifted his eyes to hers, slowly, wretchedly. 'Alright then. Maybe you *should* go to France for the summer. Perhaps you're the one who needs some time to decide what you really want.'

Caroline insisted on coming to meet them at the station on the mainland. 'Don't worry. I need to come to buy materials for the new gallery in any case: I've moved to bigger premises, in Saint Martin on the harbour-side. It's a better location, as well as having more space; more tourists pass by there than in Sainte Marie. So I'll be coming over anyway and I don't want you and the children to have to trail from the train to the ferry with all your luggage. It'll be even more of an adventure for them, taking the car across.'

Ella almost wept when she saw her old friend standing on the platform. She lifted Robbie down from the train while Rhona struggled to help with the bags. Caroline enfolded her in an embrace that felt at once so strange and so welcome that Ella truly had to fight back the tears.

She was still reeling from the shock of discovering Angus's affair and from the strain of the past few weeks. They'd put on an act for the children, although Rhona, always sensitive to the undercurrents of emotion that flowed between her parents, had become more anxious than ever, her wide, serious blue eyes watching her parents' every move as she tried to make sense of the atmosphere of anger and pain that hung in the air like the smell of something burning. 'I want you to come too, Daddy,' she'd begged, clinging to him as he saw them on to the train at Waverley.

'Come on, Rhona. Mummy needs you to help her. Now, you're going to send me a postcard every week, remember? And take lots of photos to show me. I'll be here when you get back, waiting for you all.' He'd met Ella's eyes as he'd spoken that final sentence, the lightness of his tone belying the strength of his message to her. Then he'd kissed her, awkwardly, on the cheek and watched his wife and children climb into the carriage of the train that would take them away from him for the summer.

Ella felt strangely off balance, and not just as a result of their long journey. Once they'd stowed their luggage in the boot of Caroline's car and driven the short distance to the ferry embarkation point, she was overwhelmed by a flood of emotions that surged through her as the Île de Ré came into view. The children bounced with excitement on the back seat as they saw the boat approaching, reminding Ella of the day when she'd stood in this same place, watching the boat that was coming to carry her across the water to the island.

Memories crowded back, of impressions and sensations and the voices of Marianne and Monsieur Martet, both now gone. Memories of Christophe. She wondered what his life in Paris was like these days, but there would be time to ask Caroline. She settled back in the passenger seat, easing her back, which was stiff from sitting on trains for so long. She took a deep breath of the sea air and felt the tension in her shoulders ease a little. She seemed to have been carrying herself so carefully for so long, trying to hold it all together, as if she would splinter into tiny pieces if she relaxed for one second. But now, away from home, away from Angus's wounded, guilty eyes, the luxury of the long summer holidays stretched before her. She looked forward to introducing the island to her children in the coming weeks; and she hoped it would be a time of healing so that she could find a way to carry on, somehow, the life that seemed to have come to a dead stop.

'How does the car get on to the boat?' Robbie asked, leaning forward between the front seats to watch as the ferry drew up alongside the quay. A smell of diesel mingled with the salt tang of the sea on the warm air that wafted in through the open windows of the car.

'There, look.' Caroline pointed. 'They will put ramps in place. Once all those cars have come off, we will drive on.'

'Can we take a picture? I want to show Daddy that we went on the ferry.'

'Here, give me the camera and I'll take one of the three of you. Stand a little closer, there, that's good, now smile!' Caroline handed the camera back to Ella and then helped Robbie climb back into the car again. 'Come on now. We don't want to be left behind! We'll be on the island in a hop and a skip and a jump.'

Ella joined Caroline where she sat on the terrace. The table had been cleared whilst she was upstairs putting the children to bed and now all that was left was the remainder of the bottle of white wine that had accompanied the evening meal and their two glasses, sitting alongside a pitcher of white roses whose petals were illuminated in the glow from a candle lantern.

'Here.' Caroline topped up one of the glasses and pushed it towards Ella. 'Did they go down okay?'

Ella nodded. 'It's hard to tell whether they're more excited or exhausted. Robbie's out for the count already. He asked me when we can go and see the boat that we're going to do the sailing in, but by the time I finished answering he'd already fallen asleep! And Rhona can hardly keep her eyes open, although she's determined to read another chapter of her book before she turns out the light. She loves the room, especially the vase of flowers on the dressing-table. And they both absolutely adore you already. I knew they would.'

'Well, the feeling is entirely mutual, I can assure you. And since it looks increasingly unlikely that I will ever have any children of my own, I think I shall borrow yours instead.'

'Have you not met anyone?'

'There's an artist I see from time to time, when it suits us both. But he's definitely not a family man.' Caroline paused, taking another sip of her wine. And then she said, 'And, to tell you the truth, I'm not sure I have the strength to bring children into a world where there are people capable of doing what they did to my mother. And to Agnès and her children. No, I'm a career woman and it's better this way. It's my choice. Don't feel sorry for me. I'm content and fulfilled. And I shall very much enjoy being a special "aunt" to Rhona and Robbie.'

Caroline reached out and held Ella's hand briefly, before releasing it to take another sip from her own glass.

'So. We have many weeks in which to catch up, although after all these years maybe even that won't be enough time. But perhaps we should begin with you. Do you want to tell me what happened to make you change your mind and come to the island for the summer after all?' She shot Ella an astute glance. 'I'm guessing whatever it was may be the cause of those dark circles beneath your eyes.'

They talked late into the night. They scarcely noticed as the candle in the lantern burned low and then guttered in a pool of its own wax, flickering twice before finally dying, to the disappointment of the moths that had gathered on the glass.

'Oh, Ella, I'm so sorry that you are suffering this way.' Caroline picked up a petal that had dropped softly on to the table from one of the roses, stroking its silken softness with her finger. 'In my solitary state, I have often envied you your husband and your family. But I do see that it's not all plain sailing. I remember my mother saying once, when we were out in *Bijou*, that the secret to making a marriage work is a lot like sailing a boat: if you have too much anchor and no sail then you will feel trapped; but if there is too much sail and not enough anchor, that doesn't work either. You need to try to find the balance between the two and then steer a course that is true. And, she said, the way you do that is with the compass of your morality and the rudder of your soul.'

Ella smiled. 'It sounds complicated. But then marriage *is* complicated, as I've found.'

'Well, I hope this summer will give you the time and the space you need in order to get yours back on to an even keel.'

Caroline paused, raising the rose petal to inhale its rich scent.

'But Ella, there is something I must tell you. When I first wrote suggesting you come for the holidays, I told you that Christophe would be in Paris. Well, in the end his plans changed, before we knew that your own would as well. He is on the island.'

Ella kept her eyes downcast, running a fingertip around the rim of her wine-glass. But her hand trembled and so she dropped it, quickly, into her lap, hoping that Caroline hadn't noticed.

'Where is he?'

'Don't worry. He will not come to the house, unless you say it is alright for him to do so. He's staying above the new gallery in Saint Martin – there's an apartment there. He's perfectly comfortable, there's space for him to work, and *Bijou* is moored in the harbour just in front of the building, so it's ideal for him. He and I have discussed your visit. He realises it could be awkward for you. With the children here . . . and we'd wondered whether Angus might come too, after all, at least for some of the summer. Although I don't know whether that would have made it more or less awkward. Christophe would love to see you all, but only if it's what you want.'

Ella was silent for a few moments. Then she turned to Caroline, her expression unreadable in the shadows. 'Of course, I'd love to see him. And I'd love the children to meet him too. I've told them all about the Martet family, what good friends you all were to me when I was here for the first time nearly twenty years ago. I just wish that they could have met your parents as well.'

Caroline nodded. 'Very well.'

The tone of their words was nonchalant, but carefully so.

In the darkness, something seemed to have shifted. It was hard to say what, exactly. Perhaps it was just a change in the breeze, which caused the white rose in the pitcher to release its remaining petals on to the table all at once; perhaps it was the delicate wash of light that flooded the darkened garden suddenly, as the full face of the moon appeared above the dunes beyond the whitewashed wall.

Or perhaps it was something less tangible: a barely perceptible awareness in each of the two women that fate, like the swinging needle of a compass, had turned to point towards the possibility of another path. One that, until that moment, had been unimaginable.

'Good morning! Hello? *Coucou!* Where are you all hiding?' The house was still and silent as Ella came downstairs the next morning. She'd slept soundly, for once, worn out by all that travelling. And, having closed her bedroom shutters, she'd not realised how late it was.

A note sat in the middle of the kitchen table, weighted down by the fruit bowl: *'Mummy. We have gone to have breckfast at a caffy. In Saint Martin. We will bring you back a crussent. Or Caroline says you can come and find us on a bike at the gallery. Love from Robbie XXX'*

For a moment, Ella toyed with the idea of staying put and enjoying the peace while Caroline entertained her children. But she couldn't resist the thought of joining them, not wanting to miss out on the children's excitement. And the thought of a croissant and a *café au lait*, sitting in the sunshine on the quayside, was just too tempting.

She hadn't been on a bike for years, and wobbled slightly as she set off up the sandy track between the neat rows of vines. But she quickly regained her confidence and was soon pedalling along the road that led to the north of the island. The roadside was lined with wildflowers, a *petit point* of Delft blue, magenta and silver-grey against the raw sienna of the grasses. The ever-present ocean breeze made the hem of her sundress flutter about her knees and lifted her hair from her shoulders, cooling the smooth skin of her neck even as the sun warmed her cheeks and forehead.

'Oops, I'll get freckles,' she thought, remembering her seventeen-year-old self's preoccupation and smiling as she did so.

Reaching Saint Martin, she rattled across the cobbles in the Place de la République and then turned into one of the steep, hollyhock-clustered streets that ran down to the port between whitewashed houses. The shops and cafés were already abustle with holidaymakers. She got off and wheeled her bike, taking in the snug harbour filled with boats and looking out for Caroline and the children in case they were sitting at a table outside one of the cafés. It was easy to spot the gallery, which faced her from the other side of the stone bridge that separated the two *bassins* of the harbour, with Caroline's name painted on the canvas awning that shaded its windows from the sun. And her breath caught for a moment when she saw *Bijou*, just as Caroline had said, moored in front of it.

She propped the bicycle against one of the iron stanchions holding the chain that encircled the harbour's edge and stepped into the coolness of the gallery, a bell sounding faintly from an inner room as she crossed the threshold.

She stood stock still, gazing round at the paintings that lined the walls. They were all Christophe's work: sea-scapes and beach-scapes, interspersed with portraits of fishermen, a woman leading a donkey, workers in the salt-pans. In one corner was a separate display of several fine ceramics, alongside works by a sculptor – a local man, she later read in the accompanying catalogue – which sat on individual plinths.

She turned back to look more closely at one of the paintings, of wind-blown grasses in the dunes, clouds scudding across a summer's sky.

And then she became aware of another presence in the room: a quality in the silence of the holding of a breath; the sensation of a pair of eyes upon her.

She turned.

He stood in the archway that led to the inner room. Watching her.

Without a word, she stepped swiftly across the space between them and put her arms around him. He hesitated. Then she felt him embrace her back.

When she could speak, she stepped back to look at him properly, blinking the tears away. 'There you are. The man who came back from the dead.'

His face was thinner, lined now, and his hair was dusted with silver. His eyes were dark as the ocean deeps, and as hard to read.

He smiled, but it was one of the saddest smiles she had ever seen. 'Ella. You have grown even more beautiful over the years. How I have longed for this moment, and how I have dreaded it. Knowing that it would be impossible to see you, and impossible not to.'

'Sometimes I think life itself is impossible,' she replied. She raised a trembling hand to her chest, as if to try to calm her heart which was beating so fast.

Then she noticed the pictures beyond the archway, within the inner room of the gallery. They were all portraits and her breath caught as she recognised Marianne. She stepped towards the painting. 'This is wonderful, Christophe,' she said quietly. 'You have captured her very essence.'

There was another silence between them then, filled with the sound of grief, as loud as the soft roar of a sea-shell held against the ear.

The bell pinged faintly and voices in the doorway of the gallery broke the spell.

'*Coucou*, we're back!' Caroline called.

'Mummy, you're here! Did you ride the bike? We had breakfast in a café and then we had an ice cream straight away afterwards. It was made of salty caramel which sounds like it's not going to be very nice, but it's absolutely delicious!'

Ella stooped to hug her son. 'Why Robbie, you're not wearing your brace!'

'I don't think I need it when I'm on holiday. It's easy because here on the island everything is flat. And Caroline says ice cream is very good for building up my strength. I think I might need to have one every single day.'

'Oh, does she indeed?' Ella laughed. 'Well, she is a very wise woman, so that must be true.'

'We got you a croissant, Mummy.' Rhona handed her a crumpled paper bag. 'And we bought some soap made with milk from a lady donkey. It makes your skin lovely and soft, Caroline says.'

'It's called an ass. Some people think that's a rude word, only you're allowed to say it because it's not rude when you mean a donkey, is it Caroline? Ass, ass, asses' milk.' Robbie was clearly enjoying exploring all sorts of new-found liberties.

'My goodness, what a lot of adventures you've had and it's only the first morning of your holidays! I'm sorry I slept in and missed so much.'

'That's alright. We've saved some adventures for you too. Like going out in the sailing boat. It's called *Bijou* and it's a she.'

'That's right, Robbie,' said Caroline, with a smile. 'And now, let me introduce you to her captain. This is Christophe, my brother.'

'Hello.' Robbie shook Christophe's hand, man-to-man. 'I'm Robbie Dalrymple and this is Rhona. She's my sister.'

Christophe nodded, the light in his eyes belying his grave expression. 'I've heard a lot about you both and I'm very pleased to meet you.' As he crossed to shake Rhona by the hand, his pronounced limp became apparent. Robbie eyed him, appraisingly.

'Have you had polio too?'

'No, Robbie. I encountered a German shell one fine morning. And then I spent several years in a prison camp, which didn't help matters much.'

'Coo, that's ripping! Can you tell me all about it?'

Just then the bell sounded again as a couple of tourists stepped over the threshold.

'Maybe we should save that for later?' Ella intervened gently. 'I think we'd better leave Caroline and Christophe in peace for a little while as they have work to do. I need a coffee and my breakfast.' She held up the paper bag. 'And then we can go to the covered market to buy some things for lunch.'

'Alright.' Robbie lifted his hand in salute. 'See you soon then, Caroline. Christophe, will you come and have lunch with us too? And, Mummy, we can show you the ice-cream shop.'

The island worked its magic on them all. As the weeks passed, Robbie grew stronger in the sunshine and sea air – and perhaps the daily *caramel au beurre salé* ice creams helped too. His discarded brace rusted in a corner of his bedroom whilst he cycled and swam and ran through the dunes to build fortresses of damp sand on the beach. His favourite game was to build Stalag Luft VIII-A, the prisoner-of-war camp that Christophe had told him so much about, and then to dig tunnels with an oyster shell to allow the hermit-crab prisoners incarcerated there to escape back into the sea.

Rhona's cheeks grew rosy, with a scattering of freckles just like her mother's. The wind teased waves into her sand-gold hair, ruffling it out of its usual severe Alice band so that it curled in soft tendrils about her face. She followed Caroline like a miniature shadow and loved helping out at the gallery, her confidence growing to the point where she could even speak a few words of French to the clients who stepped in out of the heat of the day to browse amongst the artworks.

Ella settled back into the rhythm of the Île de Ré, the busyness and constant clock-watching of life back in Edinburgh dissolving in the holiday atmosphere of the island. Slowly but surely, she began to feel more relaxed, less burdened, her tension and unhappiness melting away into the background. Once again, the narrow strip of water separating the island from the mainland became a gulf so wide that the realities of life slipped from view, Edinburgh lying far beyond the horizon. She knew it was just a brief interlude, as ephemeral as the sunlit dreams that illuminated her nights as she slept, but she let herself sink ever deeper into that summer, luxuriating in the beauty of the place, comforted by the wondrous memories of those other times, not allowing herself to think about the journey back to their real lives that awaited them in a few weeks' time. In place of sadness, she chose joy, finding the beauty once again, even amidst the pain and the anguish.

Best of all were the days when they loaded a picnic basket into *Bijou* and headed out between the high stone walls of Saint Martin's harbour into the ocean.

One day, as the summer was nearing its end, Christophe showed the children how to sail her, letting Robbie haul in the sheets and Rhona take the tiller, as they tacked westwards on a broad reach towards the far tip of the island. Ella's eyes met Christophe's above her children's heads and she smiled her gratitude to him. When they moored up for lunch in the *Fier d'Ars*, the shallow lagoon that borders the salt-pans, he pulled out a sketch pad and tore off a sheet of paper for each child. 'Right, we're going to do some drawing now. What shall we sketch?'

'Let's draw Mummy!' Robbie pointed to where Ella sat watching the three of them, resting her head against the doorway to the cabin.

Ella blushed. 'I think you should find something else . . . the beach perhaps?' The thought of forcing Christophe to look at her made her feel uncomfortable. There was still an awkwardness between them, a sense that they shouldn't let one another get too close.

'No, that's much too difficult, Mummy. We're going to draw you, so you have to sit very still.'

'Yes, Ella, sit very still please.' He was teasing her now, sensing her embarrassment and trying to put her at her ease. He handed each of them a pencil and they began to draw her.

'No rubbing out, Rhona.' he stopped her as she tutted and reached for his tin of pencils. 'Use the line you've already made and correct it. You see, like this. You can draw several light lines until you start to build up the right shape. That's it, good. Now go over that one and make it a little darker . . .'

Caroline wasn't with them that day; she had stayed behind at the gallery to prepare for a drinks reception that she was holding that evening to launch an exhibition of her brother's latest work. They'd promised to come back early and lend a hand polishing glasses and folding napkins. All at once, Ella felt self-conscious about being without their chaperone. *How ridiculous*, she thought, *as if I were seventeen again. It's not as if anything can possibly happen between him and me.* She sat still, as directed, gazing out to sea, all the while conscious of his eyes skimming her eyes, her lips, her throat as he drew her.

They presented her with the three sketches. 'Very good. What a brilliant drawing, Robbie. And, Rhona, yours really is excellent.'

'I'm going to keep it and send it to Daddy.' Rhona took hers back and put it in the bag that contained her sun-hat and sandals.

Ella handed back the other two drawings, noticing that Christophe tucked his between the pages of his sketch-book before starting to unpack the lunch things. Would he keep it? Or would it just be thrown away when he got home?

And why, all of a sudden, did that seem to matter so very much to her?

'I'm sorry. Have we been introduced? Why, Rhona and Robbie, it's *you*! I didn't recognise you in your smart clothes.' Caroline, looking radiant herself in a black cocktail dress, with her hair piled up in a loose *chignon*, stooped to hug the children.

'Your team of helpers, reporting for duty.' Ella gave a mock salute. 'Give us our orders.'

'Robbie, can you go and find Christophe upstairs? He's filling ice buckets to chill the wine and I think he might need a hand breaking up the ice block with a hammer and chisel. Make sure he doesn't do any lasting damage either to himself or to the kitchen. And, Rhona, please could you finish folding these catalogues – like this – and then lay out a few piles of them here and there?'

'It looks wonderful, Caroline.' Ella admired the newly displayed exhibits.

Caroline nodded. 'His work gets better and better, doesn't it? I hope it will be well received. We have quite a number of my Parisian clients coming this evening – the island is becoming such a fashionable place to holiday these days. If they like what they see, they could be influential in spreading the word back in the city. His work is starting to command Parisian prices, even on the Île de Ré.'

As the evening shadows began to lengthen across the cobble-stones, the first guests started to arrive.

The children handed round glasses of chilled Sancerre and were exclaimed over and proclaimed '*charmants*'. The two rooms of the gallery were soon filled with an elegant and sophisticated crowd, and Ella circulated, eavesdropping on the guests' appreciative comments and admiring remarks about the artist and his work. Caroline introduced her to a former colleague from the Louvre, who regaled her with anecdotes from the museum during the war years and reassured her that all the artworks that had been hidden in safe locations around France had survived and had now been returned to their rightful home.

As Ella leaned closer, to catch the man's stories above the rising hubbub, she was aware that Christophe seemed to be watching her rather than listening to the chatter of the group that surrounded him.

Her children approached, and Christophe continued to watch her as she introduced them. She noticed a look of pain, fleeting as a flicker of lightning, that pulsed in his eyes as she drew her children close to her side, and she wondered whether it had been a mistake to come back to the Île de Ré after all. Perhaps she should have let it be, allowed time to dissolve the bond of their friendship rather than perpetuating it across the years. Despite the clarity of the opalescent sky above the roofs of Saint Martin, where swallows dipped and soared beyond the church tower on the hillside across the harbour, she had a sudden foreboding, as heavy as gathering storm-clouds. What would happen in a week's time when the holidays came to an end and it was time to board the train that would carry them away from the island and back to their lives in Edinburgh? It would be impossible to get on that train. It would be impossible not to.

'There you go.' Christophe carried Robbie up the stairs and deposited him gently on the bed, so as not to wake him.

'Thank you,' whispered Ella. He watched from the bedroom doorway as she eased off her son's shoes and drew the covers over him, stooping to brush the hair from his forehead and plant a kiss there. Christophe turned away and, without a word, went back downstairs, his limp making his footsteps thud unevenly on alternate steps.

'Goodnight.' Ella kissed Rhona and tucked her in, moving across the room to pull the shutters to. The night breeze stirred the muslin curtains, soft as the breath of sleep. 'You were a wonderful help at Caroline's party tonight, my grown-up girl.'

'Thank you. And Mummy?'

'Yes, Rhona?'

'It's only one more week to go until we see Daddy again, isn't it?'

Ella nodded.

'That's good. I think he must be missing us, don't you?'

She nodded again. 'Night, night. Off to sleep now.'

Rhona yawned, then tuned on to her side, pulling her pillow close and wriggling into a more comfortable position. Her mother hesitated for a moment, watching as Rhona's eyes closed, her lashes fluttering, delicate as butterfly wings against the roses of her cheeks. And then Ella turned and left the room.

Christophe sat on the terrace, his head tilted back, watching the stars. She sat down on the chair beside his and followed suit, gazing into the night sky.

Caroline had gone home with her artist at the end of the evening. 'Are you sure you'll be alright?' she'd asked Ella, holding her at arm's length and scrutinising her face. 'I can easily put him off for another time.'

Ella had laughed. 'Don't you dare! We'll be fine. I don't want to be the one to get in the way of your love life – I feel we've probably been a bit of a hindrance on that front already this summer.'

They'd found Robbie curled up behind Caroline's desk, sound asleep. 'Here,' offered Christophe. 'I'll carry him to the car. Let me drive you home. You'll need a hand at the other end.'

So they were alone together. Ella wondered fleetingly if it had been engineered? And, if so, by whom? Caroline? Christophe? Or by Ella herself, who could, after all, have turned down the offer of help and driven the children home on her own. Was it all three of them, conspiring together? Or could she blame it on something else? On Angus's affair? Or was it just fate?

Above them, the Milky Way was a river of light, flowing through the blackness of the night. As she watched, Ella felt as though she were being pulled into its stream, swept along, unresisting suddenly.

And then she knew, with utter certainty, that leaving Christophe again was impossible. That, in a life filled with impossibilities, this single truth was the only one that mattered. She and the children would stay here on the island and they would make a life together with him.

Without a word, she stood and held out her hand to him. He looked up at her, pain and fear clouding his expression, and shook his head.

She took his hand in hers, then nodded, her eyes still locked on his, her smile calm and clear.

She pulled him to his feet and they walked, hand in hand, to the dunes, which gathered them once more into their hidden embrace, secreting them away from the world of impossibilities, in a place where the only certainty was love.

When she woke, just as the blue mist of dawn crept across the beach, he was no longer lying beside her. She turned, drowsily, and saw him there, his pencil whispering across the page of his sketch-book as he drew her. When he lifted his eyes to glance at her again, she was smiling at him.

'This will be my greatest masterpiece, Ella. All these years, it has been waiting to be created. But now is the time.' He sketched a few more lines, then carefully closed his sketch-book and stood, holding out his hand to her.

They brushed the sand from their clothes and, hand still clasping hand, walked back to the house before the children awoke.

It seemed that Caroline sensed something had changed the moment she saw them together. She drove Christophe back to the apartment above the gallery after lunch and on her return she suggested that they all go down to the beach to collect shells.

She and Ella sat against the soft flank of the dunes, watching Rhona and Robbie as they pottered up and down the strand-line, busy as sand-pipers, each with a bucket to fill.

'Ella,' Caroline said, gazing out towards the sea, unable to look her friend in the eye. 'I know. Christophe has told me, about your decision last night to leave Angus. Tell me, please, that in the clear light of day you have reconsidered.'

Ella shook her head. 'No. If anything, I'm more determined than ever. There is so much for me here – a life with Christophe, the possibility of happiness, freedom too. I have none of that back home in Edinburgh.'

'I know it's hard, Ella. But think of your children. What is going to happen to them?'

'I'll keep them here. You've said yourself how happy and well they look now. I know it'll be a big adjustment for them, but they'll adapt. Children do.'

'But Angus? Rhona, especially, will never forgive you. She talks about her daddy constantly. It will be a terrible wrench for her.'

'Angus should have thought of that before he embarked on his affair,' Ella retorted angrily, seared by guilt which she tried to block out. 'He is the one who initiated all this. He is as much responsible for the outcome as I am.' She brushed away furious tears that suddenly blurred her vision as she watched the two small figures at the water's edge, heads bent over their latest find.

'Two wrongs don't make a right. You know that, Ella.' Caroline's voice was gentle, carefully non-judgemental. 'But Angus won't give up his children without a fight. Are you prepared to lose them? Because it may come to that. If you choose to leave your marriage, the court may rule that the children must stay with their father. And you have only experienced the Île de Ré in the summer. It's entirely different in wintertime when the Atlantic gales lash the island. What about schooling for your children? What if Robbie needs more medical attention sometime? All of these questions will be taken into account when some judge is deciding which of you gets to keep Rhona and Robbie. It will tear you apart, Ella. It will tear them apart.'

'No. You're wrong, Caroline. People make their lives here, children grow up here. We can too. I know it will be painful for a while, but when Angus sees how strong Robbie has grown, how well they are both looking, he will have to admit this is the best place for them.' She held up a hand to silence Caroline's next objection. 'Please. Don't make this harder than it already is. I need you to help me through it, not to try to talk me out of it.'

Ella stood up and dusted the sand from her skirt. She walked away, up the beach towards the children.

Christophe arrived the next morning and scooped them all into the car. 'Come on. I'm taking you to one of the wilder beaches today. It's a beach I want to paint. There are some good waves there.' He pulled a sun-umbrella and a heavy wooden surfboard down from the rafters of the shed. 'Let's take this with us.'

'Ripping! Is it yours?' Robbie asked.

'No, it belongs to an American friend. I'm storing it for him while he's in Paris.'

'Can you stand up on it?'

Christophe laughed. 'No, Robbie, not with my bad leg. But I'll teach you how to body surf if you like, it's really good fun. And then, if you get tired of jumping in the big waves, you can float on it instead.'

They drove along the south side of the island, then turned down a sandy track, leading to a stretch of golden sand which followed a straight course for a mile or so before curving into a point like a fish-hook in the distance. Breakers washed ashore in a tumble of foam.

'The trick to this beach,' Christophe explained to the children, 'is to understand its shape. If we stay up at this end, where the waves are white, we'll be fine. This is where it's shallower. But be careful, because the water gets deeper suddenly, just there, you see, where the waves are still travelling in, unbroken. That's where the channel is.'

'Are you sure it's safe?' Rhona asked, anxious.

'Don't worry, darling, Christophe wouldn't bring you anywhere that wasn't.'

'You'll be fine, Rhona. The tide is coming in at the moment so it's perfectly safe. And I'll be with you in the water all the time.'

Soon they were splashing happily, jumping in the waves and whooping as they soared towards the beach on the surfboard.

Ella came out of the water first, shivering despite the heat of the sun. The Atlantic was bracing, to say the least, but she warmed up again quickly, sitting on her beach towel and basking like a seal. Completely waterlogged, Rhona came running to find her own towel. 'It's so much fun, Mummy,' she gasped, breathless with exhilaration. 'I'm going to go back in!'

'Alright. But tell Christophe and Robbie ten more minutes and then it's time for lunch.'

They were all starving and devoured the baguettes that Christophe had brought. Juice ran down their chins from the peaches he pulled out of a paper bag for afters.

'Can we go back in? Can we, Mummy?' Robbie was impatient to get back to the water.

'No. We need to let our lunch go down for at least an hour. You know that, Robbie. Have a snooze. Or go and look for some more shells to add to your collection.'

Annoyed, he curled up in his towel. Five minutes later he was asleep, and Ella carefully repositioned the sun-umbrella to protect his face from the sun. Sleepy with food and sunshine and worn out by the churning power of the sea, Rhona lay down too.

'This is how it will be,' Ella thought. 'Days like this, the four of us, perfectly content.' She smiled at Christophe and then curled up next to her children.

He bent down close to her. 'I'm going to head over that way to sketch.' She nodded, already drowsy. 'Back soon.'

It was Rhona's scream that woke Ella.

In a split second she was up and running, racing to the water's edge. Beyond the white water, Robbie was just visible. He was lying on the surfboard, trying desperately to turn it back to shore. But the tide had turned whilst they slept and a strong rip current had seized him in its grip and was carrying him out to sea.

Without stopping to think, Ella plunged into the water. Dimly, from far off, she could hear shouting voices, Christophe's amongst them. But all she could see was her son, his new-found strength ebbing from him fast as he struggled against the power of the sea.

She felt the water seize her, the current in the channel sweeping her out. But she didn't care, it was carrying her to Robbie. She had to reach him before he fell off the board and the waves claimed him. She swam strongly, not fighting against the rip but using its power.

She reached the surfboard. 'Hold on tight, Robbie. I've got you now. But you have to stay on the board, alright?' He nodded, his face white with exhaustion and panic beneath his tan. She held the back of the board and tried to kick, to turn them out of the current. But the surfboard tilted sickeningly, the rip refusing to relinquish its grip, and Robbie screamed as he nearly fell into the water. Choppy waves washed over her head and she swallowed salt water, choking and gasping as she turned the board back into line with the flow. She glanced back over one shoulder. They were far out now, the figures on the beach receding rapidly. She hoped Christophe had got Rhona, making sure she wouldn't try to swim out after them.

She clung desperately to the end of the board, trying to tread water so that she wouldn't weigh it down and make Robbie slide off. Suddenly she realised she couldn't feel her legs. The icy waters out this deep were sucking the warmth from her body, draining her.

She tried again to turn the board out of the current, but again it tipped. There was nothing for it but to let the rip carry them out even further. She just had to hope it would eventually slacken off enough to allow her to turn the board. But would she have the energy to steer them back to shore when it did?

She clung on. 'Please, God.' The thought was loud in her head. Louder even than the roar of the wind and the slap of the waves. 'Please, God, don't let him die.' As the current swept them onwards, a feeling of calm crept over her, the numbness seeping upwards from her limbs into her brain.

And, suddenly, she saw it all so clearly. Like the current, her plan to stay on the island was a terrible, destructive force. One that would carry them far from the life they had known; one that would sweep them all away.

It was madness.

She would lose her children.

She would wreck their lives. And how could her own remain undamaged therefore? She would drown, and she would carry Angus and Robbie and Rhona, and Christophe too, down with her.

As she and her fragile son were swept ever onwards, she began to bargain with a god that she wasn't even sure she believed in. 'Please, God. Let us live. I'll go back. I promise. I won't stay on the island. Just let us live.' Her fingers were numb now and she felt her hands beginning to slip from the board, unable to grip.

'Mummy?' At the sound of Robbie's voice, weakening now, a surge of strength jolted through her, a sudden heat flooding her veins like quicksilver.

'Hold on as tight as you can, Robbie.' She kicked out, with every ounce of strength that remained. And the board turned, slowly, ponderously, as the current relinquished its grip. Up ahead, miraculously, she saw the spit of sand, like the tip of a fish-hook, that projected from the beach. Christophe was running and hobbling along it, waving to attract her attention, calling her in. And then he splashed into the breaking waves himself and swam out to them, catching Robbie as he slipped from the board.

'Can you make it?' he shouted to her.

'Yes,' she gasped, able to hold the board more tightly now, using it to propel herself forward. 'Just get him to safety!'

Then there were strong arms reaching for her, pulling her on to the beach. A dry towel draped around her shoulders. Rhona sobbing, clinging to her. Robbie, grey and shivering with shock, being wrapped in more towels.

And the look in Christophe's eyes as he read her exhausted expression and he realised what she now knew. That she would always, *always* save her children first.

2014, Edinburgh

We were supposed to be going to The Balmoral – as the North British Hotel is called nowadays – for tea in the Palm Court. That was going to be my Christmas present to Ella. But, in the end, she wasn't up to it. There are more and more days now, the nurses tell me, when she doesn't get out of bed at all. Like the days when I arrive to find her deeply asleep as she drifts further from this world, the tide of her life ebbing away, leaving behind a scattering of memories and a few white shells.

So, instead, I've brought Christmas tea to her. Propped against her pillows, she smiles and gives my hand a squeeze as I place the tray before her. 'This is just splendid, Kendra dear.' I can see she's tired, but she's making an effort to get into the festive spirit for my sake.

'Well, we're celebrating the end of term as well as Christmas. Two of my favourite things! Finn helped make the mince pies – he cut out the stars for the tops. He made this card too. And Dan sends love.'

Ella peers at the card, bringing it closer to the light, and then smiles broadly.

'I know,' I say, 'it's not exactly seasonal.' Finn has drawn the shed at the allotment, in perfect detail. And if you look closely enough you can just make out that the honeysuckle that grows up the side of it is in full bloom, each petal carefully coloured pale yellow.

'I love it. And I get the message. Your beautiful boy always does my old heart good. It's well drawn too. He has talent.'

I pour the tea, then settle myself in the chair at her bedside.

I feel awkward and self-conscious, wanting to ask my grandmother a hundred questions and yet wanting to be sensitive about the intimacy of all that happened between her and Christophe – as well as between her and my grandfather – during that pivotal summer of 1957. And I wonder, too, how much my mother knew about it all. Was she aware, at the time, how close to the wind they were all sailing? Could she sense the dangers that threatened them? The emotional storms that were raging and the rocks that lurked just beneath the surface of her family life? Is that why she won't see her mother now?

As if she can read my mind, Ella dabs her lips with a holly-sprigged paper napkin and says, 'Rhona and Robbie were oblivious. They were both shaken by the incident at the beach, of course. But they didn't know how close I came to leaving Angus. Damage limitation. We always try to protect our children, as you know.'

'It must have been so hard, though, leaving the island at the end of the summer. I can't imagine how you must have felt.'

She nods. 'I did a lot of thinking on the homeward journey. But I never looked back. I knew what I had to do and I got on and did it. I don't think I felt very much for a while, but eventually, when my heart began to thaw out again, I suppose what I felt most of all was guilt. Guilt that I hadn't loved Angus well enough, that I had betrayed him – long before he betrayed me – every time I thought of Christophe; every time the demands of motherhood and domesticity and your grandfather's career grated on my nerves. The distraction of a fantasy can make reality seem harder to bear, I suppose.'

She pauses to take a sip of tea. 'You know, I think the biggest mistake I made was not to see that the imperfect reality was worth so much more than the perfect dream.'

I nod slowly, considering this. 'So, is it wrong to dream, to want the things we don't have?'

'No, my darling, never give up your dreams. But just make sure they don't distract you too much from the good things that there are in your day-to-day life, even if that life is by no means perfect. Because there always *are* good things' – she picks up Finn's honeysuckle Christmas card again – 'but sometimes you have to concentrate to be able to see them.'

PART 3

1970, Edinburgh

Ella and Angus took their seats in the painted splendour of the McEwan Hall and Ella fished in her handbag for her glasses so that she could find Robbie's name in the programme, amongst the hundreds of others who would be graduating that day.

'Here.' She handed Angus her cardigan. 'Use this to keep a seat for Rhona.'

He smiled at her. 'Quite a thing to have them both finish their education. Finally! It's been a long haul.'

Ella nodded and smiled, although, sitting here now, the years seemed to have flown past all too quickly. In a few days' time Robbie would be setting off to drive to Spain with two of his friends, making the most of his last few weeks of freedom. He'd only be back long enough to pack up his things and then he was off to London to start his job in the City. Thank goodness they'd still have Rhona living at home, or she'd have been utterly bereft. Even if she did only catch fleeting glimpses of her daughter these days. Rhona often only returned home from work long enough to get changed before going out with her friends in town or meeting up with her boyfriend to go to the cinema.

Where had all those years gone? After that summer on the Île de Ré, she'd returned to Angus with no word of explanation. He'd asked for none, either. He was simply relieved to have her back. He never asked her any questions about those weeks that they'd spent apart.

The children, oblivious to how close to breaking up the family had come that summer, had prattled on happily, telling their daddy about days on the beach, sailing expeditions with Christophe, helping Caroline in the gallery, and the superhuman quantities of the ice cream they'd consumed. Angus had exclaimed over Robbie's new-found strength and the fact that he walked with scarcely any trace of a limp now; and he told Rhona that she'd grown at least two inches taller over the summer, as he'd ruffled her sun-streaked hair; he'd admired their collection of shells and pored over the photographs with them; and he kept the paperweight in the shape of a donkey wearing striped cotton trousers in pride of place on the desk in his study, on top of Rhona's sketch of Ella on the boat.

Only when Robbie recounted the story of being swept out to sea on the surfboard, and the way Ella had rescued him, did Angus meet her eye. 'She's an extremely brave woman, your mother. Brave and strong. Luckily for us all.'

For her own part, Ella never wasted time regretting the decision she'd made to return. In fact, she rarely allowed herself to think of it at all. It was safer not to revisit her memories of those weeks on the island. She kept them locked away in a part of her mind that she would not – could not – visit. On the train that had carried them home, the Île de Ré receding into the distance with every clatter of the wheels over the tracks, she'd come to see that she had two choices: she could let her feelings of bitterness and loss define her marriage from here on in, allowing resentment and self-pity to corrode her heart and reduce her to a sad shadow; or she could accept the situation with grace and equanimity, whole-heartedly immersing herself in the life that she'd chosen, fighting to stay in the light instead of allowing the darkness of despair to drag her under.

She knew it would take all her strength and determination to make her marriage work after everything she and Angus had been through. Perhaps, despite all the challenges she had faced, this would be her greatest test yet. She only hoped she had it in her to face the prospect of trying to love again with a heart that felt like it had been shattered into a thousand pieces.

She and Angus had been careful with one another, considerate and thoughtful, conscious of the fragile trust that needed to be nurtured daily if it wasn't to be destroyed again. They had each upheld their side of the relationship, as good parents and loyal spouses. But, despite Ella recommitting to the relationship, they'd never managed to recreate the closeness that had existed in their courting days and in those first, precious weeks of their marriage before the arrival of Caroline's letter had changed everything.

Sitting in the grand gilt hall of the university now, a flicker of anxiety fluttered briefly in Ella's chest: what would happen when they no longer had either of their children at home? What would life be like when it was just the two of them left, she wondered, without the welcome distractions that Robbie and Rhona brought to their daily lives, distractions which filled the silences and papered over the cracks?

She shrugged it off. That they were still together twenty-five years on was no small achievement. And if their marriage was lacking in some ways, there was still friendship in it and a mutual respect for one another, which was more than you could say for some of the people they knew. The blossoming of flower power and free love in the sixties had resulted in several of their friends' marriages imploding: the so-called Dawning of the Age of Aquarius had turned out, in many cases, to be the Dawning of the Age of Devastation and Divorce. At least she and Angus had managed to avoid inflicting that on their children. And, in fact, she was grateful to him for providing her with so much. They'd moved to Morningside ten years ago, to be closer to schools and Angus's work as well as to Ella's ageing parents. She felt she'd come full circle, treading in her own mother's footsteps as a homemaker.

But she hadn't been content just to sit at home as the children grew more independent; she'd become a volunteer fund-raiser for the children's hospital which had been such a focal point of their lives during Robbie's illness and she was now Chairwoman of the committee. So, as she raised her eyes to the illumination of the domed ceiling far above her, she sent up a silent message of thanks for all that she had. And, once again, she deliberately refused to think of that other path which her life might have taken instead.

'Hello, Mum, Dad.' Rhona slipped into her seat alongside Angus, kissing him on the cheek. 'Phew, just in time. It was a bit tricky getting away from the office.'

As the organ struck up 'Gaudeamus Igitur' and the new graduands processed in, Ella eagerly sought out Robbie. Angus nudged her, pointing him out amidst the black-gowned ranks, and Ella had to grope in her handbag for a handkerchief as her eyes overflowed suddenly, the enormity of this achievement overwhelming her – not her son's graduation but the simple fact that the four of them were there, together still.

It was early September and, as always seemed to happen, they were enjoying a spell of good weather just when the schools had started back and everyone was incarcerated in their classrooms and offices once again.

Ella was working in the garden, dead-heading roses and cutting back the exhausted end-of-summer growth in the borders. After raking the fallen leaves from the front lawn, she'd propped open the side gate, making it easier to manoeuvre the wheelbarrow as she carted the damp, loam-scented piles to the compost heap in the far corner of the back garden. So, it should have been a peaceful scene that Angus came home to, his wife finishing off her work amidst the serenity of the newly ordered flowerbeds.

And yet, he sensed her aura of anguish even before he greeted her.

He set his briefcase down on the path and watched her tip out the last barrow-load of leaves with an angry energy which seemed to charge the atmosphere with invisible crackles of electricity.

As she turned towards him, her face was contorted, tears streaming from her eyes which were red and swollen. She wiped her nose and mouth with the sleeve of her shirt, leaving a smear which gleamed on her cuff like the silver snail trails which criss-crossed the stone slabs at his feet. Wretchedness hung heavy on the autumn air, mingling with the smoke from a bonfire in a neighbouring garden.

Wordlessly, he crossed to her and wrapped his arms around her. He waited as she pressed her wet face against his suit jacket.

Finally, when she was calm enough to speak, she pulled away from his encircling arms and turned her back on him, on the pretext of picking up the rake that she'd discarded on the ground.

'He's dying.' She threw the tools into the wheelbarrow with a clatter, knowing that she had to keep moving because otherwise her grief would catch up with her and overwhelm her completely.

Angus stood there, unable to reach her, excluded from her distress. Because how could he comfort her about this?

She wiped her nose with her sleeve again, then pulled a folded letter from her cardigan pocket. 'Caroline wrote. Christophe has just a few weeks to live, the doctors say.'

'What are you going to do?' Angus's misery made his voice low, his throat constricting with helplessness. He had always been a man who got things done, who resolved problems logically and methodically, so she knew that he loathed this emotional tangle.

She didn't reply.

'What are you going to do?' he repeated, the words coming out more forcefully than before and with a raw edge of bitterness and fear.

Neither of them noticed Rhona, who'd seen the open gate and heard voices in the back garden. She stood, frozen, taking in the scene before her: the angry, stooped posture of her mother; the defeated, despairing attitude of her father as he spoke those words.

'I'm going to him. Don't try to stop me. All these years I've stayed away. But I have to go to him now. One last time.'

Ella heard Rhona then. Her gasp. Then her shriek, like an animal in pain.

Angus moved towards her, but she held her hands up as if to fend him off and turned away from both her parents, running to the house, leaving them both standing there in the dusk with the smell of smoke hanging in the air, as if it was the aftermath of the explosion of truth that had just been detonated.

Ella turned too and walked slowly to the back door. Very deliberately, numb with a grief for so much that she now saw was lost, she climbed the stairs to her bedroom and began to pack.

Suddenly, Rhona stood in the doorway, her face a white mask of fury. 'I understand it all now.' She spat the words at her mother, her voice shaking with anger. 'You were never here for us really, were you? All through my childhood I felt I could never get your attention. I put it down to Robbie's illness, made a thousand excuses, blamed myself for being unlovable . . . I thought it was my fault. But now I see what was really going on. That summer in France, you were having an affair with him, weren't you? That man?' She couldn't bring herself to say his name. 'It all makes sense now. How could you have betrayed us in that way? How could you have betrayed Dad?'

Ella stood, the blouse she'd been folding hanging limply in her hands, and looked at Rhona wearily. She knew there was no point telling her that Angus, too, had had an affair. All that would accomplish would be the girl's complete and utter devastation, her disillusionment with both of her parents. To take the father she so adored from her would be cruelty itself. The explanations, the blame and counter-blame, all seemed hopeless now; they could only cause more destruction.

All these years, she'd protected her children; all she could do now was carry on trying to do so. So she held her tongue and looked her daughter in the eye.

'I'm sorry.'

'That's all you can say?' Rhona's eyes opened wide in incredulity. 'Well, I'm sorry too. Sorry you weren't able to be a better mother to me. You always paid attention to Robbie, never to me.' Pain and resentment poured out of her now that the dam of her emotions had been breached.

Ella tried to explain. 'But that's because you were the strong one. You're like me, Rhona – you had the strength and the resilience to carry on. Robbie needed my strength more than you did.'

'You're wrong! I longed for you to love me and look after me the way you did him. I was just a child. You expected too much of me, but always made allowances for him. Perhaps you taught me to expect too much of you. But that's all gone now. Don't expect me to be here when you come crawling back – if you ever do. I never want to see you again!'

Ella caught a taxi from the boat, asking the driver to take her to the gallery in Saint Martin. She knew that was where Caroline would be. Christophe too, perhaps? She had no idea whether he still had the strength to work.

Caroline rose from behind the desk as Ella stood in the doorway.

'You came! I didn't know whether you would.'

The two women hugged, each supporting the other for a long moment. 'Tell me,' Ella said.

Caroline shook her head. 'It's not good, Ella. I must warn you. He's going fast now. Sandrine's daughter takes care of him when I'm not there. It happened so quickly. One day he was alright – just a little tired – then the next he was bent double with the pain. The doctor says the cancer seems to have spread very fast. It's in his bones. He suffers a great deal. There is nothing more to be done, so they have let him come home from the hospital. He'll be pleased to see you. Let me just finish up here and then we'll go to him.'

Ella sank down on to a chair to wait. Her eye was caught by a blue bowl, sitting on its own in a niche set into the wall. The delicate ceramic looked as if it had been broken into several pieces and then fixed back together with a vein of purest gold, which shot through the piece like a lightning strike against a sky of midnight blue. She reached out a finger and touched the rim. The join was perfect: her fingertip sensed only the very slightest catch where the gold met the clay, invisible to the eye.

Caroline appeared beside her, pulling on her jacket. 'Beautiful, isn't it? It's a technique called *kintsukuroi*. Japanese in style, although this piece was made by a local potter. I love the philosophy behind it: that something which is so unique and irreplaceable is worth mending with pure gold, so that the cracks and flaws themselves become part of the beauty of the piece.'

Ella nodded, moved.

'And have you seen this?' Caroline took her gently by the elbow and turned her so that she was facing the wall on the other side of the gallery.

Ella froze.

In the centre of the wall hung a single painting, larger than any of Christophe's other works. A woman lay sleeping amongst the sand-dunes, one arm curving above her head in utter abandon, her gold-streaked hair mingling with the beach grass that bowed in the ocean breeze. A faint smile played over her lips. Her other hand, the fingers curving softly open, held a hinged white clamshell.

'It's entitled *Neptune's Locket*,' Caroline said. 'Everyone who sees it asks "What is she dreaming of?" Her smile has the same mesmeric, elusive quality of the *Mona Lisa's* smile; and yet she looks more like one of Botticelli's subjects. Many, many people have asked the price, but it is never for sale. It's become famous. People come to the Île de Ré just to see it. "Why don't you put it in a gallery in Paris?" they ask. But Christophe refuses. It is to stay here, where he can see it; and where I can look after it.

'And now, dry your eyes,' Caroline handed Ella a tissue. 'You must be strong and cheerful for Christophe. Your being here will be the best medicine possible for him.' She closed the metal shutters over the gallery's windows and locked the door carefully behind her.

The bedroom was dark, the shutters pulled to, allowing just a sliver of light through to bisect the shadows. The muslin curtains stirred languidly in the evening breeze, but beneath the mineral breath of the sea Ella detected something else: the sickly-stale smell of illness overlain by the chemical tang of medications and disinfectant. Caroline held a finger to her lips and motioned Ella to come closer to the bed. Christophe lay, propped on pillows, his gaunt face peaceful, for the moment at least. At first his breathing seemed almost normal. But, as she listened, she noticed something in its quality – a catch here and there, a faint wheeziness on the in-breath – that spoke of troubled currents running just beneath the surface.

Caroline made as if to take his hand and waken him, but Ella stopped her. Every minute he spent asleep must surely be sparing him from the pain that wracked his emaciated body in his waking moments. She gestured to a chair at the bedside, eyebrows raised, asking a soundless question. Caroline nodded and left Ella sitting there, waiting for him to awaken of his own accord.

Eventually, his eyelids fluttered and his face creased as another wave of pain washed through him. She took his hand and his eyes opened, struggling to focus.

He licked his cracked lips and she leaned closer to hear what he said: 'Either I am dreaming, or I have died and am now in heaven.'

She smiled and shook her head, gently squeezing his hand in hers. 'Neither. I'm here. I won't leave you.'

'In that case,' he was smiling too now, 'I intend hanging on for as long as I possibly can.'

He fell silent again and she sat holding his hand, willing some of her strength to flow into his wasted body.

'Do you remember that night at the inn, with the *Mona Lisa* illuminating that drab little room?'

She laughed. 'Of course! How could I ever forget?'

'When I was in the prison camp, I kept a drawing I'd done of you under my pillow. It was the same principle. You were my *Mona Lisa*, my reminder that truth and beauty existed even in that dismal place. And here you are again now, in my hour of need. In real life this time. How lucky I am to have known this.'

She leant over and kissed his forehead as he drifted off to sleep again, the faint smile still creasing his face.

'Your being here is certainly doing him good.' Caroline bustled into the kitchen carrying a breakfast tray. 'He's eaten a little this morning. Says he slept well. He seems to have a bit more strength today.'

The two women helped him out of bed and, with a robe draped over his shoulders, carefully escorted him downstairs and into the garden. They propped him on pillows on a *chaise longue* where the jasmine dropped its last flowers of the season like fallen stars. He lifted his face to the sun and sighed. 'I can already feel it doing me good.'

The early autumn light set a cluster of golden coneflowers ablaze and warmed the last of the year's roses so that they readily released their sweet, musky perfume. It seemed to Ella that she saw every petal, every scarlet leaf and every blade of emerald grass, her senses heightened by the feeling that she must hold on to each one of these precious moments before they slipped away forever. She sat beside him, reading to him from a book of French poetry, feeding him a verse at a time in order not to tire him out.

Caroline worked quietly in the background, using the opportunity to air his bedroom and change his crumpled sheets, occasionally bringing him his pain medication or another glass of water to sip. He reached up to catch her hand. '*Merci, ma soeur.* You have always been the most wonderful sister, Caroline. The other half of me: my twin.'

He drifted in and out of sleep as the day wore on, but one or other of the women was always at his side when he woke again. Time slowed and, as the light softened and the shadows lengthened in the garden, the three of them discovered a new-found sense of deep peace.

And it seemed to Ella that this was enough: to be here, the three of them together again at last, in their own small world, removed from everyday realities. Alive. It was everything. Her contentment could not be disturbed by thoughts of her family, thoughts of Angus, thoughts of the world beyond the island. The fortress that she and Caroline created to protect Christophe's final days was impregnable.

'What a perfect day.' Christophe raised his face to receive Ella's kiss. 'You know, I do believe I feel a little stronger this morning. Let's take

Bijou out. The breeze is just right, if we set off from Saint Martin we can tack westwards and then it'll be a smooth run for home when we turn.'

Ella glanced at Caroline, who shook her head almost imperceptibly. 'Why don't we wait and see how you feel tomorrow?' she said, gently brushing a strand of hair back from his forehead.

'Please? Surely this good weather can't last much longer? It may be the final chance we have to take her out this season.'

His words hung in the air, deceptively light. Ella knew that there was a more sombre implication. His last summer. His last outing . . . his last sail.

She glanced again at Caroline, who shrugged, giving in.

'Good idea.' Ella matched her tone to his. 'If you're sure you're strong enough? It really is a glorious day. A true Indian summer. Come, Caroline. I'll help you pack the picnic basket.'

They drove him to the harbour and Caroline brought the boat round to a place where they could help him step, with relative ease, down on to the deck. Ella wrapped rugs around him and placed cushions behind his back so that he was well supported. 'I feel like one of your precious sculptures being wrapped up for dispatch to a client.' He smiled at his sister as she made the boat ready and cast off from the quayside.

He really did look a little better today, Ella thought. Perhaps the fresh air and sunshine he'd been enjoying in the garden were helping hold back the progress of his disease, giving his weakened body the strength to fight back again. Maybe he'd rally a little and there would be more opportunities to sail after all. Her spirits lifted as hope stirred in her heart.

The breeze was soft and languid, a gentle caress, which seemed to respect their wish to make the day last, savouring every moment as they tacked up the island's coastline to the lagoon of the *Fier d'Ars*. They saw very few other boats: the holidaymakers had long since returned to their busy lives in the city, leaving the sea to the island's year-round inhabitants; and the fishing fleet had set out earlier that morning, making the most of the spell of unseasonably benign weather to venture far out into the ocean where richer pickings were to be found.

'It feels as though this day has been created for us alone,' Ella remarked, smiling at Christophe as she squeezed his hand gently.

He smiled back at her and for a moment her breath caught as she glimpsed the boy she had first met on the dock all those years before, his dark eyes flashing with humour and passion, his high cheek bones casting shade across the contours of his handsome face.

'Right here, right now, I am perfectly happy,' he said. 'How fortunate I am, to have had this day.'

Caroline judged the final tack perfectly and eased *Bijou* into the shallow lagoon flanked by dunes of pale gold sand. The water was mirror-calm in the bay as they lowered the sails and dropped anchor, allowing the boat to swing quietly on its mooring. The sunlight's attenuated autumnal rays saturated the air with quiet warmth and Christophe lay watching the last swallows darting through the sky above him, preparing themselves for their long flight as they followed summer's journey south.

They ate little, none of them having much appetite for the food Caroline had packed into the picnic basket. Ella fed grapes to Christophe and helped him sip water from a cup, which she held to his cracked lips. The two women packed the food back into the basket when they'd finished and then kept a silent vigil while Christophe slept, the peace of the afternoon and the gentle drifting of the boat on her mooring soothing his pain-wracked body for a spell.

They let him sleep on, loath to wake him, listening to the quiet sighing of his breath, like the sound of waves breaking on a far-distant shore.

The air was still warm when they hoisted the sails and turned *Bijou* for home, the graceful line of her hull cutting cleanly through the water's crystal-clear surface, leaving scarcely any wake to show where they'd been.

When the car pulled up in front of the house with the pale blue shutters, Christophe turned to Ella. 'It's such a balmy evening. I don't think I'll go in just yet. Come and sit with me in the garden.'

She gathered up a couple of rugs to ward off any chills, and helped him to the *chaise* where she settled him comfortably. The delicate scent of the white roses mingled with the last of the jasmine in the garden that Marianne had planted, and for a moment it seemed that she was there, her presence comforting them, as it had reassured Ella in that moment in the forest when she'd prepared to place the pill in her mouth that would have ended her life so many years ago.

A harvest moon, vast with ripe fullness, slipped above the dark line of the dunes and hoisted itself into the night sky.

Christophe murmured something and Ella bent close to hear him. He licked his lips. 'Take me to the dunes.'

Without protesting – for what could be the point of that now? – she helped him to his feet. Wrapping a rug around his shoulders, she supported his frail frame, grown so insubstantial now, as they picked their way across the path of soft sand that threaded its way through the beach-grass, their way lit by the lantern moon. At the highest point, where the crest of the dunes opened its face towards the sea, she settled him into the cradling dip of the sand, spreading another rug for them to lie on and scooping sand beneath it to make a pillow for him to rest his head.

She lay beside him, her arms around him, and felt the faint rise and fall of his chest which, once again, seemed to echo the sighing of the waves on the beach below them.

He kissed her hair gently. 'It has been perfect, hasn't it, my Ella? You and me. Our love.'

She nodded, closing her eyes to allow the hot tears to spill out and run over her temples where her pulse throbbed.

'But you know,' he went on, 'it has only been able to be perfect because it was never corrupted by reality. Imagine if we had got married, if you had come to live with me in Paris or here on the island. It would have been altered then, by the thousand daily demands of real life, by financial worries and worries about our children. Maybe even by loving our children more than we loved each other. All those things that you and Angus have weathered in your relationship.'

'I don't think he and I have a relationship any more,' she said softly. 'I think I broke it into pieces when I left to come here this time.'

She felt Christophe shake his head. 'You're wrong,' he said. 'He loves you, just as I have loved you. Perhaps even more so, as he has carried on loving you despite all that your marriage has had to endure. I may have been your first love, but he is your lasting love. Be brave, my Ella, as brave as I know you to be. When I am gone, return to him. Ask his forgiveness. Forgive him in your turn. For the sake of your children, but most of all for the sake of each other. You both deserve it. I know this, because I have seen his children. I remember how Rhona loved him and defended him. You wouldn't have had to struggle to decide between us, Ella, if he wasn't a good and loving man. Don't give up on your marriage now, even if you feel it is broken at the moment. It's still worth saving.'

He coughed, his face contorting suddenly as pain's steel fist tightened its grasp.

'Hush, there now,' she soothed him. 'Don't try to talk any more.'

'Promise me you'll go back to him, Ella? You'll try again?'

She kissed him gently in reply, trying to reassure him and yet to avoid saying again what she believed, that she'd destroyed her family, finally, in coming to him.

He fell silent, spent with exhaustion. The only sound was the sighing of the waves on the shore and the faint, plaintive cry of a curlew. His eyes fluttered closed and she wasn't sure whether he was still awake. But then he whispered, 'Talk to me, Ella. Talk to me about the beauty of this world.'

She hesitated, fear making her heart miss a beat as she sensed him slipping away from her a little further, along a path that only he could travel. She took a breath, calming herself so that her words, when she spoke, could be a steady and strong anchor for him.

'I remember that first night, when we came here and danced on the beach. You held me in your arms and told me you would rather dance with me than with the ocean. There was a path of moonlight on the water and I told you we could step out on to it and waltz together to the far horizon.'

She felt his breathing calm and deepen a little as he relaxed in her arms.

'I remember the second night, when we came here to the dunes after that night in the *auberge* with the *Mona Lisa* for company. How extraordinary both of those two nights were. You gave me that gift then. The gift of seeing beauty in the ordinary. The miracles that are all around us in the everyday and the mundane, if we only open our eyes to them.'

He smiled, the only sign that he had not yet fallen asleep.

'And I remember the third night with you, here in the dunes,' she whispered. 'When I woke, you were drawing me. And from that drawing you have made the painting that has passed on that same gift to the whole world . . .'

She tailed off as his breath slowed and deepened, the soft kindness of sleep claiming him. And as the waves whispered and sighed on the shore, she held him to her and danced with him out on to a sea of memories.

Before sunrise, when the morning star kept its lonely vigil between the setting of the moon and the first light of dawn, a stillness woke her. She sensed it even before she turned to look at him, wrapped in the rug beside her.

An absence.

She held his cold body to hers.

The darkest hour.

As the first rays of warmth stole across the beach, she lay there still, holding his lifeless body in her arms and watching the waves wash in.

Caroline came to find her. She knelt and wept warm tears into Ella's hair as she enfolded them both in her arms.

But Ella couldn't cry. Her own tears were frozen somewhere inside, buried deep. Because she knew that if they ever began to fall, they might never end. She would weep a salty river that would carve its way across the beach and flow into the waters of the Atlantic, cold and indifferent as they engulfed her pain, her loss, the tragedy of her life. She had lost everything. Christophe, Angus, her children, her home – because how could she go back now, having made the choice to come and be with Christophe? Rhona's parting words rang in her ears: 'Don't expect me to be here when you come crawling back – if you ever do. I never want to see you again.' Was that how Angus would see it too, if she went back? That she was using him, skulking home now that Christophe was gone and he was the only refuge she had left?

She felt so tired all of a sudden. Defeated. Grief wrapped her in its heavy blanket, a thick fog which saturated her body and mind with its dull, cold ache. She grieved not just for Christophe and the relationship that they had never been able to have, but for Angus too: for what he had taken on in loving her, for the years he had suffered, being married to her and knowing she could never love him completely, wholeheartedly, as he deserved, while Christophe lived. He was a good, brave, loving man, but she had inflicted terrible pain on him, she knew, and so guilt added its unbearable weight to her grief until she could endure no more. She was overwhelmed and empty.

Lost.

After the funeral, once Christophe's coffin had been lowered into the ground, Ella paused to read the inscription on the headstone alongside the freshly dug grave.

'*A la douce mémoire de Philippe Christophe Martet et sa femme adorée, Marianne. "Lève-toi, mon amie, ma belle, et viens!"*'

'Where is the quotation from?' she asked Caroline, who had taken two roses from the posy she'd picked from the garden to lay on Christophe's coffin and placed them beside her parents' stone.

'It's from the *Cantique des Cantiques*. The Song of Solomon. It's the first line of one of my mother's favourite verses. In English it would be something like, "Rise up, my love, my fair one, and come with me!" Even though *Maman* does not lie here, we wanted to commemorate her alongside *Papa*.'

'It's perfect for them.' Ella brushed the palm of her hand over the soft moss that cushioned one corner of the stone. 'I'm glad he's here beside them.' She nodded towards Christophe's grave.

Caroline shook her head suddenly, vehemently. 'He's not here!' She picked up the bunch of flowers that she'd laid to one side to be placed on Christophe's grave once the earth had been piled back. 'Come on, Ella. Let's go! Let's sail with him, one last time. That should be our goodbye, not here, not with mud and stone like this, but out on the sea, where he was most alive.'

She pulled the hat from her hair and let the curls spill over the collar of her black coat, then seized Ella's hand and the two of them ran, stumbling slightly in their formal funeral shoes, past the small crowd of mourners who were filing back towards the gate, to where the car waited beyond the graveyard walls.

They drove straight to the harbour, not bothering to go back to the house first to change. In Saint Martin they attracted a few bemused glances as they boarded *Bijou* in their funeral clothes, Caroline in a long coat with silver filigree buttons and Ella in a black shift dress and matching jacket which she'd borrowed from her friend for the day. They made ready and Ella cast off from the quayside. Caroline steered the little boat through the harbour entrance and, instead of turning westwards to follow the island's coastline as they usually did, she headed straight out towards the open ocean.

Wind-driven clouds scudded across the sky above the swell of their sails, and the waves danced about the hull, sending sparkling necklaces of spray into the air alongside them. The late-September sun illuminated their faces and painted the sea-scape with a wash of soft light that made every drop of water, each foam-capped wave and every line of the island's receding form stand out with astonishing clarity.

Ella turned to Caroline in wonder. 'You were right. He wasn't there, in the graveyard. But he is out here, all around us!'

She nodded, the anguished lines of her face relaxing into something more like her usual expression of gentle calmness. 'We are dancing with him, one last time. This is how he wanted to say goodbye. Not in a sad, muddy hole in the ground; and not weak and wasted, lying on his bed. But here, now, like this. Celebrating the beauty of life, celebrating the freedom of the ocean. Celebrating love.'

When they were far out, where the waters surrounding them were deeper and the swell of the waves became slower but more profound, they dropped the sails and let *Bijou* drift. Caroline untied the ribbon that bound the posy of garden flowers together and handed half of them to Ella. 'Let's scatter them here for him.'

And so the two women strewed the last summer flowers from Marianne's garden on to the ocean as the little boat bowed and curtsied to the waves. And as she threw the last white rose petals to the wind, Ella felt she was giving Christophe back to the sea: letting him go to be with that beautiful dancer, that other love of his life, who was drawing him into her arms.

2015, Edinburgh

Today, of all days, I want Ella to be awake. But she sleeps deeply, her breath so light that I stoop to hear it, the covers scarcely rising and falling over her heart.

'Come back,' I whisper. I want to lay my head on the crisp, white sheet and let it soak up my tears. 'Don't leave me all alone.' But she is sailing far out now, where the ocean is deep. I wonder whether she's dreaming of Angus and Christophe, reliving the memories which seem to elude her more and more in her fleetingly brief waking moments. I think of the two men, picturing Christophe's youth and vivacity and my grandfather's handsome solidity.

So now I know. Now I understand why my mother has refused to see my grandmother, unable to forgive her. But I also understand why the full story needs to be told, so that Ella can, at last, let her daughter know how much she has loved her; how she has protected her all these years; so that she can be forgiven in the end.

1970, Île de Ré

Caroline was preoccupied with work. Upon the news of Christophe's death, the art world had grown even more interested in the body of work he'd left as his legacy and she was inundated at the gallery in Saint Martin with enquiries from collectors and art galleries around the world who all wanted a Christophe Martet original to hang on their walls.

'*Non*,' she repeated time after time, into her constantly ringing phone '*je suis désolée*. The work entitled *Neptune's Locket* is not for sale. But I will send you the catalogue of the other works that we have available.'

Left alone at the house, Ella felt washed up, like flotsam, by the tide of emotion that had brought her here and then receded with Christophe's death, leaving her high and dry, discarded and unloved.

She wandered the deserted rooms of the white house with the mist-blue shutters, searching for comfort in Marianne's furnishings and Christophe's paintings, in the family photographs and the familiar creaking of the floorboards as she walked. But she felt no traces of the spirits that she sought in the emptiness. The curtains hung limply at the windows, stirred listlessly now and then by the faint drafts that found their way through the wooden frames whose paint was cracking and peeling here and there after the onslaught of summer sun and salt air. Marianne's garden was bare now, the flowers dead, leaves falling in flurries as the Atlantic began to muster the first winds of winter and hurl them at the little island, buffeting the sea-birds, which shrieked and banked against the gusts before soaring off to find shelter elsewhere. The stark, grotesquely contorted stumps of the vine stocks in the vineyard alongside the house mirrored the way her heart felt – deadened and bleak, twisted into a hard, lifeless knot of despair.

When she'd exhausted herself with her endless walking, Ella wrapped herself in a quilt and slumped on a sofa in the drawing-room, or lay motionless on her bed gazing at the blank ceiling above her, for hours on end. Her heart and her mind felt as empty as the house, filled only with sadness and the dull ache of loss.

Caroline left to go to Paris for a week, to see the lawyer for the reading of Christophe's will and to oversee the delivery of another consignment of paintings.

When she returned, she was pained and shocked to find Ella in a state of collapse. She had clearly hardly eaten in Caroline's absence and her hair hung in lank, dirty strands about her pale face. Her eyes were deadened, and seemed sunk into their sockets, which were underlined with dark half-moons of exhaustion.

'You must try to eat something,' Caroline urged, as they sat at the dinner table that evening. 'Please, Ella, just try a little, for my sake?'

But the life force, which had always burned so brightly in her friend, had been extinguished and an expression of panic crossed Caroline's face suddenly, as she registered the depth of Ella's despair. And so, the next day, she made a phone call from the gallery.

Ella sat in the dunes amongst the bowing marram grass, her hair whipped by the wind, gazing out to sea. White-capped rollers surged in from the west, crashing on to the sand before falling back, dragging dark trails of bladder-wrack in their wake.

She imagined walking out to meet them, letting the water lift her off her feet and gather her body, washing away the hurt and the sadness with its numbing chill until she would feel no more. She could see herself there, pictured the waves enfolding her in their icy embrace, but was unable to summon the energy to rise to her feet and take those final steps towards oblivion. She scarcely heard the roar of the sea, and hardly felt the chill that seeped into her numbed limbs: they were no match for the white noise of pain that rang in her ears nor the stony coldness of loss that saturated her body.

And so she didn't hear Angus until he was there, suddenly, beside her.

Without a word, he gathered her into his arms and held her tightly to him, warming her with the heat of his body, smoothing her hair back from her eyes so that he could kiss away the hot tears that she began to weep. He rocked her, as a mother gently rocks a baby, and let her cry, silently at first, but then with wrenching, guttural sobs that seemed torn from the deepest reaches of her shattered heart.

She fell silent finally, her tears spent at last. He held her still and they lay together, cradled in the dunes' embrace with the roar of the wind and the sea all around them. But she felt warm now, safe in her husband's strong arms, the blood in her veins beginning to thaw and flow again like the quiet, almost imperceptible trickle of the first streams after a long and bitter winter.

Her dry, cracked lips moved and he leant in close to hear her whispered words. And he smiled, hearing the wonderment in her voice as she echoed the words she'd said that night, so many years ago, in a dark and alien forest:

'You came to find me. I was lost and you came to find me.'

2015, Edinburgh

As I read the last words I've written, my grandmother nods and her eyes close, a smile illuminating the soft skin of her face, as worn and fragile as the powder-blue cardigan that's draped over her shoulders. (I've offered to buy her a new one to replace it, but she laughed and said, 'You'd be wasting your money, my dear Kendra. This comfortable old friend will see me out.')

Over the winter, week by week, I've untangled Ella's story from her cache of memories, the tapes and photographs and letters, and written it down the way she wanted it to be told. When I began, I'd thought it would be a simple exercise of typing out her words exactly as she'd spoken them into her tape recorder. But as I listened and pored over the neatly ordered photo albums and shuffled through the letters from Christophe and Caroline, her story had drawn me in so that I could see it through her eyes; it seemed to be writing itself, carrying me along so that I, too, fell in love with the places and the people who had filled her life with everyday miracles.

I've grown far closer to her in these last months and, instead of the chore it used to be, visiting Ella has become one of the highlights of my week. It's been a welcome escape from the realities of my own life, the draining demands of my job and the anxieties about my son and my husband. But it's more than that too. I see her differently now that I know her story. Her past has come to life and made me see what really matters in this world. I'm proud that I'm her granddaughter and I hope that I can claim some of her courage and her sense of beauty in my own genetic make-up.

As the words I've just finished reading hang in the air around us, I stroke my grandmother's age-spotted hand, the skin soft as crumpled tissue paper. I see each brown mark, each callus, each stiff, gnarled knuckle differently now. The scatterings of dark stains, which the French call 'the flowers of death', are reminders of summers spent on a sun-soaked island – more sea than land – where, for the first time, a young woman found freedom and love; the calluses tell of a sail-boat skimming across the lace-capped waves with sheets close-hauled, the ocean's wind catching each breath and tossing it into the eternity of a perfect blue sky; and the swollen joints are mementos of acts of breath-taking love and courage, these hands that clasped and held and carried, a whole history of work and motherhood: an extraordinary life.

But they are hands that had to learn to let go too, just as I will have to let go soon of this frail hand that I hold in mine.

There's a tap at the door. A nurse pops her head round and I turn to meet her bright, professional smile with a polite one of my own.

'All okay here?' she asks, her voice softer than usual, out of respect for death's hushed presence in the room. The open door allows in a waft of nursing-home air, which smells of the plug-in air-fresheners that spit a venomous, chemical scent at each passing pair of legs to mask the underlying perfume of urine and disinfectant. It mingles with the scent of the white lilies in a vase on the chest of drawers in the corner of the room. I brought another bunch with me when I last came to visit. They're past their best now, the pure white petals turning to parchment as they decay.

I nod, smile again at the nurse and turn back to my grandmother. Ella's breathing is faint, a shallow, staccato sip on the inhalation; an impossibly long pause; a faint sigh on the exhalation.

I wish I'd known Ella's story before, so that I could have been a better granddaughter to her than I have been. But at least I came to understand it before it was too late. At least her story can now be told. I hope my mother will understand too, now, before it's too late for her to make her peace.

My heart was in my mouth when I'd finished writing; the day I brought the finished manuscript to Ella's room. What would she make of it? Had I done her story justice?

She had been awake, but she asked me to read it aloud to her, saying, 'I'm too far gone these days. My eyesight is so poor, and my memory wanders so if I try to read anything myself. But they do say that hearing is the last of the senses to go. So, read it to me, my dear. Let me listen to my own story one last time.'

There's been an unspoken sense of urgency these past few days. Every time I came to visit her to read her some more of the manuscript, she'd drifted a little further away. She would fall asleep sometimes as I was reading to her and then I'd mark the place carefully and tiptoe away, hoping that she was dreaming of the Île de Ré, or the beach at Arisaig, and the two men who have loved her as she has loved them.

And this final day, with the last words read, I sit in silence, watching her smile as she lies there with her eyes closed. And my heart swells with happiness that I've done her story justice and with sadness that, now that it's told, there's a sense of another ending that sits heavily in the hot, artificially scented room.

I wonder whether I should leave her to sleep, but suddenly her eyes open wide, the misted sea-green of them clearing so that, for a few moments they are the colour of the deepest ocean once again. Viridian.

'Thank you, Kendra,' she says. 'I knew you would tell my story well. That you would understand. That you would write the truth of it all.'

'I'll give it to Mum,' I reply. 'I know she'll see things differently too when she reads the whole of the truth.'

Ella nods and then reaches her age-spotted hand towards the bedside cabinet, pointing to the fine, deep-blue ceramic bowl shot through with a vein of purest gold like a lightning bolt.

'It's the *kintsukuroi* bowl, isn't it Granny?'

'Caroline gave it to me when Angus and I left the island.' Her voice is a faint whisper now and I have to lean in close to hear what she's saying. 'She asked us to call in at the gallery on our way past, just as we were setting off for home. We walked in and when Angus saw the painting, *Neptune's Locket*, he looked at it for a good long spell. Then he nodded, and said, "He loved you the way I love you – body and soul." It felt as if he was laying to rest the spectre of Christophe that had haunted him throughout our marriage. A bit of closure, I suppose. And then Caroline said that she had something to tell us. Which was that Christophe had left the painting to me.' She frowns, struggling to remember.

'At that news, Angus's expression flickered – just the tiniest bit, but I noticed it. And in that moment I understood that his acceptance had taken courage and generosity of spirit, but that having the painting there the whole time would have been too much, even for him. So I said to Caroline that I didn't think there was room for it above the mantelpiece in Morningside. Can you imagine how out of place it would have been in that setting? I told Caroline that the painting belonged where it was, in the gallery, so that people could still come and see it. And that was the right thing to say because I saw the look of relief on Angus's face. But then he said, "And we will come back every summer to visit it, and you can show me this island which has been the other love of your life." So, that's what we did.'

'Where is the painting now, Granny?'

'Why, Kendra, it's there!' Sudden joy flickers across Ella's face. 'Caroline is still alive; she lives on the Île de Ré. She has help, of course. Do you remember Sandrine and Benoît, who used to manage the house for the Martets? Whose daughter cared for Christophe through his illness? Well, they are long gone, but their granddaughter runs the gallery in Saint Martin for Caroline. And Caroline herself still goes there most days to supervise things, despite her age. She's quite famous in the art world and still has the keen eye for beauty she always had . . .'

Ella's voice tails off and her eyes close for a moment as her memory drifts from its course. But then she opens her eyes again, focusing on my face with an effort. I sense she's struggling now.

'Anyway, where was I? Oh yes, the bowl. So, there we were in the gallery, about to come back to Edinburgh. And Caroline took it from its plinth and said, "Do you remember what I told you? About the philosophy behind this? That something which is unique has its own beauty that can never be destroyed; that it's always worth mending, even when it's broken; and that the fractures and the scars become part of the beauty too, making the piece even more remarkable, even more precious." And then she said, "Heal your heart, Ella. Let Angus help you. Mend your marriage with veins of the purest gold and remake it, better and stronger than before." And we did. Because, you see, Kendra, I fell in love with your grandfather all over again. Caroline was right: our love was worth mending. In the end, we made the scars part of the beauty of our marriage.'

She pauses, smiling, remembering. Then goes on, her voice growing a little stronger for a moment. 'And Christophe was right too. He was my first love, but Angus was my lasting love. I'd always thought I wanted a second chance with Christophe, that life had cheated me of it. But, in fact, the second chance I got was with Angus. How lucky I am, to have loved and been loved by two such good men.'

For a few moments she's lost in her thoughts again, her mind wandering where the tangled skein of her memories takes her.

But then, once more with an effort, she pulls her attention back to the bowl on the cabinet beside her bed. 'When you give Rhona the manuscript, give her the bowl as well. Tell her that I'm sorry for the damage I did, but show her that it can be mended. Tell her that I know it will be, even if it's after I'm gone.'

I pick up the bowl carefully and stir the collection of white shells that lie within it with my forefinger.

'And the shells, Granny? Is the one that Christophe gave you in here?'

She smiles again. 'But of course it is! And the one Angus gave me is too. Along with other shells I've collected on Atlantic beaches as reminders of perfect days. And shells my children found and gave me, which are some of the most treasured ones of all. Souvenirs. Memories. Such richness . . .'

Her voice is growing weaker once more, her eyes misting as her mind fades again. I bend close to her to hear the words she whispers.

'Keep them for me, Kendra. The shells. Add them to your own collection of memories and keepsakes. With Dan and Finn. To remind you to find the beauty in your life, even in the most difficult times.'

'I will. And I'll be back tomorrow, Granny,' I promise. Before I go, before I kiss her forehead one last time and smooth back the fine white hair – hair that was once the sun-kissed blonde of the grasses that grow amongst the sand-dunes on that wind-swept island – I whisper another promise to my grandmother.

'I'll tell her, Granny Ella. I'll give Mum your story to read. And I'll make sure she understands as well.'

I stand to leave, gathering up the manuscript, and the bowl of shells which I wrap in my winter scarf to keep safe.

In the doorway of her room, I hesitate for a moment, listening to her soft breathing. It's changing, slowing: a shallow sip; a pause; a sigh.

She's beyond my reach now, slipping further away with each breath. I hope she's with them, the ones who have gone before. If they are holding her in their arms again at last, then maybe I can bear to let her go.

2015, Île de Ré

There's no hint of what lies ahead as we skirt La Rochelle, passing a chaotic jumble of ugly signs advertising the offerings of the superstores that flank the city's by-pass. But then I realise that there are subtle changes all around us: there's a new freshness in the air as Dan winds down the window to let the early summer warmth wash into the car; the vegetation has changed too and the road is now lined with scrubby pines and silver-leafed shrubs that are tough enough to withstand the scouring of a salt wind. And the light is different all of a sudden. It has a clarity which heightens the colour of the tamarisk trees with their plumes of rose-pink froth and paints the heads of the bulrushes that grow in the ditches alongside the road a rich velvet brown, as they dance in the slipstream of the passing cars.

We negotiate a roundabout and pay the toll for the bridge. And then suddenly we are swept into the air on a soaring arc of concrete that, these days, spans the channel separating the Île de Ré from the mainland. For a moment I regret that there's no longer a ferry to catch; I would have enjoyed retracing that step of my grandmother's journey. Has the bridge made a difference, I wonder? Has being physically tethered to its motherland made the island lose the sense of otherworldliness, that feeling of stepping off the edge of the world and out on to the ocean that she talked about?

To our left I glimpse the serried ranks of cranes in La Rochelle's busy port, which stand to attention behind the busy to-and-fro of white-sailed yachts in and out of the harbour.

'Look, Finn, can you see the boats?' I try to distract my son from his rocking. It's been a long day's journey for him and he's never comfortable in unfamiliar surroundings.

And then I look to the right and I catch my breath. For there is the Atlantic, a sweep of green water, dappled golden over shallow-lying sandbanks, just as Ella must have seen it that first time. And far out, along the horizon, is a strip of deeper colour, a wash of green-blue that is hard to define. 'Viridian,' I murmur. 'The colour of the ocean beyond the point.'

I needn't have worried. The island – changed though it must be after all these years – is still an island. I sense it immediately. Even though it's now referred to as 'the Twenty-First *Arrondissement*' because allegedly *le Tout-Paris* comes to holiday here in its chic little towns and on its beautiful beaches, there's no way this low-lying land of salt-marshes and sand-dunes can ever be truly tamed: it will always belong more to the ocean than to the land.

We pass fields of wildflowers, where cornflowers, poppies and Queen Anne's Lace weave their own exuberant version of the French flag, and fields of purple scorpion weed abuzz with insects. The lush, fresh green of vineyards is interspersed with the old gold of cornfields, scarlet-spattered with yet more poppies. The soil at the roadside is sandy, bound by sprawling tendrils of wild vines which have escaped from the constraining trellising of the vineyards and made a bid for freedom amongst the spikes of silver sea-holly and santolina that thrive in the salty air.

Following the directions Caroline has sent, we turn off the main road and into Sainte Marie de Ré, where Dan negotiates the car through the narrow streets between rows of whitewashed houses. And hollyhocks. They are still here, just as Ella described. Tall spires of tissue-paper flowers in shades of raspberry, apricot, cream and plum.

I glance again at Caroline's letter. '*Turn left, following signs to the campsite. Pass the vineyard on your right-hand side and just beyond it you will find the house. Sandrine will leave a key on the terrace at the back, under a blue ceramic pot of geraniums. Make yourself at home. I shall be staying in the apartment above the gallery in Saint Martin, and I look forward to meeting you all the day after you arrive. Come to the gallery at midday and we will go and have some lunch together and make our plans.*'

I'm here because Ella asked me to come. When Robbie and Jenny went to collect her things from the nursing home they found a note in the drawer of her bedside cabinet, addressed to me.

It had been an emotional few days; first, the phone call from Robbie to say that she'd gone, and then the conversation I'd had with my mother, telling her about the manuscript. She'd answered the phone in her customary way, with a crisp, 'Rhona Mitchell speaking.' Her voice became a little more gentle though, softening when she realised it was me, and she'd asked as fondly as always after Finn and Dan. But when I broached the subject of Ella's funeral, that defensive tone returned.

'I don't know when I'm coming up,' she'd said. 'The timing's not very convenient. I might not even be able to get away.' There was a finality in the way she said this that allowed no room for argument, so I let her words sit there, heavy as a gravestone.

'Okay, Mum, but listen, there's something I need to give you. So, if you're really not going to come for the funeral I'll have to send it to you. And I want you to promise me you'll read it. Will you?'

'What is it?' She was suspicious now, distrustful. 'Something your grandmother's cooked up?'

'Please, Mum. Just read it. Then we can talk afterwards.'

She'd sniffed, and I wasn't entirely sure whether it was a scornful sound or an attempt to disguise the fact that she was crying.

'Are you okay?'

'Of course, I'm okay. Why shouldn't I be?' A pause . . .

Then she'd said, 'Don't go to the trouble of sending whatever it is. Of course, I'll be there. We'll stay at Robbie's. It will be a good opportunity to come and see you all as well.'

'Okay, Mum, it'll be lovely to see you.' I'd hung up the phone and let my hand rest for a moment on the *kintsukuroi* bowl which sat on the kitchen-dresser weighting down the sheets of paper that tell Ella's story. I ran my finger lightly around the rim, feeling the almost imperceptible ridge where the vein of gold joins the deep blue shards of pottery, binding them together.

'She's coming,' I'd whispered. Although I don't know who I was telling it to, standing there in my empty kitchen.

Then I'd picked up the note, written in Ella's shaky italic script, and re-read it.

My dearest Kendra,

You have been my faithful ally, writing down my story so that Rhona will finally understand. I hope that she will forgive me, although I accept that forgiveness may be too much to ask. But her understanding of the truth will be enough. So you have given me peace of mind, at last, and for that I thank you.

You've already helped me so much that I hesitate to ask more of you. But I would like you to go to the Île de Ré, sometime when you can manage it amongst the many demands of your busy life. Would you do that for me? Go to the island and find Caroline. She knows my final wishes.

I should so like you to meet her. And perhaps you might enjoy a visit to that place – I know you've grown to love it already through writing about it. I hope you will

*find some of the freedom and peace there that the island
has brought me over the years.*

*Thank you for being such a wonderful granddaugh-
ter. And thank you for telling my story.*

Your loving grandmother, Ella.

So my mother came to Scotland for the funeral and we all hugged one another and cried as Ella was laid to rest alongside Angus, her lasting love.

I gave my mother a large envelope, containing the manuscript, and a wrapped box containing the bowl. 'Open the box after you've finished reading this,' I told her.

She nodded briskly and, without giving them a second glance, stowed both envelope and box into the capacious bag in which she'd brought presents for Finn. I haven't heard from her in the past fortnight, so I don't know if she's begun to read Ella's story. Or if she's finished it and decided not to mention it yet. But I understand that she needs time. Plucking up the courage to face the truth may take a while; realising how much more there was to her mother's story – and her father's – and allowing the defences of her anger and pride to be dismantled will take considerably longer.

In the back seat of the car, Finn is growing restless. He's never been on such a long journey before and we've been nervous about how he may react to being in strange surroundings. We usually stay at home in the holidays, so that he can be in his familiar environment and stick to his usual routine. Any changes can agitate him, although it's been a while since he last had a full-blown meltdown. But Dan and I had decided that our need for a holiday outweighed Finn's need for the safety of familiarity this time, and Caroline's offer of use of the house was just too tempting to pass up.

Dan's been struggling, I know, no matter how manfully he's tried to pretend otherwise. The community garden's been closed down: government cuts, no funding. That seemed to be the final blow to his confidence. Still jobless, he's picked up bits of work here and there, doing the accounts for a couple of small local businesses, work that he does late at night once I'm home and can take over Finn's care. I know how tough it is for him, and how desperately he needs a break – in all senses of the word.

'You alright back there?' Dan glances anxiously in the rearview mirror.

'We're nearly there, Finn,' I soothe him. 'What a good boy you've been. Just a few more minutes.' As I hand him his comforter, a worn scrap of blanket he's had since he was a baby, I notice he's bitten his lips until they're cracked and bleeding. He hangs on to it tightly, bringing it close to his face to smell its reassuring scent of home.

'Look, there! That must be the house. See, Finn? The white house with the pale blue shutters.'

Dan pulls up on to the sandy verge, alongside the whitewashed wall that surrounds the house and its garden. I'd half prepared myself to be disappointed, expecting that it might be run-down now, the garden overgrown or – worse – levelled to a patch of easily maintained lawn. But Caroline and her assistant Sandrine – the granddaughter of the original Sandrine and Benoît – have looked after the property with loving care over all these years. It's just as Ella described it and I feel a sense of excitement and relief.

I hold my breath as Finn clambers out of the car at last – he'd refused at first, so we'd left him sitting in his seat as we opened up the house and began to unload the bags. He sat there with his comforter, crooning softly to himself, which is one of his self-soothing techniques when he's feeling anxious or stressed. Dan and I exchanged a guarded glance, both wondering whether this trip was going to turn out to be another horrible mistake to add to the list of abortive attempts at holidays we'd had in the early days, before we gave up trying.

I pretend to rummage in one of the bags as Finn walks up the path and stands in the doorway, his slight frame backlit against the sunshine beyond. A waft of breeze lifts the white muslin curtains on either side of the French doors in the kitchen and they billow voluminously, filling like the sails of a ship. Automatically, I tense, bracing myself for his high-pitched scream if he is panicked by this unfamiliar sight. But, to my amazement and relief, he begins to laugh. I feel my shoulders drop as they relax, and I laugh too, with joy, at his rarely heard response. Because he laughs so seldom, it's all the more precious when he does.

He points. 'Look, Mummy, it's ghosts. Friendly ones, like Casper.'

For a second I wonder whether he truly is seeing spirits, whether his mind allows him to glimpse worlds the rest of us cannot. And it seems plausible that he might, because the house feels full of friendly ghosts. It's already welcoming and familiar, even though we've only just walked into it, filled as it is with the spirit of Marianne's gentle kindness, and Monsieur Martet's love for his family, and Christophe's passionate sense of beauty. But when I turn to follow Finn's gaze, it's just the joyous, billowing dance of the curtains in the sea-breeze that is amusing him so.

'Come upstairs and see your bedroom. I think it might have curtains like that too.'

With calm acceptance, he takes my hand – another treasured rarity – and we climb the stairs together.

'I like holidays, Mummy,' he tells me as he stands on the bright rag rug in his room, watching as I open the shutters and allow the sunlight to flood in. I know better than to scoop him up in my arms and hug him tightly to me, even though, instinctively, it's still what I yearn to do. But I hold my hand up, fingers spread like a starfish, and he presses his own tiny starfish hand against mine in our agreed gesture of love.

I nod, smiling into his wide green eyes, so like the eyes of his great-grandmother in the photographs when she was young. 'I like holidays too.'

After supper, he settles under the counterpane on his unfamiliar bed without a murmur. I pull the shutters to, but leave the window open, drawing the curtains across. 'Look,' I whisper, 'the friendly ghosts are keeping you company.'

He nods, his expression grave as usual, and spreads his comforter on his pillow so that the familiar smell of home will keep his night terrors at bay.

'Good night, Finn. Sleep tight.'

I tiptoe back downstairs to the kitchen, where Dan is running water into the sink to start the washing-up. 'Leave that,' I say, handing him a towel to dry his hands. 'Let's go and sit on the terrace and finish our wine.'

He pulls me to him and I bury my face in the comforting breadth of his chest. We haven't shared a moment like this for ages. It feels good to stand here like this, together.

With his arm around my waist, he guides me back to the garden and we sit at the table picking at the cheeses and the bowl of glossy cherries that Caroline had left for our arrival, sipping the dark red wine in our glasses. Dan raises his glass to mine with a soft clink. 'Here's to Ella, who brought us here. What a paradise it is.'

'To Ella,' I echo. And I smile as I reach for my husband's hand, our fingers interlocking. We sit there in silence for a while, watching the stars come out as a crescent moon, delicate as an eyelash, drifts in the dark sky above our heads. I breathe in the honeysuckle-scented air and I remember Marianne.

I don't know whether it's the wine, or the novelty of sitting out so late in the warm night air, or perhaps it's the fact that the two of us are light-headed with relief – and not a little disbelief – that Finn seems so relaxed here and that we are finally having a family holiday. But suddenly I feel closer to Dan than I've done in ages. Years, in fact. The ten long years since Finn was born.

Sitting here beside my husband, holding his hand in the soft glow that escapes through the slats of the shutters from the lamp that lights the night in Finn's bedroom, to keep the terrors that torment him at bay, I know what a toll all of this has taken on Dan and me. But the Île de Ré seems to be weaving its subtle magic around us, just as it did around Ella and Christophe all those years ago, binding us to one another again, reminding me how much I love this man who has shared the struggle to understand our son and to try to get him the care he needs. I'm reminded of Ella's single-minded determination when it came to caring for Robbie through his battle with polio, cajoling the authorities into providing the right treatment for him. I must have inherited that gene from her, I think, and it renews my sense of purpose to think that, in some way, she will be with me to keep on fighting for Finn, whatever the future may hold. It's a frightening prospect, to put it mildly. How can we create an environment where he'll feel safe? What will happen when he outgrows the specialist school where, even now, the resources and support available for him are limited? Will he ever be able to work? To support himself? And the unthinkable thought is always there, the dread that consumes me in the sleepless hours on my worst nights: what will happen to him when we're gone?

As if he's read my mind, Dan laces his fingers over mine, and I turn to smile at him.

'It's been tough, hasn't it? You've been a star, Kendra. Keeping it all going while I'm lazing about at home.'

'It's hardly your fault you lost your job. And you never laze at home. I know what hard work Finn is. You're doing a fantastic job. He loves having you there to look after him. Look how he enjoyed the gardening project while it lasted. How he loves working with you in the allotment.'

Dan nods. 'He does, doesn't he? You know, I'm really rather proud of our vegetable patch. And the other day, after we'd visited the City Farm, he told me he wants to make it bigger and maybe get some chickens too.'

I laugh. 'Can you imagine what the neighbours would have to say about that?' Our pocket handkerchief of a suburban plot is no smallholding.

'It would be great, wouldn't it, to move to the country some day? Finn definitely seems more relaxed in a rural environment. Just look at how well he's adapted to being here. We could have a proper vegetable garden, maybe an orchard too like that one' – he waves his wine-glass towards the trees just visible beyond the gate at the far end of the garden – 'Finn could learn some proper gardening skills, maybe get a job at a plant nursery eventually, or on a farm . . .'

'Would you enjoy that, do you think? Giving up city life and moving to the country?'

He's silent for a few moments, contemplating. 'Do you know? I really think I would. I'd like to be my own boss, start some kind of project of my own, something creative that Finn could be part of. Be master of my own fate, for once, instead of reliant on other people's business for my salary. Or lack thereof!'

In the dim light, I glimpse the way his mouth turns down, a flicker of despair contorting his features briefly. But he pulls himself together, as he always does, protecting me from his sadness and his frustration, his sense of failure.

'What about you?' He squeezes my hand again gently. 'What would you do if we won the lottery?'

I laugh again. 'We'd better start buying tickets!' Then, more seriously, I say, 'I'd love it, I think, living in the country. I could write, and help with Finn, and collect the eggs from the chickens and cook you both delicious, nourishing meals with our homegrown produce.' I sip my wine. 'Isn't it a pity that the city is where the jobs are? The minor flaw in our cunning plan.'

Dan stretches, leaning against the back of his chair, raising his face to the starlight far above us. He sighs, a despondent breath of frustration. Then turns to face me again, leans in to kiss me. 'At least we are dreaming. And that, in itself, is progress. I've just realised that I stopped dreaming a long time ago. It's time we started again. Life is definitely the better for it.'

I smile, remembering my grandmother's words. 'Ella once said something very much along those lines too.'

He releases my hand and draws a finger along my jaw-line, caressing it softly. 'You have the same-shaped face as her. I only realised it when I saw the photos of her when she was young. How lucky I am. I love you, Kendra.'

And I realise in this moment that he is my first love and my lasting love. Together, we are Finn's parents. Together, we will make it work, whatever life sends our way. And that – I see suddenly – is all that matters.

My eyes meet his and I notice that they are the clear blue of a summer's sky: the sadness, the fear, the guilt and the pain that have clouded them so often of late, have all been washed away. His gaze is unequivocal.

The sighing breath of the ocean enfolds us both as we stand up and, with arms twined around each other's waists, make our way back inside. Dan leads me up the quietly creaking staircase to our bedroom where the pale muslin curtains billow towards us in the night breeze, beckoning us in silently. In the light of the moon, lulled by the hushing sound of the waves, we drift together, holding fast as we lie beneath the painting of a wind-blown boat, sailing free across an ocean lit with the light of a summer's love. And we know that we are saved.

'It must be the sea air,' comments Dan the next morning.

Finn has slept through the night and is now tucking into a second croissant, slathered with French butter and cherry jam (the latter clearly homemade, presumably by Sandrine). He pauses for a moment, licking crumbs from his fingers, to observe, 'I like eating breakfast in the garden,' then focuses his full attention on manoeuvring another spoonful of jam on to his plate.

'Me too,' grins Dan and I notice his hand lift slightly, as if to reach out and ruffle his son's hair; but he catches himself in time and lets his hand rest on the table between them instead. It's going to be a day of unknown challenges for Finn as it is. We can't risk any extra upsets.

Some days – rare, precious days – he'll let us touch him, hold his hand, help him get dressed. But we have to wait for those moments, read the signals carefully, let him come to us, or else we risk invoking the tempest of his rage and panic which will splinter our fragile little family group into distraught fragments until we are all fraught with exhaustion once again.

But today is a good day and, so far, the risk that we've taken coming on holiday has paid off. So we proceed with caution, taking tiny, tentative steps into this new territory, holding our breath and hoping – as we spend our whole lives doing – for signs of progress.

I keep my voice light. 'Today Mummy's going to go and meet a friend in a town near here. She's the lady who owns this house. There are boats in the town. I wonder whether you would like to see the boats, Finn?'

He ignores me and carries on picking up the flakes of buttery pastry that freckle his plate with his sticky finger, intent on transferring every last one into his mouth. I know better than to push for a reply. The three of us sit in silence, Dan and I carefully sipping our coffee. No pressure.

Once the very last crumb has been picked up, Finn regards his perfectly clean plate, his expression unchanging. 'I would like to see the lady,' he says. 'And perhaps the boats as well.'

The sun is high and hot as midday approaches, shrinking our shadows to dark puddles beneath our feet on the cobbles of the quayside. Mercifully, Saint Martin isn't too busy as it's still early in the season and I thank my lucky stars, as well as the Scottish education system, that the school broke up well before most of the rest of Europe does. Dan and I flank Finn, automatically trying to create a buffer between him and a world that his mind can find so confusing and terrifying. We're always trying to second-guess his reactions, although usually we fail. 'It's not that his mind is misinterpreting the world,' the psychiatrist once explained. 'It's just interpreting it differently. Who's to say – perhaps he's the one who's getting it right and it's the rest of us that are wrong. It all makes perfect sense to him, the way he reacts. We just need to try to see things through his eyes.'

I glance at him, anxious that the sudden onslaught of noise and colour and people in the busy harbour might panic him. But he's using one of his coping strategies, focusing hard on his feet, looking at patterns in the cobble-stones, intent on tracing a path across them that allows him to feel secure in this strange new environment. Any other child his age would be looking around, exclaiming over the boats on their moorings, and the ice-cream shop, the cafés with their bright umbrellas and the smell of hot sugar from the crêpe stall on the quay. But he knows that if he can just stay focused then the demons that lurk within these new sights and sounds can't get to him. So, he plods on, biting his lip as he places his jelly sandals carefully on those stones that look safe to him, not looking left or right until we have crossed the bridge that links the two sides of the harbour and are standing in front of the gallery.

We step over the threshold into the gallery's outer room, where matte grey walls are hung with a series of bright-coloured abstracts, shaded by the awning which keeps the sun's bleaching rays at bay. Finn surveys the paintings gravely and then his face splits into his widest grin. 'Look, Mummy, there are the boats.' And I realise he's right. What look like abstract geometric shapes resolve themselves, seen through his eyes, into a regatta of sail-boats splashing through a sparkling sea.

'My child, you are absolutely correct.' A woman appears in the archway that leads through to the gallery's inner room. She is very old, her pure white hair drawn into a soft *chignon*, at the nape of her neck, her dark eyes hooded; but she stands upright and her features are still elegant in her lined face. 'Those are indeed the boats. Not everyone can see them. You clearly have an eye for art.'

Finn turns his serious, wide-eyed gaze upon her. 'Are you the lady?'

'You know, I do believe I must be. Caroline Martet, very pleased to meet you. And I think you are Finn, *n'est-ce pas?*'

She holds out a hand towards him and I tense, expecting him to cringe from it, or to slap it away as he has done to other strangers who've attempted to shake his hand before now. But, to my surprise and relief, he reaches out his own small hand and clasps hers briefly.

'Did you paint the boat pictures?'

'No, my child. I wish I had, but I was not given that talent. My brother was the artist in our family. Although he didn't paint these particular pictures. They are by a friend of mine.'

'Which ones did your brother paint? Can I see them?'

'I have just one of his left here in the gallery. The others have all been sold. But you might have noticed the paintings in the house?' Finn nods. 'Well, most of those were painted by him.'

Finn continues to survey her gravely, but, where most people would be disconcerted, she meets his gaze with a calmness and wisdom that seem to reassure him. 'I like the one of the boat on the sea best. It's in Mummy and Daddy's bedroom.'

'I know the one to which you refer,' Caroline smiles. 'That is indeed one of his. It was one of your great-grandmother's favourites too. She had one quite like it, also by him, in her home in Edinburgh, so perhaps you are reminded of it by the one in the house here. You are clearly a young man of discerning tastes, Finn. And these must be your parents, I suppose?'

She embraces me tightly, then holds me at arm's length. 'Kendra. It is good to meet you at last. You have Ella's complexion . . . the shape of her face too.' She touches my cheek softly, her fingers knotted and arthritic. 'But you, Finn' – she turns to him again – 'have her eyes.'

'Can we see the painting?' he asks. 'The one your brother did that you have left?'

'Come,' she beckons. 'It's through here.'

Dan and I follow the unlikely pair of art-lovers into the back room. And then my breath catches and I have to stifle the sob that rises in my throat.

My fragile son stands, gazing upwards, dwarfed by the canvas which almost fills one wall of the inner room, lit by a single spotlight. His straight, gold-streaked hair is the same as the woman's in the painting, the colour of the beach-grass that blows in the dunes. Her eyes are closed, watching her dreams behind the veil of sleep, but I know if they were to open they would be the same colour as his, the colour of the deepest ocean, out beyond the point. Her beauty has the same ethereal quality as his. A Botticelli *Venus* with a *Mona Lisa* smile.

Tears spill from my eyes. Dan reaches for my hand and I sense that he, too, is as overcome as I am. It's not just the juxtaposition of Finn, our tiny, delicate son, beside his great-grandmother's portrait. It's the realisation that this is more than just a painting . . .

In this moment, I see my grandmother for who she truly was – a pure force of beauty, love, joy and compassion. And I see, too, that that is all that matters: it is everything. If I can try to live my life with this in mind, then I know that I will be happy, wherever I may be and no matter what challenges surround me.

'Do you like the painting, Finn?' Caroline asks gently.

'I think it is a very good one.'

'And why is that?'

'Because she looks like she is dreaming a good dream. Not a horrible nightmare with monsters that chase you and try to make you be someone different than who you are.'

'You're right, Finn. She looks very peaceful, perfectly contented being who she really is. As we all should be.'

He nods. Then says, 'I think I would like to go and look at the real boats now.'

'Well, that can certainly be arranged. In fact, I think it's lunch-time, so why don't we go and find a table beside the harbour? That way we can look at the boats and eat at the same time.'

Caroline closes the gallery and leads us along the quayside towards the harbour-master's offices, to a quiet corner where there are fewer people milling about. We settle ourselves at a table shaded by a broad canvas umbrella, from where we have a good view of the boats, and order *moules-frites* along with a chilled bottle of Sancerre.

'Here, Finn, have a piece of bread to keep you going.' Caroline proffers the basket of crusty baguette. '*Et voilà* – here is your Orangina. That should keep the hunger at bay until our food arrives.'

Finn sips his drink through a white paper straw, rhythmically swinging his feet below his chair, his attention focused entirely on the boats safely moored in the calm waters of the harbour.

'*Santé!*' Caroline raises her glass. 'What a joy it is to have Ella's relations here. It does my heart such good to see you. I trust you have found everything you need at the house?'

'It's perfect, thank you, Caroline. I can see why Ella fell so deeply in love with this place. Everything's just as she described it. Seeing the painting this morning was a real treat too.'

'I'm very glad you like the picture so much.' Caroline pauses, taking a sip of her wine. 'Very glad, indeed. Because, Kendra, it is yours. I have a letter here for you, from your grandmother. That is why she wanted you to come here. Not just to visit the Île de Ré in her memory, but to see your inheritance.'

As if in slow motion, I lower my glass back on to the table. And then I realise that my mouth is hanging open in amazement and shut it quickly. Both Dan and I are staring at Caroline, scarcely able to believe what she's just announced so casually, whilst Finn, who is oblivious, still swings his jelly sandals beneath his chair, rocking to and fro as he counts the forest of masts in the harbour, softly under his breath.

Caroline reaches into her capacious handbag and pulls out an envelope. 'Here it is.' She hands it across to me and my hands tremble as I open it, the sight of Ella's shaky handwriting making my vision swim.

My dear Kendra,
So you have finally made it to the island, and I hope it has lived up to your expectations. I'm sorry I'm not there with you. But I derive great pleasure from the thought that perhaps it will become a place of magical memories for you and your family as it was for me throughout my life, firstly with Christophe and then with Angus.

As Caroline will have told you, Neptune's Locket is yours. It's my way of saying thank you for telling my story. In these, my final days, you have given me back my memories; and in addition you have given me the hope that Rhona will, at last, forgive me. These two gifts are beyond anything I could have asked for: you gave me peace, at the end.

In return, I should like you to have peace in your own life: the peace that comes from having choices; the peace that comes of being financially secure; and, above all, the peace of knowing that your beautiful boy's future is assured, whatever care and support he may need.

Caroline will help secure a suitable buyer for the painting. She knows exactly what to do, and I believe she already has some of her contacts lined up. I should love to think of it on display in a portrait gallery in London, Paris or Edinburgh – somewhere you can go and visit it from time to time perhaps, but somewhere where it will be accessible to a wider audience too. Christophe's finest work deserves that.

Use the money to secure the future for you and Dan and Finn. Use it to allow you to live your lives surrounded by the beauty and peace that will be best for your child. It gives me great joy to think of that.

With my love,

Ella

My hand is trembling even more violently as I look up from reading the letter. Dan reaches over to place his hand on top of mine, to steady me with his own solid, reassuring strength that has always been there, even in the hardest times during these past difficult months when I know he's often felt the bleakness of his own despair.

I grip his hand tightly and look across at our son who is still rocking and counting and sipping his drink.

In the clear summer light that dazzles as it dances on the water, casting sunbeams on to Finn's face, suddenly I dare to dream of a future stretching ahead of us that is filled with hope and joy instead of darkness and worry. I see a little house in the country, where we can grow vegetables and raise chickens; where Finn can find peace and feel safe; where I can write and Dan can know the dignity of being his own master again.

And I see holidays, when we will travel as a family to a wild, low-lying island moored in a sea of light.

And then I turn to my husband, my eyes brimming with an overwhelming sense of amazement at the miracle of this life.

The everyday miracle that is love.

AUTHOR'S NOTE

Thank you for reading *Sea of Memories*. I do hope you've enjoyed Ella's story. Wherever possible I have kept the historical background as accurate as possible, following the key events and dates of the Second World War. However, in one or two areas I have taken certain liberties, following Mark Twain's advice to 'never let the truth stand in the way of a good story'! I hope my readers will forgive me.

If you have enjoyed this book, I'd be very grateful if you would consider writing a review. I love getting feedback, and I know reviews have played a big part in other readers discovering my books.

Merci, et à bientôt,
Fiona

ACKNOWLEDGMENTS

I'm grateful to everyone at the Madeleine Milburn Literary Agency for their belief in my writing and their encouragement (and especially to Maddy and Hayley). Heartfelt thanks, too, to the team at Amazon Publishing for all their support, in particular my editors, Sammia Hamer, Victoria Pepe, Mike Jones and Marie Selwood, as well as Bekah Graham.

I've dedicated *Sea of Memories* to the memory of my Scottish grandmother, Milly Macdonald. Some aspects of the story are based on her recollections of life in Edinburgh. She is certainly not Ella, but I like to think she might well have been a neighbour and a friend.

To my sons, James and Alastair, who are stars as ever, and to all the friends – old and new – who have walked the path beside me over rough and stony ground, I send my love.

ABOUT THE AUTHOR

Fiona Valpy spent seven years living in France, having moved there from the UK in 2007. She and her family renovated an old, rambling farmhouse in the Bordeaux winelands, during which time she developed new-found skills in cement-mixing, interior decorating and wine-tasting.

All of these inspirations, along with a love for the place, the people and their history, have found their way into the books she's written, which have been translated into German, Norwegian, Czech and Turkish.

Fiona now lives in Scotland, but enjoys regular visits to France in search of the sun.